Published by Accent Press Ltd 2016

ISBN 9781783759286

Pica

Jeff Gardiner

Dedicated to Emily and Bethany.

Acknowledgements

I'd like to thank Samantha Curtis and Lorraine Mace for their support and encouragement, plus my editors at Accent Press, Rebecca Lloyd and Alex Davies, for their wise advice.

Chapter One

This new planet possessed the familiar signs of life – oceans, continents, oxygen, carbon-based life-forms, and an inhabitable climate. Within seconds, my avatar hovered over the lush, green world where I could see jungles, mountain streams, and vast plains, like the Serengeti, all teeming with wildlife. A quick scan showed the planet contained over four thousand species of mammal, plus tens of thousands of species of birds alone. An eco-system of such incredible biodiversity deserved just one response. I pressed the button to release a monstrous tongue of napalm flame.

Trees blazed into an inferno immediately; miles of forest wiped out in a single blow. Creatures stampeded in swathes. Clouds of birds erupted into the air, fleeing the conflagration; some already ablaze or singed. Then I carefully aimed two nuclear missiles with such accuracy that they blew away all visible greenery, and using heat-seeking weaponry I chased and finished off the dwindling flocks of birds, picking off stragglers one by one. I waited until the entire landscape on each horizon became a black desert of ash before landing my ship.

Beaming down to the planet's surface in nanoseconds, I found myself sitting behind the wheel of the most powerful, indestructible, pimped up, ultra-modified super tank, which possessed unlimited weapons including laser, flamethrower, missiles, and an even greater nuclear capacity than I'd used so far. It protected me from the still-spreading radioactive fallout. As an amphibian vehicle it could also turn into a submarine or full-on warship; on dry land, though, it reached speeds of over four hundred miles an hour. Awesome.

My mission was to take over the entire planet, but before I could fully lay claim to this dominion I was forced to stop on seeing hordes of strange, ugly rhinoceros-lizard hybrid creatures charge towards me. They had survived the nuclear blast. I had to think quickly. Pressing the accelerator, I crushed hundreds of them under my ten tons. Others flew off the spiked bumpers of my vehicle in various directions, spattering blood around randomly. With a simple press of a button I scattered a few smart bombs and watched as limbs and gore spiralled before my bulletproof windscreen.

I kill mercilessly and drop a hundred chemical bombs to pollute the rivers, kill off all vegetation, and poison all living species, which left the planet wiped of life and finally belonging to me. This world will be mine! Or at least it will after completing level twenty of *Organik Apokalypse*. Bring it on.

'Luke? Dinner's ready.' Mum's voice could just be heard over the explosions. I activated a series of chemical bombs to ensure the extinction of all existing lifeforms.

'I said dinner's ready!' Mum called again.

A herd of giant scarlet bovine creatures suddenly came into view. I wiped them out with a single gigantic flame. That felt good. Now I had to find a place to begin building the megalopolis – my giant city of concrete and chrome skyscrapers. My army of autominions were ready to be released. They would hunt down and kill off any surviving creatures, begin to build my giant cities, then colonise the entire planet, with me as their master – the conqueror of yet another world.

'Luke! Did you hear me?'

'Yeah, in a minute.'

'No, Luke, now. We have guests.'

How annoying. I was nearly there. Mission almost complete.

'I just need to save where I am. Hang on.'

'Luke! Come down. Now!' I heard Dad shout. 'The food is getting cold and we're all waiting for you.'

Yeah, yeah. Whatever.

Parents just don't understand these things. All because adults can't wait a few moments and prefer food that burns their mouths. What consideration did they have for me, exactly? I pushed my chair away with the back of my legs in contempt,

2

hoping they'd hear it fall to the floor. Then some noisy stomping down the stairs would show them my feelings on the matter.

I still felt angry when I walked into the silent dining room. Three strange faces sat around the table – a boy sat in my place and an elderly couple offering me fake smiles. Dad sat in his usual chair and Mum stood serving a pile of plates. I checked out the boy. He looked a bit of a freak. You know the sort – a saddo. Not a geeky type or a boff – more a bit of a loner ... a victim. His clothes looked slightly grubby and his hair was totally uncool; greasy and parted down the middle. I had to hold my nose to stop myself from sniggering. This was going to be one very dull meal.

Mum sat down and lifted the lid off the casserole dish.

'Right, then. Please help yourself to vegetables.'

The meal began with awkward silence then stupid small talk about the weather. The boy was introduced to me as Guy. Crappy name if you ask me. Don't guys get burnt on bonfires? I made an indistinct grunting noise and nodded in his direction without really catching his eye – mainly because I couldn't bear looking at his hideous hair and grubby shirt. The stupid git needed a bath and some deodorant too. It turned out the couple were his foster parents, looking after him because his mum was ill.

'Guy will be living round the corner for the foreseeable future, Luke, so perhaps you'd be willing to show him around and be generally friendly,' Dad said with some emphasis, before speaking through gritted teeth. 'I realise that doesn't always come naturally to you.'

I contorted my face into a sneering smile which seemed good enough for my parents. They were so easy to con.

'We'd appreciate that greatly,' said the man, smiling through his grey toothbrush moustache. 'Wouldn't we, Celia?' His wife nodded enthusiastically before reaching out to pinch Guy's cheek.

'We want what's best for our little poppet. Don't we, duckie?'

When Guy looked back with big cute Disney eyes and

nodded sweetly, I felt a huge urge to regurgitate my dinner.

After a completely tedious half an hour of being forced to smile politely at the inane conversation and answer dumb questions about school, I finally asked if I could leave the table.

'We haven't all finished eating, yet, young man,' growled Dad. I mumbled inaudibly, but with enough gusto for everyone to see my displeasure. It was vital Guy should see who was boss around here. 'What's with the attitude, exactly?' Dad went on, intent on ruining my street cred. 'Just sit quietly and show some manners.'

I rolled my eyes because I knew it annoyed him.

'Well, if he's finished, dear, he might as well leave us to it.' Mum was obviously keen to avoid a confrontation in front of our guests.

'Right. Thank you,' I said, wanting to make my point clear. I made sure I only looked at Mum, avoiding Dad's usual scowl.

'Go on then, dear.'

I was aware of Dad tutting as I strutted triumphantly out of the room, then he mumbled something to Mum about undermining his authority. She replied about him being too tough on me. Before I'd reached the top of the stairs the visitors made some excuse to leave early even before Mum could offer them coffee and chocolate mints.

Safely back in my room, I clicked on to the icon for *Organik Apokalypse* and spent about an hour choosing locations for each city. I watched as my autominions, now reproduced in their billions, began the large-scale building process. What once had been jungle, river, and plains was now filled with shining towers and concrete blocks. Cities soon joined together to make mega-regions, until the entire planet became a mass of concrete; one giant urban conurbation ready to be filled with humans who would bow down to me as the master of their world. Now the planet was nearly fully transformed my work was almost done.

I strode majestically amongst my autominions, overseeing the whole process of building tower blocks and ultra-cities, as spaceships, miles long, brought the planet's new human population to settle here. I had to think of a name for this planet, one that reflected the courage and heroism of its founding

Emperor – me.

A flashing display on the bottom right of my visor warned me that a native lifeform had been detected. What?! I thought I'd obliterated all life-forms, so I checked my weapon belt and sprinted off in the direction of the alert. These battles gave me a great deal of satisfaction – the thrill of the hunt.

I selected a rocket launcher with a laser harpoon attachment and ran towards the last piece of natural, albeit decimated, wasteland left on the planet. A quick scan showed nothing but giant rock formations; a deep gully. I strode stealthily towards the first outcrop, expecting something to leap out at me. Nothing.

Enjoying the challenge of one-to-one combat I switched off all scanners and radar, which required skill and swift reactions – something I'd mastered from hours of gameplay and the reason I was worshipped like a god on so many planets. I was invincible.

The initial warning came as a sound. A snort? Having found attack to be the best form of defence I ran wildly towards the sound. I took a sharp left after a giant boulder and came face to face with the creature.

About ten feet high, it had the solid legs and massive tail of a lizard, but the head of an insect with mandible pincers that snapped together from side to side. It spat what seemed to be acidic venom, which I avoided deftly with a series of jumps and rolls.

Using the laser harpoon, I hit it in the chest but it hardly seemed to notice. I charged the rocket-launcher, hoping to aim it squarely between the eyes.

A loud screech from behind me made me jump.

I let go the controls of my game and whipped my head round, perplexed.

There on my windowsill stood a damn bird.

The top, small window pane was still open on its hook, and I hadn't bothered to close my curtains yet. The stupid idiot must have hopped through the opening and come into my room. What was that all about?

It was black and white with a long tail flicking up and down.

5

A magpie. I'd never taken a great deal of interest in birds, but Dad always bored me senseless by telling me their stupid names when we went for crappy walks in the countryside.

Now a bloody magpie was in my bedroom checking me out. I stayed in my seat and stared back at it, wondering what the hell I was supposed to do. I considered jumping up and waving my arms, to scare it back out the window. But that might only panic it and send it flapping round my head. Perhaps I should creep towards the window and open it before shooing it out. That sounded the best plan, but what if the bugger pecked me if I got too close? It had a long, black beak and sharp claws. My instinct told me to call for Dad, but I wasn't a baby any more who needed Mummy and Daddy to help me every time.

This was a freakingly bizarre standoff.

It shrieked again. Loudly.

'Piss off, you stupid dumb bird.' I couldn't move. I wasn't thinking quickly enough here.

Just then, a scrabbling sound to my left distracted me and my door opened. At first I assumed Mum or Dad had come up to investigate the noise, but in shot a familiar small shape; Frisky, our cat. He hissed and leapt straight towards the magpie, which immediately spread its wings and squawked in self-defence. Frisky took a swipe at the bird and landed on the floor. The bird flapped its way around my room, swooping at me and the cat. I ducked like a coward, and even Frisky seemed a bit shocked at this counter-attack.

I wondered if we were going to get pecked to death. Serve my parents right if they came up to find my still-bleeding corpse. Then they'd realise how much they should've appreciated me. With nothing to lose, I jumped up and waved my arms manically.

'Sod off, you gimp!'

The magpie landed back on the windowsill and I froze, ready to reach out to open the larger window. The magpie, however, seemed to have had enough. It hopped up towards the small opening, and looked back at me with a sideways stare. Its black eye seemed to blink. Then with one last shriek, it ducked its head and disappeared.

As soon as it had gone, I closed the window.

What the hell?

For a moment I sat on my bed trying to work out what exactly had just happened. My next thought returned to my game. Glancing at the screen, I watched my avatar getting bludgeoned to death by the humanoid-insect's whiplash tail. I could only look on helplessly as it played sadistically with my dying body. The hideous thing leaned towards me to bite off my head in its razor-toothed jaw, leaving several other creatures to squabble over the remains of my innards and carcass, until the screen went red and offered me a return to a previously saved level. I'd have to begin level twenty all over again.

Then I remembered Frisky, looking sorry for himself, sat in the middle of my carpet. I got down on my knees to stroke his soft fur.

'Thanks for trying, buddy. That was a bit weird, eh?'

As I tickled his chin to console him, he bit me, sinking his teeth into my finger and clawing the back of my hand.

'You bastard!'

I whipped my hands firmly around the cat's middle. I tucked him under my left arm, with that hand grasping both back paws; my right hand firmly holding both of Frisky's front paws. Unfortunately, this left my right hand exposed to the cat's sharp teeth. He struggled, but had to content himself with giving me a sharp nip. Ignoring the pain, I rapidly changed my hold until I got the stupid creature in a tight bear hug. I got a few scratches through my jumper, but it seemed worth the hassle. In this position I inched towards the window. Then in one swift movement I opened it outwards and threw Frisky out into the darkness. There followed a thud and a yowl. I'd heard cats always land on their feet, so what was the problem?

Perhaps the magpie was out there waiting for him. On the other hand, why did I care?

Finally succumbing to tiredness, I went to bed.

Chapter Two

Just after nine a.m. Dad woke me up by opening the curtains and plonking down a cup of tea on the bedside cabinet. I hated tea in the morning – especially the way Dad made it; way too milky to start, then as it got cold it always grew a thick, rubbery skin that looked like dried glue. More often than not I'd chuck it down the loo when Dad wasn't looking. This time he actually spoke to me as he set the mug down.

'Have you seen Frisky? He's not in here with you, is he?'

'Uh-uh,' I replied, yawning heartily. It didn't twig at first.

'It's just that he didn't appear for his breakfast. We can't find him anywhere. You didn't let him out, did you?' Then my brain caught up with my ears.

'Nope.' I made a big pantomime of stretching nonchalantly and then scratching my head as if in deep thought. 'Perhaps he found a way outside and went exploring.'

'Mmm, possibly. It's just not like him, that's all.' This was true. He was an old house cat – hardly ever went outside. 'He needs his tablet too.' Dad finally left the room muttering to himself.

Hell! I'd forgotten about Frisky's heart murmur. Now I felt really guilty. Pushing back the duvet, I jumped up, put on my blue fluffy dressing gown and moccasin slippers, and went to help search for Frisky.

Please be there, Frisky. Don't let anything have happened to him …

Mum and Dad were lifting up the furniture and looking in cupboards.

'Was a window left open last night? Perhaps he got out?'

'Oh, I don't think so,' Mum answered, deep in thought.

'The bathroom window was left open. I just closed it,' I lied. 'I heard a noise last night. Maybe Frisky jumped out the bathroom window. Shall I go and look outside?'

'I suppose it's worth a try,' Mum said, looking puzzled. 'I could've sworn I checked the bathroom.'

I began to unlock the back door and hope my burning face didn't give me away.

'Not in your slippers, Luke!' my mum shrieked, as if I was about to inject myself with heroin. 'Honestly, you'll get mud on them. I'll go.'

Mum stepped outside, calling out, 'Frisky!' Not wanting to look too soppy, or give the game away, I had to hide my relief when the stupid moggie suddenly appeared from behind the shed.

'It's OK Luke, Frisky's here. You were right – he was outside.'

'Of course I was right,' I said coolly. 'Aren't I always?'

Seeing the old flea-bag calmed me down. Frisky was about the only animal I could get to like. Maybe. He was OK when he let me tickle his tummy.

School was its usual tedious treadmill of uninspiring lessons – something to endure until they released us at 3.30.

What made this day even worse than usual was that the weirdo who came to my house with his foster parents did indeed appear at school. When I first saw him I almost approached him, yet at the sight of his greasy hair and shabby uniform with trousers that didn't quite reach his shoes but flapped halfway down his leg to reveal grubby white socks, I turned immediately and pretended I hadn't spotted him. My fear that he'd be a natural victim came true when I saw Guy being taunted by a large group of year elevens from a distance.

He wasn't in any of my lessons, which luckily meant I didn't have to sit next to him. I worried that he might tell a teacher he knew me and that I'd be forced to 'look after him'. During the lunch break I kept half an eye out for him – purely as a means of self-protection – because if, for some hideous reason, he recognised me and made for me, I'd need some way of escape or a damn good excuse to preserve my own reputation. Word in the playground reached me that he hadn't survived the whole day and had been sent home snivelling like a baby. For some reason I felt a shiver of dread ripple through me. Why had my stupid parents been so flipping kind to his foster parents? Why did these things always happen to me?

To be honest, I was just glad to get home unscathed that day. Frisky slept on my bed as I played *Organik Apokalypse*.

The next day was yet another on the hamster wheel. Each lesson completed was one less to attend in my life. Every day at 3.30 I mentally ticked off how much closer I was to leaving school, and though I didn't like to think too much about how I was wishing my own life away, I couldn't help thinking there had to be a better way of enjoying my childhood than this. I walked slowly back to my educational prison. How I longed for the day when I could leave this dumb place, once and for all. Being an adult must me great with no school to go to. Having said that, my parents never seemed particularly happy – but then again, I wouldn't make the mistakes they have made. This thought made me smile.

Guy appeared a few times at school and one particularly horrible moment involved me walking past him in the corridor. Simon and I were dawdling to our IT lesson when I suddenly looked up and saw Guy smiling at me. Something in his eyes looked lost and forlorn. For a millisecond I considered acknowledging him, but how could I explain this behaviour to my mates? If I associated myself with him then it would be like sticking a 'punch me' sign around my neck so I looked away without a flicker of expression and moved on. It just got worse.

During Maths the whole class rushed to the window to watch what seemed like a riot going on during a PE lesson outside. A teacher managed to break up the inevitable crowding and scatter the pupils back to their various activities, before crouching down to help a pupil who was curled up in the foetal position with his hands over his ears.

'That's the new kid,' someone shouted. Our Maths teacher, Mr Winkler, seemed as nosy as the rest of us. Indeed, there was Guy lying in the mud, presumably having just been tackled or fouled.

'He's a freak,' someone else called. This caused a great deal of hilarity, which I joined in.

'What's his name?'

'Guy,' I said, keen to seem knowledgeable.

'Right! Show's over,' old Winkler called out, realising he'd lost control of us. 'Let's get back to our seats.' The likelihood of us getting back to any semblance of work or concentration now was a big fat zero.

'Is he your mate then, Luke?' Connor called out as we slowly and grudgingly tore ourselves away from the spectacle. Connor remained at the window longer than the rest of us and had to be told a second time to sit down.

'No!' I replied as emphatically as I could without sounding fake. Protesting too much would get me caught out.

I got away with it.

The rest of the lesson involved us chatting and doing very little of the dull exercise placed before us.

We managed to watch a bit more of the football lesson outside as our Maths class was downstairs, overlooking the sports field. Guy kept running away from the ball. Then one time, when he did try to stop the opposition striker from getting past him by standing his ground, the on-coming player whacked the ball straight into his face. It must have really hurt, but we all laughed and squealed with pleasure. Old Winkler managed to get us back into our seats again.

I indicated to Connor and the others when Guy walked right past our classroom accompanied by the PE teacher. Guy's face was contorted into a howl of agony – red and covered in muddy tear stains. His high-pitched squeals seemed amplified by the window glass as he continued screaming like a little girl.

The timing of it couldn't have been more perfect. Our whole class laughed and even our teacher had to suppress a chuckle.

That night I ate my dinner quickly and locked myself in my bedroom, after promising the oldies I'd complete all my homework. Instead, I played *Organik Apokalypse* for a while before wasting a number of hours on the Internet, messaging mates and posting inane messages on people's profiles. Just before going to bed, I felt the urge to go to my tall cupboard and bring out my number one, carefully hidden, prized possession – my air pistol. It fitted perfectly in my grip as if it had been designed for me – a Desert Eagle .44 Magnum replica BB gun, loaded with twenty-five 6mm ball bearings. It was a top-quality copy with easy cocking, spring action, and a range of fifteen metres, in a chrome finish with black grip. It had cost £19.95 on Amazon and I'd used Dad's debit card with no problem. My only concern at the time had been that Mum or Dad would be in when it arrived, but as luck would have it I answered the door on delivery while home alone. My parents never check their bank statements, so I'd got away with the whole escapade scot-free. Laying it on my left palm I examined it from different angles, admiring what one review had called 'the sleek shape and the economy of design'. This classic Magnum remained the most powerful semi-automatic in the world, and used in so many Hollywood films. Eventually, I placed the air pistol under my pillow and got ready for bed. Anyone daring to break into this house or attack my family would get a nasty surprise.

I often woke up early and the next morning saw me rouse at 4.09 a.m. With a sudden burst of vigour I threw back the duvet and padded over to the window, where it was an easy matter to flick the curtains over my head and get a good view of the back garden. With careful fingers I propped open the corner of the net curtain, slipping one hand underneath until it reached the window catch. Noiselessly, I managed to open it four or five inches, shuddering at the sudden cold blast of air. As I peeked through the gap, keeping my head to windowsill level, there was enough light to make out the familiar shapes and dusky colours of the garden in the morning gloom. In the middle was the whirly-gig washing line, folded under its green canvas cover. The rockery displayed various shrubs that merged into a larger herbaceous border. Further down, the buddleia was still in its purplish bloom and white daisies poked through the green and brown, patchy lawn. The shed at the end had gone yellow with age underneath its black wonky roof.

Putting my hand slowly on the pistol tucked under my pillow I raised the treasured object towards the gap in the window, where I wedged it between the frames and steadied it with both hands. Knowing it to be fully loaded, I closed my left eye and tried to aim it with a sniper's precision. All I had to do was wait for a suitable target.

After only a few minutes of staring into the washed-out early morning light I saw a movement in next door's oak tree. A magpie flapped down from the branches and landed on the fence just below my window. Its long, black tail twitched as it stood still momentarily. Was it the same one? I stared at it with pure hatred.

I steadied my grip and felt my trigger finger twitch. Hold still. Squeeze slowly. The shot still made me jump. The magpie cracked its wings and flew away, shrieking and chattering loudly. I stayed stock still for a long time, worried the noise might disturb my parents. Lucky it wasn't a real Magnum or the whole street would have woken from the explosive report, whilst the recoil would have blown me backwards across the room.

But nobody stirred.

Damn! I could've sworn I'd hit the stupid thing.

Suddenly, a squirrel bounded across the top of the fence and threw itself at the tree, sticking to the bark as if it had Velcro on its paws. It disappeared up the tree in a spiral. It didn't remain still long enough for me to take a proper shot.

About five minutes later the magpie returned – or at least, I assumed it was the same bird. It landed on the lawn and began pecking the ground. This time I knelt up higher, hoping the people in the houses opposite wouldn't spot me – if they were even awake. I'd remembered not to put any lights on, but still had to be careful.

The black feathers of the magpie flashed with iridescent blue. It stayed still for quite a few moments entirely within the gun's sight. The nozzle of the pistol went right through the open window as I rested my arm on the bottom window frame.

Hold still. Ready. Squeeze. Got him! Yaaay.

The magpie attempted to fly away, but had been injured enough to stop from taking off. Instead, the momentum of the pellet knocked it sideways onto the path, where it lay flapping pathetically. I made sure I closed the window as quietly as possible.

Chapter Three

You could only approach the huge roundabout via the flyover, which took me over the dual carriageway that led to the motorway slip-road. The roundabout, or at least the junction, was known locally as Coney Island because it always teemed with rabbits. It was hardly New York, although the giant pillars made me think of the term 'concrete jungle'. You saw the rabbits best at night if you drove past in the darkness; your headlights caught all the red eyes and millions of them scampered around the grassy outer edges of the big roundabout. The middle of the island was a gigantic tangle of bushes and trees which reached right up to the road crossing directly above it, just touching it with its branches.

I patted my jacket pocket to check the whereabouts of my trusty Magnum Desert Eagle.

I'd often wondered what else lived in that overgrown wilderness – perhaps some new species or weird hybrid animal? Or a family of psychotic cannibal mutants who only came out at night to hunt down unsuspecting victims? As I approached Coney Island, a lyric from an Elvis Presley song came into my head. 'You ain't never caught a rabbit and you ain't no friend of mine.' My parents were obsessed with the so-called King of Rock'n'Roll, and even choreographed embarrassing dances to his songs. The idea of catching a rabbit appealed to me at that moment. They were pests – vermin – weren't they? Farmers shot them all the time, right? I felt strangely drawn to the wilderness of the roundabout. No rabbits were visible just then, but I felt compelled to sneak in and see if I could at least see one, if not shoot it.

I ignored the beeping horns as I sprinted across the dual carriageway, and only just avoided the cars approaching at ninety miles per hour. I scrambled onto the grassy edge of the roundabout, aware of dirty looks from drivers passing closely by, jogged over to the first tree, and hid behind it. I hunkered down with my back to the trunk, determined to stay hidden from the cars. Nobody would care about me being here. Most people were in too much of a rush to reach their own destination to bother about some kid messing about on a roundabout.

It really was a dense wilderness. While the strip all around the edge was neatly mown and dotted with wild flowers, the middle section was a jungle. Grass grew taller than me; brambles made the way through look impossible; bushes and trees wove their unwelcoming branches into an impenetrable fortress. The first thing to do was complete a recce of this uncharted land to find any openings.

I wanted to get as deep into it as I could. Right to the middle. Away from the civilised edge. Crouching down on the floor to avoid being seen, I found I could get quite far by wriggling on my elbows and knees, like a lizard skittering through the undergrowth. No obvious entrance existed on this side. If the other side proved the same then I'd be forced to get a stick and hack my way through. In this prone position I became aware of millions of irritating flies and insects trying to get into my mouth or up my nose. My throat began to itch and go dry, but I was determined to continue. Down here I also got a close-up view on the round, pebble-like scatterings of rabbit poo. It was impossible to move without squashing some against my clothing. I tried to keep my hands away from it.

As I slithered further round I reached the gigantic concrete plinth which held up the flyover overhead. Once I'd inched between its gravelly wall and a big, spiky bush I could scrabble to my feet and stand without being seen at all. With my back against this wall I felt completely hidden and free to move, knowing I'd be completely invisible now to the outside world. Past the bush I reached a little clearing – after being covered in strands of spider web, which I had to wipe from my face and hair. On the patchy grass lay a few beer cans, torn wrappers, and bits of plastic – evidence that I wasn't the first explorer here. I quickly got over the disappointment. The cans looked rusty and had probably been there for a number of years.

I sat down against the concrete wall. Through my back I felt the vibrations and rumblings of the traffic zooming above my head. I hoped the noise might conceal my presence from the rabbits. Where did those stupid fluffy bastards hang out? I took out my Magnum. With that in my hand, I would be the king of Coney Island.

A scream to my left startled me. My heart pounded and I nearly tumbled over a tree root, but I held my nerve and stayed still, trembling. I saw a magpie hop into my grassy space – as if the space belonged to him. He didn't look too happy to see me, and I wondered if it had come to exact revenge upon me. It stared at me with hateful eyes; its head cocked sideways as birds do, then flapped its wings and screeched like a demented maraca – 'Chacker chacker chacker!' – before hopping away and flying off. Bloody bird! I'd have been happy to empty a whole magazine of pellets into it.

So where were these sodding rabbits then? I needed to penetrate the undergrowth; reach the heart of darkness. There must be a whole colony of them in there somewhere. Of course – rabbits burrowed down, so they would be right underneath my feet. I was probably standing on thousands of them right then. I tried to imagine the intricate maze of tunnels underground, filled with hot-blooded little vermin, and began to formulate methods and list various apparatus that might be required for complete decimation of the warren.

I decided to push further into the undergrowth, trying to ignore the presence of nettles and thorny spiked bushes. Pulling my hand into the sleeve of my sweatshirt, I gripped the cuff inside my clenched fingers for use as a makeshift machete. I karate chopped at the twigs, branches, and brambles that appeared in my way above waist height, and even more rabbit poo became evident.

As I slowly progressed inwards I considered what an amazing place this would be to have a den. No-one would ever find it. It would be a place just for me when I needed to escape from the endlessly sad reality of life. Clouds of midges swarmed into my eyes and mouth. I had to keep my hand in front of my face as I moved as much for the spider webs as the branches and bramble runners. My sleeve was already absolutely covered in goosegrass – those pesky little spiked seeds which are impossible to pull off woolly clothes.

I couldn't imagine there was far to get to the middle now, although the diameter of the roundabout was clearly bigger than I'd first envisaged. To my surprise the undergrowth thinned out, leaving a glade which looked like it had been purposefully created. Just left to nature it would surely be overgrown with weeds and bushes. Instead I found myself looking into an almost perfectly spherical hole – as if I'd just climbed inside a giant ball. Not much light reached in this far, so I found myself squinting slightly to judge its dimensions: I reckoned it was a similar size to my bedroom.

At first I stayed where I was; hidden behind a bush and peering into the hole. As my eyes got used to the partial gloom I could see that the ground was covered in short, lush grass. Just then, a movement attracted my attention up ahead. A rabbit! The little creature had crept out of the undergrowth opposite to casually nibble the grass. The sound of me scratching my chin was enough to alert the rabbit into sitting bolt upright, where it sniffed the air and turned its head each way four or five times. Then it released a string of brown pellets from under its tufty white tail. The rabbit seemed to be aware of me, but perhaps did not consider me a threat, because it returned to its nibbling; by which time half a dozen more rabbits appeared from nowhere. I sat stock still, content now simply to observe.

I slowly raised the gun to my eye line.

Just as I began to wonder if one would come close enough for me to shoot it, I heard a different sound; one I recognised but couldn't pin down. Breathing? Something moving behind me? I looked around for movements. But how long should I stand still, waiting for the thing to move again? After a long pause I decided I was being a wimp, so I moved onwards.

Then a crack sounded. Was that me or something following me? I turned my head slowly round, but could only see a thick tangle of branches and leaves. I thought I saw a movement then but it could've been a shadow.

Stop being such a nonce.

As I stepped on it occurred to me that here in the thick undergrowth there were no shadows. So what had I seen?

The next noise was definitely not my imagination. Something lay in wait for me up ahead; no doubt about it. Was that a dark figure crouching over there? I stared at it, with my confidence draining, but the more I stared, the more I could see it was only a mound of earth.

I started to regret being trapped in here now, but I couldn't give in. What sort of man would that make me? Get a grip.

Realising I'd been holding my breath, I let it out slowly and continued towards where I hoped the rabbits were.

Breathing. There it was again. Then something moved to my left. It was large too. Another snapping sound made me start to feel scared. A fleeting movement made me turn to the right. And a short grunt reached me. Was that an animal or human sound? I prepared myself to run. Or to run as quickly as I could through this undergrowth. But I mustn't panic. I could do this.

Then a sigh sounded directly in my ear. I felt the breath on my neck.

I'd been caught. I froze petrified. My mind struggled between the instinct to get up, fight, and bolt, or to remain calm and turn around, slowly and with confident control. My earlier idea about cannibals came back to haunt me. Or what if it was some huge beast? I remained locked with my back now to whoever – or whatever – it was. Should I flick my head around, or not? I clenched my fists in readiness. I kept expecting to hear a noise or feel a hand clamp down on me. Eventually I summoned up the strength to count silently to three. On three I whipped my head around and brought my gun up to defend myself. No-one there…

I'd spooked myself out for nothing, and I returned the Magnum to my jacket pocket.

Berating myself with a hiss – half laugh, half sigh of relief, I shook my head and turned back to watch the rabbits.

Shit!

There – just a few inches in front of me – was Guy.

I felt his hot breath. It smelt stale and its reek clung to the insides of my nostrils. But still I couldn't move. His black hair fell in matted curls around his eyes and his teeth were yellow and jagged. To my horror he leaned in until his nose touched my cheek. And then he sniffed me. I swear it. He sniffed me! Like he was some kind of dog testing to see if I was friend or foe. His cold blue eyes scanned my entire face; covered the whole area only a few centimetres from my skin. And then he suddenly pulled his head away from me and scampered back to the middle of the glade now filled with rabbits.

What the...?

Bloody freak! He's more of a nut-job than I first thought. Part of me screamed to leave right then, another part of me wanted to find out more about this weirdo. Was he some kind of pikey? I was annoyed that he'd clearly found this place first. I stayed where I was for a while, confused and intrigued.

He didn't give me a second look after the very close inspection. Instead I watched him with mounting curiosity. What the hell was he doing here? How had he got there without me hearing him?

My fascination grew as Guy fell over playfully onto the grass. The rabbits swarmed over the clearing. He lay on his back and the rabbits came to him. They clambered on top of him, nuzzling his hands and face and hopping out the way happily when he shifted or rolled over. He played with them as if it were the most natural thing in the world. They appeared to respond to his every movement and sound. The rabbits crowded the space in their hundreds and yet all their movements were synchronised like liquid, flowing this way and that.

I watched him interacting with the rabbits until I wondered why the hell I was still there. Why was I so intent on watching this freak frolicking about? Had I suddenly turned into some kind of wimp who loved fluffy bunnies? Or worse ... watching boys roll around in the grass? Hell! What was happening to me?

One part of me wanted to leap forward and punch this saddo really hard in the face. Maybe I could stomp on a few rabbits for good measure. Watch their guts and brains ooze out under my shoe, whose soles I could then wipe clean on Guy's shirt. That would be an awesome virtual reality computer game:

Rabbit Stomper – with sensor pads on your feet, squishing hundreds of bunny brains. I could make millions ...

Actually, there was something entirely interesting and mysterious about him. His incredibly strange behaviour was both intriguing and embarrassing at the same time. Certainly, if the others at school knew my parents were friends of his I'd never hear the end of it and might just as well commit suicide. It would surely be social suicide to actually hang out with him.

Without really thinking it through I stepped out into the clearing, but as I did so, all the nearby rabbits skittered away. Instead I just found a place to stand, and waited.

Guy jumped up with impressive agility and walked boldly towards me. His eyes darted around, as if checking different parts of me randomly before putting all the images together in his mind. I was grateful he didn't sniff me again, but his lips definitely twitched into a smile.

Then he put out a hand – more in greeting than in intimacy. I offered mine cautiously and they gripped each other. His skin felt surprisingly gnarled and hard. I pulled my hand away quickly and began to retreat. He didn't react, he just watched me with a look of curiosity as I backed off.

Deciding not to look back again, I shoulder barged my way through the thicket in a direct line. It wasn't the same way I had entered, but I just wanted to find my way outside as quickly as possible. I burst through the final section of undergrowth, feeling something scratch my cheek as I found myself back on the grassy edge, surrounded by speeding cars.

Waiting for a gap in the traffic, I put my head down and ran across the two lanes, pumping my arms wildly. Nobody hooted at me this time. The bank looked really steep now, but I hauled myself up it by gripping clumps of weeds until I reached the flyover. Then it proved a simple matter of leaping over the barrier, crossing that road, and then jogging home without stopping.

Chapter Four

Maths again. I lose count how many times we have to suffer the torture of Maths lessons. It seems like we have to study it about seven times a day. I know that can't be right, but it would explain why I wasn't very good at the subject. Actually, I'm OK – I can do the sums – I just don't understand what it's for or why. Maths was invented to stop young people getting bored and causing trouble. I can't see any other useful application for most of it. It's hard to care what the value of x might be. When a teacher asks me I feel like shouting, 'If you're so bothered then work it out for yourself!' I must admit though, I haven't actually summoned up the courage to do it yet, but imagining myself doing it gets me through the hour-long lessons.

This was at least my third maths lesson of the week and we gave a big cheer when we saw we would have a cover teacher instead of old Wrinkly Winkler. This cover teacher looked even older than Mr Winkler. She had obviously dyed red hair and way too much make-up for an old bag in at least her sixties. Connor turned round and gave me and Simon a smirk as she screamed for us all to be quiet. This was going to be fun.

She tried her best, bless her, but she clearly wasn't a Maths teacher, and she appeared to hate teenagers; which seemed odd for someone in her chosen profession. To be fair, she never stood a chance with us. Connor did his 'I don't understand the work' routine, claiming to have special educational needs – which was untrue – and therefore wasn't expected to get through the work as quickly as everyone else.

Cheryl and her cronies point blank refused to work and sat with their arms folded instead.

'But it's well boring, miss. You can't make me do it. You're not allowed to touch me. What you gonna do about it? You come near me, I'll sue you.'

The poor old dear tried reasoning with them but Cheryl just got more and more stroppy and half the class went on strike. The cover teacher decided to ignore those not working and help the dozen or so keenos who were keeping their heads down and doing as they were told. Connor, Simon, and I chatted merrily without being bothered or told to keep quiet. As a class we were making quite a racket, and the old bag had mostly given up on us, returning to her desk and frequently checking her watch. I waited for the right moment to perform my party trick.

Exactly halfway through the lesson I raised my hand, but she was trying to pretend we weren't there and was staring absently out of the window. I stood up and waved my hands wildly as if on a clifftop, trying to attract the attention of strangers many miles away.

'Yoo-hoo! Hello! Miss Cover Teacher! Are you alive?'

She suddenly came to when we all laughed, and she scowled on seeing me waving manically and pulling such exaggerated faces.

'Sit down, boy, and stop being so silly.' She got up and came over to sort out the situation. I really think she was now just hoping it would end quickly. She obviously wanted to get through it without any major incident, but I was now ruining this hope.

I remained standing. 'But miss, I need to go to the toilet.'

'You know as well as I do that's against the school rules.' She stood in front of me with her arms folded.

'But I've got a medical condition with my bladder.'

She paused for a few seconds to consider this option.

'So you'll have a medical pass then?' She smiled triumphantly and raised her eyebrows as if waiting for my response.

'I've lost it, miss. I swear. I think I left it at home today, but you can check with my tutor if you want.'

Connor suddenly decided to join in.

'It's true, miss, he has. I can vouch for him. He always goes to the loo. He's got this pass thingy …'

'Excuse me, young man, but this has nothing to do with you.'

She gave him an evil stare and Connor sucked his teeth loudly before turning back to his desk.

'Miss, I'm desperate. I'll be really quick.'

'No.'

'But I really can't control it.'

'Which part of "no" are you struggling with, exactly? Is it the "n" or the "o"?'

It was a classic stand-off. Who'd buckle first? I brought out my trump card.

'Please, miss, I need you to believe me. The doctor diagnosed me as having prostatitis with suspected interstitial cystitis. It's also known as BPS – Bladder Pain Syndrome. I have to take tablets twice a day, a combination of amitriptyline and antihistamine – which helps rebuild the wall of the bladder.'

It always worked. It deserved to after spending so many hours on various websites finding information about it.

The cover teacher's face puckered up for a moment as she stared through slitted eyes.

'Be as fast as you can. I'm timing you. If you take longer than three minutes I'll keep you behind. And I suggest you don't leave your medical pass behind again. I might not feel so kind next time.'

She swept round and marched back to her desk. As she did so I jogged out of the class, high-fiving Connor, Simon, and then Pete who sat at the front by the door.

I went to the back of the school and hung around for a while out of sight of any classrooms and waited ten minutes, texting Connor and Simon. By the time I returned, nobody in the class was doing any work. The poor old dear had completely given up and was reading her book at the desk while practically everyone else was furtively throwing around a tennis ball. The game was to chuck it a little further and harder each time without her looking up. Those not involved in the game either chatted or checked their phones.

It was while the tennis ball game was in full swing that Simon brought up the subject of Guy.

'That new kid – you know, the well skanky one – I had to sit

27

next to him in ICT, yeah. Man, he stinks. He is rank. Have you seen his clothes? He kept getting closer to me and touching me. I had to push his chair away like this – and keep one hand over my nose so I didn't have to breathe in his stink, you know? What a loser.'

Connor pulled a face. 'Yeah, if that saddo comes anywhere near me again I'll smash his face in. He needs to understand respect. You know what I mean? Don't you think?' He turned to me directly.

'Yeah!' I nodded with a frown. 'What a sad loser he is, man. He needs to get a life. He's always crying like a baby.'

'He probably wets his bed, too,' Simon chortled.

'Yeah, I heard he wet himself in a lesson,' I heard myself say. Why the hell did I do that? I'd just told a big fat lie merely to look cool and in-the-know with my mates. It was too late to turn back now.

'Really? What happened?' Now half the class were listening in on our conversation.

'Um, yeah, definitely. I can't remember what lesson it was now. But the teacher asked him a question and he literally wet himself.'

'Eurgghh!'

I began enjoying the limelight.

'He was just standing there in the middle of the class with pee running down his leg and he was wading in this massive puddle.'

Three or four girls were shrieking now. 'Oh gross!'

'Talk about taking the piss,' Simon quipped. 'You don't need to take it out of him because it's already on the floor.'

Luckily, nobody seemed too bothered about the details; like when it had happened, why nobody else had spoken about it, and why no-one in the room had been present at the incident or even knew anyone who had been. The story was too good to disbelieve and was exactly what everyone wanted to hear – so it must be true. In fact whether it was true or not seemed irrelevant. I enjoyed the attention, and being considered an expert on the matter.

Only Cheryl responded differently.

'The little love. I think he's sweet.'

Suddenly all the girls changed their minds and started saying how he needed a hug and was 'really sweet … ah, bless.'

This reaction upset Connor. 'That little freak is even taking away our bitches now.'

'We is not bitches!' Cheryl screeched. 'We's ladies.'

This caused a great deal of hilarity. The cover teacher looked up gingerly, shook her head, and returned to the safety of her book.

With only a few minutes left to go of the lesson, Connor got up, called for the tennis ball which he caught in one hand, stood exactly in the middle of the classroom and threw the ball really hard at the wall about a metre above the cover teacher's head. It hit the wall with a loud crack and flew back into his hands.

The cover teacher looked up slightly confused, checked her watch, smiled, packed up her things, and walked out without another word.

My story about Guy spread through the school like a stink-bomb. I heard it from at least four other people and it had even developed a few extra details. In one version he'd done a poo on the floor, which didn't make any sense, but the chance to laugh at someone other than yourself was too much for us all to resist.

Chapter Five

I always walked faster going home than I did to school. That afternoon I found Mum weeding the front garden flowerbeds as part of her 'big tidy up'. Once a year she 'blitzed' the house and garden, generating about ten full-to-the-brim black bin bags, which I always had to help empty at the local recycling centre.

'Hi, Luke,' Mum called as I pushed open the gate. 'There's a spare pair of gardening gloves here for you.'

'Oh, um, sorry ... I've got lots of homework to do,' I improvised, hoping to scurry past and up to my room.

'I've done most of the front and back and just have the house to complete now.' She stood up and took off her gloves as she faced me. It would have been rude to just walk away. 'How was school?'

'Yeah – the usual.'

'I keep meaning to ask how Guy is getting on.'

'Great, yeah. He's doing great.'

'Hope you're helping him settle in properly. He needs a friend right now. Poor thing with his mum so ill.'

'He seems fine. He's making friends and stuff.' I tried to sound casual.

'Oh, good. We must get them round again soon.'

'Great,' I said with a fixed neutral expression. 'Hey, you look like you need a cup of tea. Shall I put the kettle on?'

'Er ... yes. Wow. Thank you. Sounds wonderful.'

'You look like you deserve one after all this hard work.'

'Thank you, Luke. That's incredibly kind of you.'

I tried to ignore the faces of confusion and suspicion she pulled as she watched me enter the house to begin my good deed. OK, so I don't usually volunteer to make drinks ... that often ... or at all, actually.

31

Frisky met me in the kitchen, yowling for food. I put some cat biscuits into his bowl.

Then Mum decided to follow me into the kitchen and at first I thought she might be checking that I really was going to boil the kettle. Instead she insisted on asking me questions while I got the tea bags and mugs out.

'So you think he'll be OK then?'

'Who?' I asked, genuinely confused.

'Guy.'

She wasn't going to let it go. Did she know more than she was letting on? Perhaps his foster parents had already spoken to her and dobbed me in as being useless. I was a complete disappointment to my parents, anyway – and here was yet another reason to confirm their greatest fears.

'Sure. It's always tough starting somewhere new, but he'll be fine.'

'And you promise to look out for him? Help him out?'

'Yeah. 'Course.'

To my horror she pulled me in for a hug.

'Thanks, darling. I knew I could rely on you. He's got special needs, you understand, and must be treated with care. His mother is very ill. You see, he doesn't find it easy going to school. He's what's known as "school-phobic". I know some children can be quite mean to lads like him, but I hope you'll be different. He needs a friend, and people to be kind to him.'

What the hell was I supposed to do now? Talk about a guilt trip.

My mum always had these little pet projects; people she liked to help out. It was clear that Guy and his foster parents were her latest 'project' and she was relying on me. Great.

I stayed silent and let her squeeze me tightly and sway with me from side to side. She then held me at arm's length and smiled at me, waiting for me to do the same.

As soon as I could I escaped her clutches and continued with the tea-making.

'Oh, you'll never guess what I found today,' Mum said, sitting down at the breakfast bar. 'A dead magpie. Grief, it was disgusting. Must have been killed by a fox or something. It was stiff and yucky. Eugh! Just thinking about it now makes my skin crawl.'

'Gross,' I said, adding the milk. 'In the front garden?' My eyes blinked innocently as I tried not to react in a manner that would give me away.

'No – the back. I think I uncovered an ants' nest too. I'll have to get your dad on to that or else they'll get into the house like they did last year.'

'Where is the magpie now?'

'I put it on the compost heap. Used a shovel.'

She shivered again.

I was relieved that she hadn't noticed the pellet wounds in the magpie and had just put it down to nature's scheme of things. I finished the cups of tea, which we drank in the kitchen, while discussing Mum's cleaning plans. She had what she called 'wacky, exciting' ideas about rearranging the cupboards and their contents, so I had to spend about half an hour nodding and pretending to listen, worried that I'd nod when I should shake my head. I got away with it.

Eventually, Dad returned home and I went with him to the recycling centre – really just a new name for the dump – before it closed. My life really is a never-ending rollercoaster! Funny thing was I went to find the dead magpie but it wasn't there – perhaps Frisky had eaten it.

Then my worst nightmare came true. I was hanging about in the locker area with Simon and Pete when Simon nudged me. I turned my head in the direction he was looking and there stood Guy. I checked the other two weren't suspicious about his presence and gave Guy a snarling, dirty look. He just smiled and gave me a really camp wave, his elbow tucked in against his ribs and a quick shake of his floppy hand as if he was about three years old.

'Who the hell are you lookin' at, incontinence boy?' Simon hissed aggressively. He turned to me to check my reaction. I couldn't be seen to be anything other than against this boy who had so quickly become the laughing stock of the entire school.

'Yeah! Sod off, you weirdo,' I said with as much conviction

as I could manage.

Seeing his face redden and his eyes moisten made me angry. Something inside me really made me want to hit him. Survival instincts, I guess.

'I can't see any wet patches yet, can you?' Pete laughed.

'No,' Simon giggled, 'but if we stay near him much longer we'll be paddling in his piss.'

'The whole school'll be flooded,' Pete snorted.

'Yeah,' I said with half a smile. 'And we ain't got our scuba gear on. Let's go.'

I pulled the other two away, so that the teasing would stop and I wouldn't have to look Guy in the face any more.

The other two came with me as I pulled them, although Simon just could not resist having the final word.

'Don't cwy, wickle baby,' he said in a stupid voice, pretending to rub both eyes with his fists. 'Mummy will give oo some yummy milk and wock oo to sleep.'

We walked off laughing, although I felt guilty about the reference to his mum. Pete kept repeating the name 'incontinence boy' and that's how we referred to him from then on. Simon later took to calling him 'that wee lad' in a bad Scottish accent – followed by a self-approving snigger.

Later that same day I was in the dinner queue with Connor when Guy brushed past me with his tray.

'Oi, watch it!' Connor shouted on my behalf.

Guy looked up shyly. 'S-sorry. It was an accident.' Then he saw me. 'Oh, hi, Luke. How are you?' His whiny, high-pitched voice made the incident even worse.

Connor stared at me. 'Do you know this tosser? Is he your friend or something?'

It felt as though the entire school had stopped to watch me; like I'd been sucked into a momentary vacuum of silence and anticipation.

'Friend?' I sneered. 'He ain't no friggin' friend of mine. Get lost, piss-pants.' The world carried on as usual, except for Guy who continued looking directly at me; his eyes boring into my very being. Then he broke away and walked off without looking back. I struggled to concentrate in French that afternoon.

Chapter Six

That night I remember suddenly sitting up in bed. I reached out gingerly for the glass of water I'd brought up with me. Lifting it to my lips I took a big gulp. Something hard rolled between my tongue and teeth, forcing me to spit out the water in a wide spray. Water dribbled down my chin, but I'd managed to eject the small, unidentified object. What was it? A spider? What would've happened if I'd swallowed it? It could have laid millions of eggs inside me which would hatch into creatures ready to consume my whole body slowly from the inside out. I even managed to spook myself out with the thought.

After creeping out of bed, I sneered at my own stupidity and retrieved the sacred Desert Eagle, reloading it with fresh ball-bearings. Through the already open window I scanned the garden for moving targets. Nothing stirred in the large oak tree, still visible against the light of the moon and stars. Then I heard the sound I'd been waiting for, like a girl screaming. It was a vixen. That was my dream prey – a fox. I ran the film through my head; of me shooting it, cutting off the brush tail, and taking it into school to impress the lads and scare the girls. It would be like in the old days when hunters brought back the heads of lions and antelopes as trophies and stuck them on the wall. How cool would that be?

And then ... from behind the back fence I saw a shadow – exactly fox sized and shaped. Yes! Luck favoured me, it seemed. I could just make out the fox's form slinking round the edges of the garden, sniffing out for rubbish and things to scavenge. Now it was mine. I held the pistol firmly until the shadow was squarely in my sights. Squeeze gently. Stay calm. No sudden movement. Was this what it was like to be a sniper? A cold-hearted killer? There must be no emotion, just a thorough, swift job. No trail or clue left behind. The repeater mechanism allowed me to pump half a dozen pellets into the soft flesh. No mercy ... no surrender. Take no prisoners: shoot first, ask questions later.

I donned yesterday's jeans and T-shirt and tiptoed cautiously out of my bedroom, taking care not to tread on the two squeaky steps on the stairs. Luckily, Mum and Dad were heavy sleepers. Once I'd negotiated the stairs it was an easy job to get to the kitchen, grab the carving knife from the wooden block, pocket a small torch, and unlock the back door. I slipped on my dad's wellies – which was a mistake as they were way too big and I had to arch my toes up as I walked to stop them falling off.

What the hell was I supposed to do with the body? Hell! – I hadn't really thought this one through properly. Would I get away with chucking it over the fence and pleading ignorant? Probably not. Wait, behind the shed was a whole pile of rotten waste, now a compost heap. It reeked because Dad never got round to sorting it out. It wouldn't be found in there – or by the time it had, it would be just a skeleton. No one would be any the wiser.

Gripping the knife tightly, I took a deep breath and shuffled in the big boots towards the back fence. I could make out a crumpled, furry body just ahead of me in the scant light of the half-moon. I felt a moment of pathos. Here was death, that big scary thing everybody feared the most. I was in the presence of death. And yet I didn't feel scared. It was just a load of bones in a fur coat. Then I remembered that there might be blood. Would I actually have the courage to touch it? It felt like a rite of passage, one of those moments in my life when I might finally be growing up and really becoming independent.

As I inched forward I bent down, close to the furry heap. I squinted a little in the gloom and stared at my night's work. Something was wrong. I fumbled in my pocket for the torch and flicked it on, looked again at the body, and switched it off abruptly.

I snatched up the soft, still-warm heap and gasped. No! Surely not! I brought it nearer to my face and cursed myself. It wasn't a fox at all.

Frisky! I'd killed Frisky! I fell to my knees.

Limp and inert. Now I recognised the beautiful tabby markings. What the hell had I done? Dropping the dead cat, I jammed my hand over my mouth and silently sobbed. Convulsions took over my body.

What was going on?

What the hell was he doing outside? He never went outside. The family pet had been a part of my life for ten years. This was worse than terrible. My whole body shook uncontrollably. How would I ever be able to explain this? I couldn't leave the body there – I'd be found out. I had to think quickly.

In the shed was a spade and fortunately Mum and Dad's bedroom was round the front, so they wouldn't hear a thing. Quickly finding it, I took it behind the shed where there was a metre gap between it and the fence. The sickly sweet stink filled my nostrils. Hot and hampered by the darkness, I quickly cleared a little space. As I pulled back old twigs and rotten grass cuttings, I felt something scamper over my boot. A rat? It spooked me out so much that in the end I didn't bother digging a hole. Instead, I used the spade to open up the compost heap about halfway down, then picking up the dead cat, dropped it in and pushed the top back down again. Soon Frisky's body was well hidden, not only in the compost heap, but by all the debris cluttering up that space, where I could only desperately hope nobody would investigate in the near future.

Now I had to consider what to do when Frisky was discovered to be missing. Cats often disappear. I would offer to design a lost cat poster and be forced to play-act for several days.

Remembering to replace the spade in the shed, I picked up the knife and returned to the kitchen, locking the back door carefully. I washed and dried the knife, then crept stealthily upstairs. Back in my room I realised I'd stupidly left the BB gun openly on my bed. Thank God neither Mum nor Dad had come in. I scrambled out of my jeans and T-shirt and climbed back into bed, cradling the Desert Eagle to my chest, having switched on the safety catch.

My head began to throb. A pain behind my eyes slowly spread to my temples and then to my neck. The pain became more acute and stopped me from sleeping. I just lay there in a panic. How stupid am I? There was nobody else to blame this time. Frisky's death was my fault. I'd have to live with it, haunting me forever.

So I lay awake all night. By the time the radio alarm went off I felt drained and ached all over. I heard Mum coming to check I was awake as she always did on the way to the shower. As the door opened I realised I still held the air pistol, so I rapidly shoved it under the pillow.

'I don't feel too good today,' I croaked, attempting to sound pathetic.

'Come on, Luke, you can't miss school just because you feel tired. Your father and I have got things to do and we can't stay at home to look after you. You'll be fine once you're up and washed. Please don't give us hassle.'

'You need to man up, son,' came Dad's voice from the landing.

I heard Dad go downstairs. I waited. Had I left any clues of my night-time adventure? But I could only hear Dad whistling above the noise of the kettle.

Once I got into the shower, I heard through the open window Dad calling for Frisky and my heart sank as I thought through the potential consequences of my stupidity. Then I heard Mum and Dad had an animated discussion about the cat. I scrubbed my face and got ready for my award-winning performance in the role of 'innocent young kid'.

I'd never told quite so many lies before breakfast, but I held my nerve as so far, no clues could possibly lead to me. Could they? I'd covered my tracks pretty well. When Mum started crying I felt truly awful and considered blurting out the truth, but I knew I mustn't weaken and that things would soon blow over. Not yet, but in a few days' time I might suggest the possibility of getting a cute, fluffy little kitten. That should distract my parents' attention away from me.

Pulling my school bag over my shoulder, I resigned myself to another day's complete boredom in the classroom. I turned to say goodbye.

'Oh, it looks like another sunny day today. I think I'll wash the bed sheets. Can you make sure all whites are in the basket, please.'

The image of Mum stripping my bed suddenly made me panic. The gun! It was under my pillow!

'Oh, I'll do my bed for you, Mum.'

Mum was, understandably, taken aback. 'Oh, thanks. That would be kind.'

'Well, I know you're busy and I'd hate to cause you extra trouble.'

'Sure. You carry on. I'll be up in a sec to help.'

I'd never run up the stairs so quickly. I dashed into the room, slid my hand under the pillow, grasped the gun, and slotted it into the small opening in the zip of my schoolbag. Once that was done I wheeled round just as Mum reached the top of the stairs.

'Wow. This is a first – someone helping me to do some housework. More than your father does.' She'd already ripped off the duvet and untucked the fitted sheet. I pulled the pillows from their cases and helped to peel the duvet from its covering.

'Thank you very much, sir,' said Mum in her still-surprised tone. 'Please feel free at any time whatsoever to help me again.'

I saluted, patted my bag, and scarpered.

Chapter Seven

No Guy at school. In fact, he didn't come in for the rest of the week. It could have been because he was ill, but more likely it had something to do with what Mum said – that he was school-phobic. Phobia means fear, so that must mean Guy was scared of going to school, which sounded a bit wimpy to me. Sometimes in life you've got to get a grip; man up, grit your teeth, and get on with it. Then I wondered if I could be school-phobic for a while and have some time off, because on the face of it, it actually sounded like a good plan. Maybe Guy wasn't such an idiot after all.

As usual Simon was waiting for me by the front gates, slightly away from the older group of stoners who stood by the tree on the corner smoking. As I walked past them, I saw the roll-up being handed around, and wondered what it was like to sit through double science in a stoned haze. Perhaps it made Mrs Blewitt's lessons slightly more interesting. After all, they usually ruined my Friday morning. She even managed to make sex sound dull; according to her, human reproduction is merely functional and slightly unpleasant. It almost put me off thinking about it.

The smokers, older kids I didn't really know, approached me with snarls and vicious expletives, generally translating as advice to move away swiftly and not return in the foreseeable future. Simon and I gladly obliged them.

'Got something to show you, Si,' I gestured secretively, as we dawdled into the school grounds. Simon looked round in the manner of a spy scanning the area for enemy agents.

'What is it, mate?'

'Here,' I said, opening my bag surreptitiously. 'Look but don't touch.'

Simon craned his neck and peered into the darkness of the

sports bag.

'Bloody hell, Luke! You going to shoot the teachers? Bit of a drastic way of avoiding doing work, isn't it?' Simon's face contorted comically. 'Have you lost the plot or what?'

'I'm not actually going to use it, you prat.' I frowned, upset by this negative reaction.

'Why'd you bring it school then?' Simon still looked at me in disbelief.

'It's a long story. Cool though, eh?'

'Er ... suppose so. Yeah,' Simon replied. His continued lack of enthusiasm was really irritating.

'But it's a Desert Eagle ... Magnum.'

'Is it?'

'Oh, flippin' hell man, you're no good. All the big Hollywood action stars use this gun – Arnie, Stallone, Van Damme, Will Smith. Angelina Jolie. Haven't you seen *The Matrix*? Agent Smith uses one.' I took a position and changed my expression as I attempted an impression of the character. 'Mr Anderson – we meet again.''

Simon laughed politely to show his recognition and when I pretended to shoot him with his fingers Simon performed the classic slow-mo 'bullet-time' reaction – bending backwards until almost in the crab position.

'What are you two nonces up to now?'

I zipped up my bag and slung it swiftly over my shoulder before spinning round to see Connor approaching.

'You wusses working out a dance routine, are you? Come and play football ... or are you too scared to join in a real man's game?' His laugh sounded like the hiss of a punctured tyre.

'Yeah, OK,' Simon said, nodding in resignation. Connor always enjoyed tackling the opposition heavily on the tarmac, usually winding them and bruising a few ribs with his pointy elbows. Well, we'd have to give back as much as he gave. I nodded wryly.

'Great,' Connor chuckled. 'We need your bags as goalposts.'

I hoped I'd remembered to put on the safety catch.

Science was predictably dull. Mrs Blewitt showed us the

different parts of an insect: head, thorax, and abdomen. We labelled an expanded picture of a stag beetle; a gigantic beast – which I thought would look great in a jam jar. I copied the word 'antennae' from the text book, then, freehanded, drew a shaky line towards one of the feelers protruding from the photocopied beetle.

'Miss,' I called out without putting up my hand. 'Why can't we have real insects in the lab? You could keep them in a tank, you know, breed 'em. Then we could pin one down and dissect it.'

'Yeurgh!' shrieked two of the girls, turning around to scowl at me.

'What's wrong with that?' I asked shrugging. 'My dad said he used to dissect rats, frogs, and fish in his science lessons. Why can't we do something cool like that?'

'Oh, gross!'

'Be quiet, Luke,' Miss Blewitt called out from her desk. 'If you don't like the way we teach you then write a letter to the Minister for Education. I'm sure he'd be fascinated by your proposals.'

With a tut and sigh, which the teacher ignored, I sat back on my stool and looked around at everyone else working diligently.

Eventually, the bell went and I scarpered to my locker to grab my French book and sling in the science stuff.

Chapter Eight

As I trudged through the doorway of the Languages classroom, my way became blocked by the tall, dark-suited figure of Mr Saddler, the Deputy Head.

'Go and wait in my office,' he told me, then muttered something to the French teacher, who nodded earnestly and tapped something into the register on his laptop. Somewhat bemused, I turned slowly around and trudged back, then left towards the front offices. I'd done nothing wrong today, there was no need to worry. I stopped outside the door bearing his name and rank.

'Sit there.' He opened the door and pointed to a grey plastic chair.

I did as I was told and waited until I was spoken to. Saddler shut the door abruptly and sat at his desk with his back to me. I tried to imagine why I'd been summoned – perhaps as a witness to something? After a few moments Saddler swung around on his red, padded swivel chair and stared directly at me without blinking. The silence grew unbearable. I thought back through my recent behaviour, which I felt sure had been acceptable, unless that old bag Blewitt dobbed me in for calling out, but that hadn't been bad. I'd been talking about the work after all.

'You're in serious trouble, son.'

Silence.

'Sir?'

'You're going to wish you'd never been born.' The sinister calm of his voice caused my throat to dry and lungs to burst, as if I was about to have an asthma attack.

My head spun as I considered all the possibilities. Surely this was a case of mistaken identity?

Saddler spun around, then took a key from his jacket pocket and unlocked a drawer below the desktop. Something clattered on the papers but was obscured from my line of vision. Saddler turned back to face me with that snake-like stare.

'Do you recognise this?'

He pushed himself to one side, allowing me to finally see the small silver and black object lying inert on some official files and papers. My Desert Eagle! But that was safely in my bag inside my locker. I slowly closed my eyes and rubbed my eyebrows with the heel of my palm. Hell!

Saddler was enjoying every second. He finally had his man.

There was no point in lying. Saddler had obviously looked in my locker and struck gold, so denying it would merely make things worse – if they could be worse.

'You're a damn fool, lad.' Saddler shook his head sorrowfully. I could see the Deputy Head was beyond being angry; his tone was now pitiful. This was worse than being shouted at.

'Do your parents know you have this dangerous weapon?'

I shook my head. What else could I do? I felt an uncomfortable heat rising to my face.

'Sorry, I can't quite hear you.'

'No, sir.'

'Is there an age limit to owning one of these? Do you need a licence?'

'It's only an air pistol –'

'Yes, I know what it is, son, I'm not an idiot. It's still a serious offence to bring firearms to school. What the hell were you thinking?'

I let my head droop further.

'Personally, I think it's a matter for the police.'

This made me jump. Police? What was I being accused of? Murder?

'However, the Head prefers not to involve the police, so there we go. It's not my decision.' He checked his watch and signalled for me to stand up.

'I've already called your parents and we're going now to meet them at Mrs Fuller's office. You can explain your actions to me, and to them.'

Bile rose to my throat and I had to suppress the urge to gag. I tried to imagine my parents' reaction when they were phoned. They would be sitting in the Head's office now, listening politely as Mrs Fuller explained to them that their son was a psycho.

When I got there it was worse than I imagined. Mum sat weeping in the corner, balancing a cup of coffee on her trembling knee, and Dad was prowling in front of her, pacing up and down like a frustrated lion in a cage. As soon as I entered, ushered forcefully in by Mr Saddler, I heard Dad snarl and Mum speak through sobs.

'Oh, Luke. What have we done to deserve this?'

Dad comforted her with a hand on her shoulder. 'It's those bleedin' computer games he plays.'

Mrs Fuller motioned for Mr Saddler and me to sit on the two remaining chairs, so I slumped onto the nearest one.

'Move over. Now!' I'd never heard Mrs Fuller shout and was shocked by her ferocity. 'And sit up!' Saddler shoved me onto the chair by Dad but I refused to look at my parents.

'Now then. Where do we start?' Mrs Fuller began to chair the meeting with her usual efficiency and natural air of authority. 'Mr Saddler, perhaps you could furnish us with the facts.'

'Yes, thank you.' Saddler cleared his throat like a barrister summing up. 'This morning we had a tip off that some students were using cannabis outside the school. We located some of the main culprits by watching them on CCTV cameras installed outside the front of the school where they tend to congregate. Unfortunately, some of them couldn't be identified because of their hoods and hats. We closely observed their actions this morning and Luke here was one of the few that we did identify –'

'I've never taken drugs –' I spluttered.

'You be quiet! Let Mr Saddler finish and then you can have your say,' Mrs Fuller growled, her eyebrows angled down towards her nose.

'Thank you.' Mr Saddler was clearly enjoying himself and relishing the groans and tuts coming from my parents. 'Because of this video evidence we then decided to check those pupils'

47

lockers. While no illegal substances or evidence to that nature were uncovered, we did discover this object in his bag.' He fished the Desert Eagle from his jacket pocket and placed it on the Head's desk. 'This is quite clearly unacceptable behaviour and I recommend that he is permanently excluded. Our school has a zero tolerance procedure where drugs and weapons are concerned.'

I knew permanent exclusion meant being expelled, no second chance. This was serious.

'Thank you, Mr Saddler,' Mrs Fuller said. 'Now then, Luke, what do you have to say for yourself?'

After squirming in my seat, I sat up and attempted to speak as confidently as I could.

'I've never done drugs. I was with a friend outside the gate this morning, but I'm not part of that gang.' In desperation I turned to my parents, attempting to stay calm. 'Honest. I've not touched the stuff. I walked past them and they shouted at me. That's all.'

'So you know the students involved? You could name them?' Mrs Fuller narrowed her eyes as if formulating a new scheme. She seemed to be asking me to become a super grass. 'You understand that you're in deep trouble here?'

'Why, Luke?' Dad suddenly joined in the conversation. His words set off Mum again, who sipped the rest of her coffee between sniffs and coughs. 'Where the hell did you get a gun from?'

The stillness echoed in the confined space of the office. With my head dully throbbing, I had no answer to offer the four gawping adults. Instead I let out a lengthy sigh and gripped my temples with my thumb and middle finger.

'Silence is often a sign of guilt,' Saddler piped up immediately. 'I don't see why we should put up with such rude behaviour.'

'Luke,' Mrs Fuller said, ignoring Saddler. 'Possessing a weapon in school is a major infringement of the rules and I'm sure the governors would support me if I applied for your permanent exclusion. It would be upheld. Do you understand me so far?' She looked first at me and then at my parents. I nodded in my humiliation. 'The police would also be very interested, as would the local papers. However, I am willing to negotiate as this is your first offence.' She looked at Saddler, daring him to argue, but he sat back in his chair, folded his arms, and sighed. I realised that a chink existed here – however tiny. 'If you could identify the students involved with drugs, or at least the ringleaders, then I am willing to change your punishment to just a week's exclusion. Obviously that will look better on your record and for future references for jobs or colleges.'

Before I could reply, Dad spoke out.

'He's very grateful to you, Mrs Fuller, and he's more than willing to comply with your very reasonable request, aren't you?'

There was nothing else for it.

'Yes, miss.'

'Splendid. I'll leave you with a form to fill in, then your parents will take you home.' She spoke directly to them now in a sympathetic voice. 'Could you bring him back a week on Monday, shall we say at 8.45, to my office for his readmission interview?'

My parents stood up and nodded.

'And would you like me to destroy this evidence?' She waved towards my precious Desert Eagle.

'Thank you,' Dad replied, sounding more than grateful.

Then Mrs Fuller turned to me. 'I will need complete reassurance that this was a stupid, one-off error never to be repeated. I need to be convinced that you are sorry and will come back with a changed attitude. You'll report directly to me, and Mr Saddler will keep me informed of your daily progress. Over this next week you need to do some serious thinking about how to change for the better. You will also be expected to catch up on all missed work. Now go with Mr Saddler, who will give you the form. Shut the door behind you.'

As I re-entered the Deputy Head's office, I noticed Saddler's eyes glinting in a smug and somewhat sinister fashion.

Chapter Nine

A whole week off school. Result! On the face of it, this seemed an exciting prospect, but as I remembered the major black mark on my record and how I would have to continue doing work school sent by email, I gradually realised that being suspended might not be as great as it sounded. All my mates would be at school.

I finally explained to Dad how I got the gun and he decided to dock all future spending money until I'd paid him back in full. I was given loads of jobs to do around the house. And then my parents made a momentous decision.

'We'll be removing your games console from your bedroom today, Luke.'

'What? You can't do that –'

'Um, I think you'll find we can, actually,' Mum replied sharply. 'Who paid for that damn machine in the first place? Was it you? Hmm, let me think now. Oh, wait, it was us.'

I'd never heard Mum using sarcasm before. This was more unnerving than one of Saddler's lectures.

'Don't you start telling me what I can and can't do, either. Your father and I have had enough of your stupidity. I felt so ashamed sitting there in your school office. What sort of parents must they think we are?' She looked to her husband for support. He stood up and changed his expression to one of disgust.

'You heard what your mother said. No more blasted computer games, so stop arguing. You're going to catch up with all coursework and get on quietly. You stay out of trouble, do you hear?'

Over the next few days I grew progressively more bored. Beginning in a conscientious manner, and under the watchful eye of Dad, who'd taken a few days off work to monitor me, I

51

quickly caught up with various pieces of homework and reading. But doing work all day became intensely tedious. How I longed for a quick go on *Organik Apokalypse*.

Dad took me to town one afternoon, but I wasn't allowed to buy any games, only study aids and software to help with schoolwork and exams. Instead I had to endure the monotony of visiting furniture and department stores. When I found myself in Ikea for what seemed like three days I thought I was going to die of eternal boredom; even school was more fun than queuing in this dull place.

Frisky's disappearance was still upsetting Mum. I helped put up posters, she wrote statuses on various social network sites, and regularly phoned the vets for any news.

'He's got one of those identity chips, so if he's found they'll find our number.' Each time the phone went she grimaced.

How bad did I feel?

Then Mum and Dad dragged me out for a walk in the countryside one sunny afternoon.

'Come on, Luke,' Mum insisted. 'You need some fresh air and a break.'

'Can't I just watch telly?'

'Nope, you're coming with us. You might even enjoy yourself if you don't try too hard.' She threw my trainers in my direction, and I grumbled as I laced them up. Dad wore his ridiculously sad beanie hat he always wore on holiday, as well as those stupid Bermuda shorts that showed off his hairy legs. He swung the keys around his forefinger and called out chirpily:

'Your carriage awaits, madam, monsieur.'

After forty minutes' drive I snapped out of my semi-conscious trance and saw we'd entered a forest at the foot of the downs and stopped in a small car park. As we got out of the car, I was alarmed to hear Mum announce this as an ideal spot for a picnic. Picnic? How old was I? Five? I didn't want a picnic in some crappy place with nothing to do. Probably end up sitting in stinging nettles, anyway. At that very moment my head was surrounded by a cloud of flies. A midge alighted on my right arm, so I slapped it, squashing it into a red blot on my skin.

'It's too hot,' I moaned, stretching until all my limbs splayed out in a star.

'Stop whinging and look around you,' Dad retorted wearily. 'Look how beautiful the trees are – how the sun glints through the branches. The way the flowers add sprays of colour to the clearing. Then there's all the birds: chaffinches, blue tits, collared doves all living alongside squirrels and other fauna. What's your problem exactly?'

'It's boring.' I rolled my eyes.

'No, son.' I didn't expect Dad to get so angry. 'You are boring. Your miserable, negative attitude is boring. You're a stereotype – everything's boring according to you. You live in your own selfish little fishbowl of a world and think you're the only person in it – well, you're wrong. Look around you, there's a whole world out there – millions of other people struggling like you. There's a planet with amazing things going on right under your nose and you can't be bothered to take an interest in it. It's not boring – do you see? You are the one that's boring and I've had enough of you. Now shut up and stop making my life such a misery.'

All three of us remained silent for an inordinately long time. The only sound came from the crinkling of sandwich bags, followed by munching. To my horror Mum and Dad embraced, enjoying each other's company all the while ignoring me.

There was nothing left to say. I had no idea how to respond to Dad's sudden tirade. After eating my sandwiches, I started drinking a can of cola, and grabbed a packet of crisps, got up, and wandered off without a word. I even waited for the inquisition before strolling off but it never came. It seemed my parents were keen to see the back of me. Nice. It would serve them right if I got hurt or fell off a cliff. I wandered off, making sure I was hidden from their gaze. Downing the last of the drink I looked at the can and hurled the metal cylinder at a nearby tree. It clattered against the trunk and caused a number of birds to crack their wings in hasty fright.

'That's it,' I said aloud. 'Piss off, the lot of you.' The can rolled onto a patch of dirt between the grass and glinted in the bright sun. Even though I knew it could be a fire hazard, I frankly didn't care.

'Be better if the whole bloody forest was burnt to the ground.'

One bird remained in place though – hopping casually and flicking its head to watch me through one eye and then the other. A magpie. I was getting sick of seeing those dumb birds, so I picked up a pebble and threw it directly towards it. It was a poor shot, but enough to make the magpie flap away, squawking noisily.

As I wandered further away from my parents I ate my crisps, pouring them greedily into my mouth and dropping the crisp packet, which blew away in a breeze, before getting tangled at the base of a bush.

Then to my horror I realised my parents were actually just a little way behind me. I heard their voices first before they came into view. Hand in hand, Mum and Dad dawdled, pointing to various aspects of the landscape or to a bird flying overhead. They were coming out of the forest now and towards a path leading directly up into the downs.

'Oh, you know it's the right time for early orchids now,' Mum said with a friendly smile.

'For what?' I didn't respond as she attempted to link arms. My parents, annoyingly, seemed to have forgotten what happened only a few moments ago.

'Orchids. Beautiful flowers. Some of them are quite rare, you know. I heard something on local radio. This is a prime spot for them.' Mum gave up trying to appeal to me.

Whoopee-doo. So the rest of the afternoon was going to be spent looking for flowers. Oh God. Was I going to be expected to pick a posy, skip down the hill, and take up flower arranging as a hobby? Perhaps I could press some wild flowers and make a pretty picture?

I slunk miserably behind them as they inspected likely habitats for orchids. Finally Mum gave a shriek as if she'd won the lottery.

'Here. Oh, over here. I think it's a bee orchid – I'm not entirely sure. Isn't it beautiful? Look at those delicate petals – the lovely shapes and colours. Oh, what a delight. Come on,

Luke, even you have to admit that is lovely.'

'Super,' I replied flatly, which solicited a hard stare from Dad. After photographs had been taken for later identification they decided to return to the car and head off home again.

Watching my parents stroll off hand in hand, I waited until they were out of sight, then I stepped over towards where the precious orchid displayed its colours in the midst of the browned grass. Standing directly over it, I undid my flies and directed my spray of streaming yellow liquid over its blossom and leaves. The orchid immediately flattened as several petals dropped off.

'Not so pretty now, eh?'

Chapter Ten

The next morning held better hopes. Mum and Dad would both be out as Dad had been called in with some kind of internal office emergency – which meant I'd be alone for a while.

Mum had her coat on and was looking at something on her phone.

'Oh, yes. That was a spider orchid we found yesterday. Apparently, it's very rare and a protected species. Pretty cool, huh?'

I pulled a face as she kissed me on the cheek. Maybe I shouldn't have taken my anger out on the flower. Mum left the house first.

'We're trusting you to be sensible, son,' Dad warned me sternly. 'Use the time wisely and no silly business, OK? When I get back, and I've no idea when that will be, I expect you to be here.'

'Sure, you can trust me.'

'Can we?' Dad muttered rhetorically. He closed the door and I heard the car start up, grinding gears as it pulled away and turned the corner.

Freedom! Surely I had at least a few hours to myself. A whole morning to do exactly what I wanted to! I could watch telly – except it was only naff daytime TV giving tips on choosing a new home or how to train your dog. A DVD, perhaps, except I didn't really feel like sitting still for a couple of hours. I could do anything I liked. Anything.

Why did all my options seem so lame? Now I finally had spare time I couldn't actually think of anything to do. The only thing that sounded vaguely interesting was to go into town for a while. At least I could look at computer games. I'd have to walk into town. It took about twenty minutes, but I had no other choice, apart from stealing money from Dad's cash pot. Bad idea. Even I'm not that stupid!

Town was pretty dull; full of old people walking painfully slowly on the narrow pavements. What I needed was a giant, armoured tank to sweep them out of my way and put them all out of their misery. Looking at stuff you want to buy isn't very exciting when you know you can't buy it – in fact, it's particularly frustrating. I must have spent a little too long in the shop picking things off the shelf because I eventually became aware of a man in a suit standing nearby, clearly watching me and even whispering into what I thought must be a lapel microphone. Maybe I was getting paranoid, or maybe the store detectives had tagged me as 'one to watch'. I carefully replaced all the goods I'd been holding and made a big display of showing my empty hands. I even pulled a tissue out of my pocket so they could see nothing had been secreted there, and then ambled outside. I guessed it would be best to walk out slowly as it's less likely to cause suspicion. By the time I stood outside the shop I felt hot, panicky, and guilty about nothing at all.

It would have been double Maths if I'd been at school. This cheered me up slightly. I could really get used to this type of punishment. I'd have to think of some more things to get me excluded again.

I got seriously bored alone in the house. I filled the kettle, switched it on, and while it boiled I opened the back door and stepped outside onto the patio. It was slightly windy now the sun was beginning to disappear, and more than half the garden lay in the shadow of the high fence. Near where the lawn met the paving stones of the patio, I found what I was looking for and smiled. Hearing the kettle switch off I returned to the kitchen, picking up the jug of boiling water to carry it carefully outside. Tiptoeing towards my intended target I tightened my grip on the kettle and aimed it at arm's length so as to miss my toes.

The cascading water turned the paving stone a dark brown, but more to the point, it washed away the line of ants parading on it. But it didn't just wash them away; I could swear I saw them curl up in pain as the hot liquid fried them alive. Spurred by such success I knelt down and took a closer aim at some other ants scuttling nearby. This time I could really enjoy their molten destruction.

'Die, you gimpoids!' I attempted a villainous guffaw. 'This is my garden. Die. Die. Die!'

Once I'd used up the whole kettle, most of the patio had had a good clean. It was difficult to make an accurate body count, but I'd certainly massacred a huge number of them. I knew the real trick, though, was to find where they were coming from. Seek out the lair and destroy the enemy in its own territory. My parents were always complaining about ants in the house.

Back in the kitchen I refilled the kettle then returned to the garden to hunt down the ants' nest. Careful observation – that was the key. Scanning the pathway and patio I quickly spotted the zigzag frantic movement of an ant; then another; and another. It soon became apparent that they all eventually made their way to one particular hole between two flagstones.

'Echo three six to Bravo two nine. Enemy headquarters located,' I spoke aloud into an imaginary walkie-talkie. 'Request for back up. Over.' Having grasped the newly-boiled kettle I crept stealthily back outside.

'Roger, Echo three six. Eagle squadron is ready to swoop. Here come the flood bombs.'

With precision-accuracy I poured the entire lot slowly down the small hole between the stones.

'Bravo two nine. Target destroyed. Repeat, target destroyed.'

'Roger that, Echo three six. Mission complete. Over and out.'

As I dawdled back to return the kettle I couldn't help wondering if this mission had been completely successful. Were they all dead? Had I completely destroyed the whole nest, or had some ants survived to fight back and seek revenge? It was then that a new plan occurred. Just to make sure. Under the kitchen sink I found a big blue bottle of bleach. That was supposed to kill all known germs. Wasn't it made of acid or something? I knew it was a dangerous substance anyway, so that was perfect. Deciding not to don Mum's rubber gloves I took the bottle outside. After working out how to remove the top, which isn't as easy as you might think, I found the ant-hole and crouched down over the wet paving stones. The bleach was gloopy and came out quickly. I managed to pour half the bottle into the hole. That should do it. They surely can't survive that; or at least, then the garden would be full of bleached, albino ants.

I was buzzing now. A thrilling sense of power gripped me. In this garden I am God, choosing whether these insignificant creatures should live or die. They remained at my complete and utter mercy; except that I wasn't feeling very merciful. Further up the garden there grew a buddleia bush with violet flowers, long and tapering, where butterflies dangled and danced over the shrub, vying for the blooms' nectar. I had an idea.

In the kitchen I found the recycling box and took out a small jam jar that had been washed and dried. Over the sink, like a mad professor, I emptied half the remaining content of the bleach bottle into the clear jar. With the jar held out before me in two hands I strode towards the buddleia and put it down on the floor. Unlike most insects, butterflies are relatively easy to catch with your bare hands. They might look pretty resting on a leaf, but butterflies are a bit gawky in flight, especially when taking off. It was a simple matter of waiting for one to land, before closing cupped hands above the butterfly then entrapping the fluttering wings in a loose fist. The flapping tickled a little but I didn't want to crush the stupid thing.

I pinched one of the wings between thumb and index finger, sending it into a frenzy. I grabbed the jam jar, lifting it up to eye level, then half-dropped, half-threw the frantically struggling butterfly into the thick liquid, cautious not to touch the bleach with my fingers.

Death was immediate. I swear I heard a fizzing sound as the body and wings disintegrated. Its carcass shrivelled as if compelled to take up the least space possible. Drowned in acid. What a way to go. I couldn't help sniggering.

Exploring the garden further I discovered new victims: spiders, earwigs, wood lice, ladybirds, and even a worm. I enjoyed hours of fun and amusement until there was no more room in the jar.

The only thing to spoil my amusement was when I noticed a magpie sitting on the fence. I swear it was observing me. Could it be the same one I saw the other day? Had it come to get revenge on me for shooting the other one? Then I remembered how the dead magpie had gone missing. Had it survived after all? Nah – that's stupid. Magpies are common enough birds. In my state of guilt I was probably just noticing them more than usual.

Then the sun set and the cold wind drew me back indoors after hiding all the evidence of my accomplishments in the dustbin.

It was as though the darkness of my bedroom affected my thoughts and emotions. As soon as I pulled my duvet up and reached out to switch off the bedside lamp, the darkness became a force of its own. An air of menace overcame me as if I'd witnessed my own death in a dream. Sometimes I woke feeling depressed after a terrible nightmare and that same feeling of doom gripped me at that moment.

A montage of images played in my mind's eye: Frisky rotting behind the shed; dead insects swarming and swelling in size, preparing poisoned mandibles and stings to pierce my soft flesh; orchids and flowers rising like armies – their roots extending and stretching towards me, strangling and constricting me until every breath had been choked out of my lifeless body. I saw my muscles and bones sizzling and melting in a giant vat of acid, desperate to scream but my jaw began to collapse and dissolve into a mulch, covering my useless, flapping tongue.

Reaching out with a frantic hand I managed to switch the light back on and all the crazy visions vanished. After a welcomed gulp of water, I slid my pillow behind my back and sat upright, stretching until both shoulders clicked.

Something buzzed in my ear, perhaps a mosquito. Then a large shadow moved in my peripheral vision to the left. I felt my eyes widen as all my limbs turned to lead. A spider crept a slow diagonal on the wall adjacent to the bed. Not just a spider, but one larger than my head, with legs like jump leads – except I didn't think spiders got that big in this country. How could this be? I watched as it lifted one leg and then another.

As I slowly shifted back from the approaching creature I knocked the lamp's beam away and the giant spider disappeared. Wondering if it had jumped, I patted my head, arms, and then the soft bed around my legs. The idea of that beast on my skin made me squirm and shiver. Yanking the light back into place, I jumped when the spider reappeared on the wall.

At first I couldn't work it out, but then I turned to look at the lamp. There, just inside the lamp shade, a spider was busily spinning its web. The lamp's beam had projected the outline of the tiny creature onto the wall as a giant silhouette. My laughter sounded weird and weedy.

Wide awake now, I lay back down and snuggled into my duvet. Before long the annoying buzz returned. It made a loud popping sound when I slapped my ear. A trickle of sweat ran down the side of my nose, but when I rubbed a finger over that part of my face I didn't find a wet smear. Instead, I touched something small and hard between thumb and forefinger. Pulling back I looked at it closely and saw that it was another spider. I squeezed it until it was crushed to a pulp, then I flicked the squidgy remains beyond the foot of my bed.

Chapter Eleven

'Luke?'

I heard Mum run upstairs and stand outside my bedroom. I waited. She knocked.

'Luke?'

'Yeah. Come in.' I continued tapping out my text to Simon, using both thumbs speedily.

Mum gingerly opened the door, waiting for me to look up and acknowledge her before shuffling a few feet into the room. I sent my text and looked at her expectantly.

'I've invited Celia and Ernest round again for dinner tomorrow.'

'Who?'

'Their foster son just started at your school. You remember? You were extremely rude last time they came. I've promised them you'll be more civil this time.'

So Guy was coming here once more. We'd be reunited even sooner than expected.

'You will be, won't you?'

'What?'

'More polite to them this time?' Her voice sounded irritated.

'Yes. I promise to be on my best behaviour.'

'Good. And you'll be friendly to Guy?'

'Of course.' I managed to make my voice sound slightly hurt. As if Mum had no reason to doubt me. I saw her bite her tongue and smile with a twisted mouth.

'Please don't let us, or yourself, down this time.' She closed my door and descended the stairs. I wondered how Guy would respond to me after my unpleasant behaviour towards him at school. Had he dobbed me in?

My phone beeped to alert me of Simon's reply.

That night I slept in fits and starts. It felt as though I'd lain awake all night, but in truth I probably dozed off for much longer than I imagined. It got to 4.15 a.m. when I realised my mind had become far too active, so I gave up closing my eyes and sat up. I hoicked my pillow up horizontally behind me and leaned back into its softness. Just as I wondered if I might be able to sleep after all in that position I heard a tapping sound. It was a deliberate rhythm as opposed to, say, a regular dripping sound. The taps got louder and more urgent. They were clear and crisp. The window. The noise definitely came from that direction and it sounded like something hard on a pane of glass. Someone was knocking on my window. My window ledge seemed too narrow for anyone to be sitting there – unless someone had shimmied up the drain-pipe – or used the fence dividing us from our neighbours. Someone could conceivably stand on that and reach my window with a stick.

The thought of looking out the window and seeing someone there spooked me out – a lot. I couldn't imagine Simon doing it; not his style. Guy? Doing so would make him a weird stalker, but I couldn't be certain he wouldn't. My fear was that if I pulled back the curtain and saw a face grinning back at me, I would go mental. My stupid imagination conjured up a swinging corpse, hanging upside down and swaying in the breeze.

Hazy light gave the curtains a kind of halo effect, so I knew it wasn't dark outside, and a pale face against a dark background would be much worse. A face in the daylight would be shocking, but somehow less sinister. I recalled my close encounter with Guy's face in the roundabout wilderness.

Steeling myself for a fright I whipped back the near corner of the curtain and glanced at the window pane. No face. No person stood or hung outside. Something stood there leering at me, but not a human face. On the window ledge stood a magpie. I was being haunted by a black and white bird. I dramatically pulled back both curtains hoping to scare it off with larger movements, but it stood its ground and continued pecking at the glass. Did it hope to be let in?

I put my face directly opposite the bird so my nose touched

the cold window. Its beak tapped a few centimetres away, making me glad about the double glazing separating us. I made a few faces, leaving fogged imprints and condensation on my side. The bird watched me with definite curiosity – its sideways stare like a camera trying to autofocus on me. I got the impression of it processing still-images in its tiny brain – as if it possessed a photographic memory.

Then I tried to scare it by making sudden movements and pulling faces. It hopped around impatiently, trying to get its beak in the tiny gaps of the frame, as if it was strong enough to prize the hinge open. I smiled, shook my head, and stuck two fingers up at it. The magpie flicked its tail with great agitation, and looked at me, first with its right eye and then with its left. With a harsh 'chack-chack-chack' it returned to its tapping on the window, and this time it did so with surprising vigour until I feared the glass might crack.

I lunged towards the latch and in one swift movement of the wrist I unhooked it and swung the casement outwards, knocking the stupid bird from the ledge. It flapped off angrily chattering, its wings long and white-tipped, its tail with iridescent greens and blues stuck out like a rudder steering its flight. To my amazement it wheeled around, beating its wings a few times before gliding around until it faced the house once more. I hastily pulled the window closed and twisted the latch.

And yet the damn bird was still shaping to dive bomb my window. Surely it couldn't smash through double-glazing? I watched aghast as it propelled itself at speed in my direction. I ducked away at the last second and heard a terrific thump.

Was it dead? I'd never heard of birds committing suicide before – lemmings did odd things like that, didn't they? But not birds. Not that I knew of. I surprised myself by caring what had happened to it. The stupid thing had been trying to come in, and now it might be injured or worse. What was it with bloody magpies? I wanted to know if it was the same one following me around.

I looked up, wondering what I'd see. When I saw a messy splat on the glass, I initially thought it to be the exploded innards of the bird. But closer inspection revealed the goo to be merely bird poo, a palette of white, black, and green. Just above the guano I could discern the outline of the magpie, where its head and wings had impacted on the glass. I even found a tiny imprint of the eye socket. I felt like it was still watching me, so I closed the curtains. Had my parents been woken up by the terrific thump? I waited for someone to investigate but no more sounds interrupted the quiet of the rest of that early morning.

I lay awake puzzled until my alarm clock buzzed at 6.30. I got dressed before daring to open the curtains. Maybe I'd imagined it all or dreamed of waking up.

Finally drawing the curtains slowly, I smiled wryly on seeing the bird poo and then looked closer at the ghost-image of the magpie, still clearly there. Wingtips held out questioningly; head turned sideways to show the beak in profile; and that eye boring through me and seeing inside me – delving into my very soul.

As usual, I decided not to say anything. I just hoped Mum would see it and clean it off as soon as possible.

Chapter Twelve

Our polite little dinner party turned out fine in the end. I had decided to be good and act all civil. In fact, I may even have overdone it slightly, going by some of Dad's expressions and looks directed at me; all of which I ignored.

I shook hands with Guy and his foster parents, and felt incredibly relieved when he chose not to sniff me this time. How awkward would that be? Seeing Guy in this different context felt odd and at first it proved hard to keep any kind of conversation going with him. He came across as painfully shy, often allowing his foster parents to speak for him. He also still looked a bit of a skank. I almost felt sorry for him.

'Poor thing has been a little ill and missed a few days of school,' Celia informed us over starters.

A few days? I thought. He'd been off for more than a few days. If he really felt ill then why would they let him wander off to roundabouts in the middle of dual carriageways? There was more to this boy than met the eye. He'd clearly been skiving school and not telling them. At first I considered grassing him up. I could innocently make some comment about him missing lots of school and not seeing him around much, or I could even open up about his crying at school, or catching him at Coney Island. I looked in his direction but he wouldn't meet my eye. I took this as him giving me the freedom to do as I felt best. His lack of challenge either meant he trusted me not to, or had already accepted his fate. But which? I couldn't be sure after my previous unkindness to him.

'Guy tells us you've been very good to him at school,' Ernest said with a tone of gratitude. 'Thank you, Luke. It's so difficult starting a new school and he tells us how you've made things much easier for him.' He looked at my parents and nodded. 'Seems your son has made all the difference for Guy.'

Guy kept his head down. Mum and Dad's looks and mutters of appreciation made me glow a bit inside and helped me decide my next step.

'No problem. It's a pleasure.'

'After last time, I was a little concerned ...' Celia added, but then stopped when her husband placed his hand on her arm.

'Guy's doing very well in lessons too,' Ernest said instead. 'He tells us he got top marks in a Maths test just yesterday.'

Now I knew that was a lie. I just smiled and caught Guy finally looking at me with narrowed eyes.

The rest of the meal became quite dull, with the adult couples swapping anecdotes about holidays and work – as if those two things were the only important aspects of life. A definition of modern life is, according to them, work your butt off so you have enough money to go on holiday so you can get away from the work you've been doing while getting the dosh together for the holiday in the first place. Our family holidays haven't always been the most relaxing either, and Dad always seemed grateful to go back to work after we've been away. It doesn't take him long to start complaining about the stress of work, though, until he's making comments about needing another holiday. This is the vicious cycle of adulthood.

I was last to finish my apple crumble and custard – probably because I had three portions.

'Luke, why don't you take Guy upstairs and show him your room?' Mum suggested. 'You can leave us adults to continue our boring conversation.'

What? Even more boring than the last hour, you mean? I wanted to blurt that out, but didn't.

'OK. You coming?' These were the first friendly words I had ever directly spoken to Guy. He grunted and stood up.

Taking another boy to my bedroom wasn't the coolest thing to do, but the thought of finally talking to this freak certainly intrigued me. I felt I had the advantage on my own territory. I wanted to know why he'd defended me when he'd have every right to grass me up and get me grounded for the rest of my life.

There wasn't a great deal to do without my games console, so I put on some music and let him perch on the end of my bed, while I sat sumptuously with the pillows against the headboard.

'Tell me about the rabbits then.'

He looked uncomfortable and I let him squirm through the silence for a few moments as I stared at him without blinking.

'OK then. Why are you bunking school?'

I had opportunity, at last, to study his features. His lank hair had been washed but still lay in wispy, flaccid clumps over his elongated head. Hair didn't seem to suit him particularly – in any style. His eyes were small and blue; the only part of him that ever seemed animated. His mouth's default setting was agape, giving him a gormless look, which belied his piercing gaze. Tufts of light fluff dotted his upper lip and the underside of his chin. I knew he was my age and yet there was something wizened and ancient about him. It wasn't just his rough skin or his gnarled and curled fingers but something in his demeanour or aura that seemed archaic.

'School's not for me,' he said simply in his strange high-pitched voice. His voice rasped slightly in a breathy whisper.

The more I saw and heard of Guy the more I warmed to him. If only I could not look at his gross hair and allay the image of him sniffing me. He clearly offered me no threat and I instinctively felt he liked and trusted me.

'Mmm. Respect. The question is – is it really for anyone? Just a form of torture devised by adults to get rid of us for most of the year, isn't it?'

He smiled broadly and it transformed his face entirely. He offered no other response.

'And teachers are either psychotic sadists who want to hurt children in some form of revenge, or are completely deluded idealists, brainwashed by all the other adults into believing they're doing something important. What do you think?'

'It's true that most teachers are ignorant of the truth,' he replied, staring intently at my window. The ghost outline of the magpie and its bleached guano were still there.

I got up and wandered over to it, tracing my finger around the filigree shapes left by the wing feathers.

'Must have hit hard.'

Guy's voice made me jump, having become so used to him

being silent until prompted to talk. I still hadn't got completely used to his whiny tone either.

'Yeah. So hard it shat itself.'

Guy smirked. 'Good aim though.' He nodded his head at the white smear that covered half the window pane. 'He was aiming at you and didn't see the glass.' Then, to my embarrassment, Guy folded up into squeals of laughter. I left him wheezing and gasping for some minutes with a fixed scowl on my face. Eventually Guy regained his self-control and I tried to get things back on keel with a joke that had popped into my head, inspired by the guano.

'Two chavs were walking down the road when a bird crapped on the head of one of them. The other said, "Wait here, I'll get some toilet paper". The first chav replied, "No need for that. By the time you return that bird will be miles away".'

I gazed back into the silence at Guy's mystified expression. Jokes are never improved by having to explain them. I decided to leave it.

'The rabbits seemed to like you,' I tried again. His neutral expression caused me to be unnecessarily explicit. 'The other day on that roundabout. You and the rabbits?'

'Thanks for not getting me into trouble.'

'Sure. No sweat.' Getting answers out of him would be difficult. Guy clearly wasn't the talkative type. 'You did the same for me. You could've told them I'd been a bastard.'

He didn't respond.

By this time I'd returned to the luxury of my pillows, leaving him to stare at the magpie imprint.

'Do you have any pets?' he asked out of nowhere. Was that sudden look he gave me an accusing one?

'Only my parents,' I blurted out, trying to keep the atmosphere buoyant. His slight wince at my words made me feel guilty when I remembered his mum was ill. I didn't know any details or the extent of her condition, but I racked my brain for a quick cover-up. 'And a flat magpie.' I gestured to the window. It didn't improve things. I was going to say 'ex-magpie' but that would be thoughtless and it only reminded me of my own ex-cat and my guilt.

'Have you?' I enquired, as coolly as a teenage boy sitting on his bed and talking to a frankly odd bloke could manage. I imagined he possessed a menagerie at home; his bedroom a jungle of rodents, lizards, and stick insects.

He shook his head. 'Nuh-uh.' He finally ripped himself away from the window and turned his head sidewise to read the names of my games and DVDs on the shelves of my bookcase. 'Animals and birds should never be kept in cages. Fish kept in small tanks only live half as long as wild fish. Birds need to fly.'

'Right,' I nodded, feigning interest. I kept with him for the sake of politeness, though. 'What about cats? They lead pretty great lives in the warmth, sleeping, eating, crapping, and … well, that's about it for some cats.'

'Yeah, but the problem there is that they're dependent on the owners and have lost the skill and cunning needed when living wild. They become fat and lazy.'

'Great life, though. I read something funny once: something like "cats don't have owners, they have staff".' I laughed, and I swear Guy's lip flickered slightly – or perhaps he just had a twitch.

'Maybe cats have it good,' Guy sneered in submission. 'House cats do live longer – usually because they're pampered. But dogs are often kept for the wrong reason. It seems cruel to me teaching them tricks as if they're circus clowns.'

'We had a cat but it died recently.' It felt good saying it our loud – almost like making a confession.

Guy just stared at me with serious eyes and nodded slowly.

'Does a spider count as a pet?'

'Hard to train a spider.' Guy's eyebrows dented in the middle. 'Most people want to kill them on sight.'

'Too right,' I chuckled. 'I love to feel the squirming body burst between my fingers.'

'I've never understood this human desire to destroy everything.' Guy scanned the room and made an almost imperceptible sound with his lips, as if blowing tiny bubbles. 'You've got about thirty spiders around this room in various hidey-holes.'

71

He went to my lamp, put his finger under the shade, and to my astonishment a small black spider suddenly scurried out and walked along his bony hand. My instinct was to knock it on the floor and crush it underfoot, but Guy's gaze of admiration as he followed the creature up his arm forced me to stand stock still and see what he did next. Guy smiled as if the spider had whispered something amusing in his ear. It reached his face, scampered onto the bridge of his nose and up between his eyes, and then stopped on Guy's forehead.

'Watch this,' Guy, said with a near tone of excitement.

The spider suddenly leapt off the boy's head and onto the curtain. I could just see the faint line of silk now connecting his head to the drape. Guy lifted his hand and lightly brushed away the thin thread, all the while laughing to himself.

'Luke?' The disembodied voice came from downstairs. It was Mum. 'Time for Guy to go now. Come down and say goodbye to Celia and Ernest.'

'Guess you're off then.'

Guy nodded. 'Meet me tomorrow in the roundabout.'

'Are you not going to school?'

He shook his head and exited my room without another word.

At the bottom of the stairs Celia held out Guy's coat for him to put on.

He might well be the weirdest person I've ever met, but there was something about him that really intrigued me. Perhaps it was because he was different from everyone else at school. In those few moments upstairs and at Coney Island he'd got me thinking about things. Weird.

'Well, thank you for a lovely meal. We must get you round to ours at some point.' Celia beamed at me. 'Thanks for being a friend to Guy.' Ernest patted my shoulder and the three of them left the house, walking in silence away from us.

Dad closed the front door.

'Well done, mate. Your improved manners were noted and gratefully appreciated.'

'Guy's a nice young man, isn't he? A bit shy, but seems pleasant enough.'

I stepped up onto the fifth step in one big stride.

'Yup. He's … um … interesting.'

Chapter Thirteen

So I went back to Coney Island the next day. I just had to. Guy had done enough to make me feel terrible about treating him so badly. Mum and Dad had given up on looking after me and returned to work. I should have done the schoolwork emailed to me. Those damn teachers were way too efficient and at first Dad took great pleasure in printing off the reams of paper detailing fascinating exercises and essays for me to attempt. Sod that. Even though I knew my parents would question me about it, I felt sure I could con them into believing I'd done it all as they never really looked at my books, and I remained convinced that Dad hadn't even read the sheets he'd been merrily printing for me. I even became fairly confident the teachers wouldn't remember to ask me for it either.

I ran across the dual carriageway and found the gap I'd used on my previous visit. I had to hold my hand out in front of me again to stop my face getting covered in cobwebs, but it didn't stop flies going into my eyes and up my nose. Briars and thickets scratched at my jeans; wet grass made my socks soggy. I found the hollow in the middle and there was Guy, surrounded by bunnies; holding a little one in his left hand and stroking it with two fingers.

Although I still felt wary of him, I couldn't help but be fascinated. He was certainly the strangest person I'd ever met, and at least 'strange' wasn't boring.

'The babies are called kittens – or sometimes kits. Beautiful.' Guy spoke in that odd high-pitch without even glancing at me. He lifted the little rabbit up for me to get a closer view. 'Did you know that rabbits aren't native to Britain? Probably brought over by the Normans from France and Spain, hundreds and hundreds of years ago. They've done well though. One doe can have about thirty babies a year, you know. They don't all survive, of course, with so many predators around, but that's pretty amazing survival tactics, eh?'

I'd never heard him speak for so long or so eloquently. I made a face which I hoped expressed a vague sense of interest.

'Not many people know about their eating habits. They eat their own droppings to make sure they extract all the goodness from their food. Not so cute and fluffy now, eh? It's not that different to cows and ruminants who chew the cud. Just sounds gross to ignorant humans who judge everything against their way of doing things. Nature often flies against what we've been socialised into believing.'

He put the bunny down and it hopped off towards what I assumed was its mother.

'Come on,' Guy said, climbing out of the hollow and pulling my arm. 'I want to show you something.' He held on to my sleeve and tugged me along at his own fast pace. I thought about pushing him away, but he sounded so insistent and I gave in to curiosity. Only as I looked down at my own feet, getting tangled in grass and twines, did I notice his bare feet. He seemed unaffected by any thorns or nettles and had even rolled his trousers up above his ankles.

He dragged me through bushes and thick undergrowth before coming to a sudden halt. Then he dived onto his front and with both hands, carefully made an opening in some tall grass. He looked up and indicated for me to get down next to him on the damp floor, so I resigned myself to getting wet and dirty and slid down on my knees, peering into the low opening. There, looking back at me, was a snake – a sodding huge one. This was definitely unexpected. Was it poisonous? I knew we had one poisonous snake in the UK. The adder? Or viper? This had black stripes around its bright yellow eyes. The length of it was brown-grey with black diamond patterns and behind its head was a yellow band.

Guy put his hand flat on the floor in front of it, palm upwards. The snake moved its head, flicked its long tongue over Guy's hand, and unbelievably slithered its head voluntarily over it, allowing him to lift its whole body off the ground. I couldn't believe the size of it; it must have been about a metre long.

'Grief! He's a monster,' I said, aghast.

'It's a female,' Guy replied, matter-of-factly.

'I didn't know we had snakes that big in this country.'

'Oh, yeah. She's a grass snake. Just as beautiful as the rabbit kitten – in a different way.'

'Can it hurt you? Do they bite?'

'It won't bite me.' Guy looked up at me and smiled as the snake wound itself around his arm and waist. It seemed content. 'It's unlikely to bite and it's definitely not poisonous. And before you ask, no, it's not a constrictor.'

I started to feel less nervous as Guy handled the creature like a pet. He tickled its throat and allowed the snake to dart its tongue all over his face.

'Ah, it just licked my eye!' Guy giggled with delight. I couldn't help but laugh. This was truly amazing.

'Are you OK?' I asked.

''Course. It's not actually licking me. It uses its tongue to smell and sense things.'

I looked on, stunned. The image before me of this odd, shy boy holding a massive snake made my head spin. What the hell was going on?

'What do they eat?' I heard myself ask and realised that it was a genuine interest.

'See if I can show you.'

Guy got down on his haunches and, holding the grass snake in one hand, pressed the fingers of the other hand into the soft, mulchy soil. After doing this a few times he found what he'd been looking for – a long, wriggling, pink earthworm. Guy pinched the worm between his thumb and forefinger and held it near the snake's mouth. At first the tongue sprang out and flicked over the wriggling mini-beast a few times, then the snake's mouth opened and gulped it down whole – with Guy letting go at the last millisecond.

'Awesome,' I cried out involuntarily.

'They love frogs and small birds or mice. They swallow them whole, just like that worm. I should put her back, really.'

'Can I hold her? I mean, do you think she'll let me?' I

couldn't believe what I was saying.

'I'm not sure.' Guy's forehead wrinkled somewhat. 'She might dart off suddenly, or even –'

'What?'

'Give it a try.' Guy slowly passed over the serpent. I tried to copy what he did. I placed one hand behind the snake's eyes and put the other hand under the heaviest part of its body. It wasn't slimy at all. Its skin was smooth and silky. It shifted and I could feel the tightening of muscles as it moved. I became concerned when the snake began to thrash about, as if struggling to escape my grip, and I had visions of giant fangs engulfing my face, and of venom being stabbed into my eyes, when the creature suddenly went limp and fell from my arms into an inert pile on the floor.

'Oh God! I killed it! What the hell happened? I didn't do anything. What's going on?'

I looked at Guy, who was studying me intently. I expected him to attack me and accuse me of murder, when I realised he was holding his stomach with laughter.

'What's so funny?'

'Thanatosis.'

'What?'

'Classic grass snake behaviour. It's a predation defence mechanism. It's playing dead.'

'What? Pretending?'

'Yeah. It saw you as a threat and to avoid being eaten it's now playing dead. Any sensible predator will give up and find something fresh to eat. Get closer and try smelling it.'

Without questioning him, I bent down and took in a big whiff. Big mistake. The snake smelt worse than a stink bomb.

'Oh man! That is rank.'

'It's very clever.' Guy gazed on with admiration. 'It smells like a rotting carcass. Perhaps we should leave her now so she can go back to her nest.'

'I didn't realise such amazing things happen all around us every day.'

I wasn't sure if Guy had heard me. He picked up the limp snake to put her back where he'd found her.

78

'Look at this.'

I shuffled over to him, wary of other wildlife lurking behind bushes. He stood up again, now holding something long and brown. At first I thought it was the plastic skin off a giant salami or ice pop that someone had thoughtlessly thrown away, but when Guy offered it to me to hold I could see it was the perfectly sloughed skin of a snake. The regular pattern of round scales looked like tiny bubble wrap, or honeycomb.

'See, the head was here and there are the eyes,' Guy said proudly, pointing to one end. A brown nose was apparent as were two translucent bumps, like cartoon eyes that pop out. 'It casts off the entire skin – even over the eyes – and it ends up inside out, like a rolled off stocking.'

The skin was dry and stiff.

'Would you like to keep it?' Guy asked, as if offering me a thousand pounds.

I took it from him. It seemed to be an intriguing souvenir for what had become a very strange day.

Guy walked part of the way home with me.

'I just want to show you one more thing today.' He sounded excited. We were passing an area of private allotments. 'Come on,' he said, opening the gate and holding it ajar for me.

'Are we allowed in here?' I asked.

'Oh, yeah. Ernest owns one of the patches. I often help him out with his vegetables.'

I followed him around the edges and past a corner, where a man in his fifties knelt down, doing some weeding.

'Hello, Guy.'

'All right, Frank?'

'How's Ernie? Tell him I've spotted a few caterpillars on his spinach, won't you?'

'Sure will.'

'You two come to help me, have you?' The man looked up and reached out for his flask.

'Not this time, sorry. I've brought a friend over. I wanted to show him my collection.'

'Right proud of that aren't you, son?'

Guy nodded and beckoned to me. Over in the far corner I

saw a pile of decaying logs and what I took to be a compost heap. I wondered what his collection consisted of.

'Do you know what one of the most endangered animals is in Britain?'

I thought for a moment.

'Some kind of mouse? No, I know – the natterjack toad.'

Guy pursed his lips. 'Very good. I'm impressed. They have taught you something at school. But, no. It isn't that. I have here in my log pile something very precious.'

He lifted up a log and hunted around for a few moments before delving his hand into a pile of wood chips. When he pulled his hand out, I saw something black sitting in his palm about the size of a small mobile phone. It had big horns sticking out the front of its head and sat perfectly still on Guy's hand.

'A stag beetle,' he stated proudly.

'No way!' I responded defiantly. 'There's no way we have beetles in this country that big.'

'We certainly do. You just don't see them very often. They used to be a common sight, but now there aren't so many left. They need rotten wood to feed on and we're covering everything with concrete and patios so their habitats are dwindling. I created this little space for them.' He swept his arm around like a showman. 'This is perfect for them. Dead wood and lots of decaying matter in the soil. Aren't they fantastic?'

I have to admit I was pretty impressed with this creepy-crawly. I held out my hand and Guy immediately placed the stag beetle onto it. I felt its feet tickle and even heard it clicking, but the beetle wouldn't settle on me, seeming to want to return to Guy. Why did animals not like me? What was it about Guy that made him so great?

The beetle began to get jittery and run up my arm, but luckily Guy rescued me and calmed it down again. He really did have some special kind of power. What was he? Some kind of Nature Boy? A kid brought up by wolves? It gave a new meaning to 'animal magnetism'.

Not only did he seem to respect and admire animals; they seemed to love him back. Freaky … but in a cool kind of way. I started thinking about my own responses to nature and stuff, and how ironic it was that this weirdo was showing me how to see things completely differently.

Chapter Fourteen

Early the next morning I was woken by a tapping sound. I knew, straight away, that it came from the window. I didn't feel nervous or annoyed – just intrigued. On opening the curtains I wasn't surprised to see the magpie. The mess from its previous visit had remained uncleaned.

This time I became uncertain whether its intentions were friendly or aggressive. It seemed calm and inquisitive, but I wouldn't let it into my room, however imploring a look it gave me. I wouldn't be able to explain bird poo on the carpet to Mum. I pressed my nose to the window again like last time, and the magpie mirrored my position. Could birds be that intelligent? Or was it just instinctive behaviour?

The magpie tapped a few more times but I just stared back at it without moving, until it seemed then to give up on me. I watched it for a few more minutes as it flew onto the garden fence and then off into the light-streaked morning sky.

Mum's talking about getting a kitten.

'Take my mind off losing my lovely Frisky. I do miss the little darling. What do you think?'

I pulled a face and gestured as if to say I was undecided on the matter.

'As long as you clear up all the poo and sick, my dear, go ahead,' Dad said, with his usual sensitivity.

Mum stuck her tongue out at him and turned to me.

'Is it too soon, do you think?'

I shrugged, knowing I wasn't being very helpful.

'On the other hand, I can't help thinking he's still around. I keep expecting to see him come bounding up to the back door like he did when he was younger. Is it just me, or do you keep seeing him out the corner of your eye. Every time something

83

moves I look round to see if it's him.'

I shook my head solemnly. 'No, it's just you, Mum.'

How bad do I feel?

At three in the afternoon, Guy knocked on my door.

'Come on.'

I did my best 'what-the hell-are-you-talking-about?' face.

'We're going for a walk.'

'We are?'

'Mm-hmm.'

'I don't do walks.' Even I thought I sounded pretty grumpy.

'You do now.'

'Where?'

'The park.'

'Why didn't you just text me?'

'I don't have a phone. Don't need one.' He made it sound like I'd suggested taking drugs.

I realised then I'd never seen him with one and he'd never offered me a number. I patted my pocket to check I'd put mine there and stepped outside, closing the front door behind me. I had no idea what lay in store for me. Whatever it might be, it probably beat the prospect of doing stupid schoolwork.

Hillgate Park was an expansive, grassy woodland with a small lake where I sometimes came to throw stones at ducks or play football with Simon. The playground was quite fun, with rope bridges and swings that went pretty high, however, Guy's mission appeared to be to show me a different side to the park.

He walked past the playground and the grass area, towards the lake. I knew about the rope-swing which kids often used on hot, sunny days, but he led me past that too. Eventually, Guy stopped on a fisherman's platform, a little wooden pier walkway that took you over the water's edge. As soon as he crouched down I felt a compulsion to do the same. He placed one hand on my shoulder and with the other he pointed out over the water, towards two objects floating about twenty metres away. When one of the objects suddenly disappeared I realised they were alive and assumed them to be ducks.

'Forgot to bring some bread for the quack-quacks,' I said

84

sarcastically, hitting the heel of my palm on my forehead and giving a goofy look.

'These aren't ducks!' he whispered forcefully. 'They're over there.' He pointed to my right and there indeed were a whole group of ducks and geese gathering around some children. 'These are great-crested grebe.' Guy suddenly magicked a small pair of binoculars from his pocket. 'Look at the crest and the colourful markings.'

I took the field glasses and looked through them. Everything was blurred. I swivelled the focussing dial and suddenly saw a slim, elegant bird bobbing haughtily on the water. It had a black, spiky tuft and what even looked like a lion's mane. Then, just as suddenly as before, it dived under. Gone. I scanned left and right and then picked it up a few feet away. Was it the same bird or the other one of the pair? Further inspection showed it had a silver fish in its slim, sharp beak. It flipped its maned head up a few times, shifting a fish round until only a little silver tail stuck out of its beak. Its next swift movement saw the end of the fish as it disappeared down its gullet. I had to admit – it was almost interesting.

'Let's see the ducks.' Off he strode, leaving me feeling a bit disappointed. Surely ducks are common and quite dull. They're either brown or have green heads. Sometimes a white one slipped in. But a duck is a duck is a duck, isn't it? How wrong I was.

'Most of these are mallards. You see them all the time. The brown ones are the females. But over there is a tufted duck – the black one. And here comes the best of all. That's a mandarin.'

It didn't look real. Surely someone had just made it and placed it on the water to confuse people. It had a golden, white, and green head with a red beak, and an array of other colours on its neck and back, purple, green, and lustrous black. Its wings stuck up like small pointed orange sails. It seemed incredibly out of place and smaller than the others, especially compared to the swans and geese that soon came towards us in hope of food.

Guy told me about Canada and barnacle geese before informing me there were also four types of swan – mute,

85

whooper, Bewick's, and even black ones.

'Who'da thunk it?' was the only response I felt able to give.

I followed Guy into the woods. He really had this amazing power to attract animals and birds. I watched him as he stood frozen for a while with his fingers on his lips, and I swear, after a while he had two squirrels sniffing around his feet and about ten different birds sitting on his shoulders and head. It didn't seem real and I kept my distance, amazed but also hoping one of the dickie-birds would do a crap on his hair. Then he'd be forced to wash it.

The woodland soon came to an end as we heard the constant drone of traffic on the nearby motorway.

'What are we doing here, you knob? I ain't playing chicken or throwing stones at cars.' I was grumpy about not being in control. Why was I letting this weirdo lead me about anyway?

'And those would both be very stupid things to do,' Guy said with a scowl. 'Why would I suggest doing them?' Instead, Guy started walking on the embankment the same way the traffic flowed on our side. 'I want you to meet someone.'

Guy hopped nimbly over the small fence, so I followed, snagging my fleece on the barbed wire.

He stopped and stared across all six lanes of the motorway and into the trees of the woodland opposite. Then he started making a high-pitched, inhuman sound, waving his hands in swiping circles.

'Kee-kee-kee!'

The call was shrill, but cut through the rumbling of cars and lorries. Guy repeated the strange ritual and I was left guessing what wonder I could possibly behold next. Unsure whether the shape appeared from the tree or from somewhere behind it, I noticed it first as a silhouette in the sky. A bird. Or more precisely, a bird of prey. It continued its flight straight towards us and I predicted correctly that it would land somewhere near Guy and that I had nothing to fear. The bird landed at the top of the tree nearest to us and when it screeched I realised just how accurate Guy's imitation had been.

It looked smaller than a pigeon but bigger than a blackbird. Its back was blue-grey and it had an orange throat, with stripy markings on its belly a bit like a tawny cat.

Instinctively I kept back to give boy and bird their own space. I didn't want to spoil the moment. Guy kee-kee-ed again and held out something in his hand that looked like a piece of meat. Had he been carrying it in his pocket all this time? It would explain part of the smell. Guy made the noise again and threw it up in the air.

The bird suddenly flapped and swooped down in a perfect arc, snatching the small lump in its talons with perfect precision.

'Awesome!'

'He is, isn't he?' Showing me these creatures was Guy's thing. He shone brightly again.

'What is he? A falcon?'

'*Accipiter nisus.*' The Latin words sounded magical.

'Do what?'

'Sparrowhawk.'

'You come and see him often then?' I was beginning to see why he didn't come to school now. What could they teach him exactly? This weirdo was learning more about the world than any stupid teacher could tell us.

'When I can.'

'Has he got a name?' Before Guy even replied I knew I'd said something stupid.

'He's not a pet. He's a sparrowhawk. A wild creature.'

I screwed up my face and tried to think of something else to ask, but Guy continued his rant before I could.

'I don't understand people's need to turn animals into humans. They aren't the same as us. They are closer to nature than most of us are. We've forgotten how to trust in where we came from.'

'Are they ever used in falconry?' I asked, hoping to not get snapped at. 'You said it isn't a falcon but hawks are used too, aren't they?'

'Yes. They're brilliant hunters. They like catching birds as they fly. They were used in medieval times, by priests especially.'

I waited for more information, but no more came from Guy,

who forgot about me for a while as all his attention went – justifiably – on the sparrowhawk. Eventually the bird got bored with us and returned to its hunting-ground or nest.

We spent a fun afternoon climbing trees. Unsurprisingly, Guy could climb like a monkey; if he'd had a tail he would have swung from a branch by it. A couple of foxes approached Guy confidently and I was amazed at how big they were. I'd never appreciated the beautiful colour of their coats before.

The two of us messed around on the swings and climbing frame until the sun sank down. Embarrassingly, I got a text from Mum asking where I was.

'Blimey. I should get home,' I said regretfully. Even if we didn't talk much, just 'hanging around' felt good. It gave me a chance to be still and think.

'One last thing before you go.'

What now? It was getting hard to see things too clearly – as well as becoming very chilly.

'I can see them.' Guy jumped up suddenly and ran back towards the lake edge. 'There. There. Can you see them?'

I squinted out into the gloom. I could just make out the edge of the water. The water rippled slightly and at the far end were bushes and trees dangling into the water itself. At first I wondered if he meant the grebes or ducks, but they were long gone.

I shook my head, mystified.

Guy pointed upwards and I tried to follow his hand as it came down and swung around in an arc, then changed direction again. Something flying? A sudden flicker made me turn my head, before something else moved in my peripheral vision, making me spin my head back around. Then I saw it. A shadow whipped past my line of vision. Then another flew overhead. Giant bugs? Too big.

'Are they birds?'

'Not birds. Bats.'

I watched, fascinated. As I got used to the darkness I began to see more. Lots of them swooped over my head; some skimmed across the lake, wheeling round and banking suddenly.

'They're called *pipistrelles*. Would you like to see one close up?'

He didn't wait for my answer, he just stood up on tiptoe, stretched out his right hand, and made some quick tongue clicking sounds. After a few moments he brought his hand down slowly, like a stage conjurer, to reveal a small, squirming object in his loosely closed fist. I watched Guy pet it gently and then blow on its face. He gradually opened his fist for me to see what looked like a mouse, not much bigger than the stag beetle. Its wings were folded up, making it look like it had long forearms on which to creep commando-style. Close up, and even in the waning light, I could see the details, its leathery ears and blunt nose. Carefully, Guy unfurled its wings to show me their expanse and intricate webbing. With a shake of his wrist, the bat flew off.

'What's your secret?' I asked, feeling sure I'd receive no answer. I was right. Guy smiled and walked off towards the park gates.

Chapter Fifteen

Mum and Dad took up most of my weekend with shopping trips and a visit to Dad's sister who'd just had twins, which made them my cousins, who I was supposed to go gaga over but failed to. I couldn't help feeling disappointed that my weekend was full – especially because Monday meant going back to school again. That in turn meant I couldn't spend the days with Guy – unless I skived off school. This seemed like a very bad idea, having just come back from exclusion. Old Saddler was bound to be keeping a beady eye on me.

It did feel strange returning to the usual routines of the school day. I'd started to get used to not being at school – that same lovely feeling of freedom you get in the summer holidays, with the thought of no school or homework stretching out for weeks ahead of you.

The first day back was OK in the end.

'So what did you do in your week off, you dosser?' Simon called out as he saw me approach. He and Pete were sitting on a low wall by the teachers' car park.

'All right? Er … not much really. My parents made me catch up with loads of work. Got a bit boring, to be honest.'

'Boring?' Pete said, contorting his face. 'Hell, I'd love a week off. I could go into town, go to the skateboard park, watch telly, play *Organik Apokalypse* –'

'Yeah, well I was grounded weren't I? And they've confiscated my games console,' I grumbled. Both friends shot me a look of sympathy – the kind you'd give to somebody on death row.

Simon looked pleased to see me anyway, if no one else particularly welcomed me or had even missed me. The lessons began and ended without notable incident and I did get away with not having done all the work sent to me. I still suffered from slight pangs of guilt for lying to Dad about completing all the work. I'd just shown him my book and explained that all the last half a dozen pages represented work done that week. He believed me as I never put the date on my work, which meant I could write fake ones in. I knew the teachers would never spot it; they just skim it when marking. Most of my work just says 'Good' or 'Well done' in red ink at the bottom of every other page.

I did look out for Guy at school but he didn't appear. I wondered if he'd gone to Coney Island, or maybe the park again. How did he manage to skip school without getting caught?

Then, on the Wednesday, he found me in the playground with Simon and Pete at lunchtime.

'Hi, Luke.' The high-pitched voice sounded even whinier than usual.

'All right?' I nodded and tried to look nonchalant about it. It did prove more than a little embarrassing. I hadn't spoken to anyone about Guy. The three of us were telling rude jokes when he interrupted and now he just stood there like a puppy waiting for me to throw him a stick.

'Hey, look. It's incontinence boy!' Simon spoke before I could say anything. The air immediately fizzed with bad energy – out of nowhere. I didn't know how to rescue the situation. I should have said something earlier, but I'd missed the chance.

'What do you want, wee lad?' Simon continued his taunting. 'Some rubber pants?'

Guy looked at me with an expression of confusion. I looked away.

'Sod off, piss-pants.' Pete joined in now. 'You can't stand here. It'll cost you fifty quid.'

My mates aren't bullies – they'd consider it 'banter'.

'Come on, lads,' I said with a fake grin. 'Be nice to the freak, or he might start to cry.'

The others stopped laughing and looked at each other confused. I held it together.

'He's new here. He needs someone to show him around.'

The other two stared at me. Then Simon suddenly burst into laughter.

'That's the funniest thing I've heard in years.' He held his sides in an exaggerated mime of hilarity. 'You'll tell me next he should become our new best friend. Brilliant! You crack me up sometimes.'

I joined in the laughter. Guy frowned and eventually dawdled off.

That night I lay there staring at the ceiling, unable to sleep. I found it hard to work out how I felt about Guy. Being friendly with him was clearly going to ruin my street-cred, yet there was something fascinating about him, even if the others couldn't see it. There was no doubting that Guy offered something a bit different. Just hanging around and doing the same old stuff was getting boring now. Maybe it was time to grow up and move on.

Mum trusted me to look after him and a small part of me wanted to do that for her. It kind of felt like I had a mission to accomplish, and my instincts told me that being with Guy would never be dull. His ability to attract wildlife and his weird behaviour drew me to him. He seemed interesting – even though he was ugly, and a little bit smelly. But, hell, we could work on that …

During these thoughts the tapping began. At first it jolted me out of my deep thoughts. I knew straight away what it was, and strangely, something inside me made me feel that it was completely natural. No, nothing odd about a flippin' bird tapping on your window, eh?

I got up and walked over to the curtains, which I pulled partially back. As expected, there in the dim glow of white moonlight and orange streetlamps, just the other side of the glass, stood the magpie.

And this time it felt different. Somehow. I welcomed his presence. Something about the bird made me feel calm and friendly towards it; I can't really explain why. Perhaps someone outside of me was controlling my thoughts. It was as if I understood something completely incredible, which if I put it into words would make me sound crazy.

Maybe I was going insane?

I let the magpie in. As soon as I pushed the window outwards the waiting bird hopped in, making a sound that almost equated to a tut. That can't be right. I was imagining things again. My first fear that the magpie would squawk and flap about madly was unfounded, but I still felt nervous in its unpredictable presence, and had to keep trusting it wouldn't poo on my bed.

But it didn't. In fact, it acted with excellent manners. What kind of bird was this? Wild birds don't enter houses after knocking politely. If a bird does accidently get into a house it goes completely mental and craps everywhere. This one looked at me with eyes that gleamed with intelligent understanding. It knew me. I swear, it looked at me and knew I wouldn't hurt it. In the old days I would have looked for a stick or a weapon. Now things were different, and I stared back at him with utter fascination. I moved even closer, confident I wasn't in any danger.

'You need to choose your friends more carefully, Luke.'

I stumbled slightly and had to grip the windowsill with my fingertips to hold myself up.

What the –?

The sodding bird had only gone and spoken to me. It snapped its beak, glared at me sideways, then flicked its tail.

Was that for real, or had I lost the plot? Being with Guy had obviously turned me into a nut-job.

Up to now, I'd witnessed some amazing sights – but they could all be explained in encyclopaedias. However amazing the creatures Guy showed me, each one existed in the real world. But a talking bird? Now we'd suddenly jumped into a different dimension.

And it had used my name.

Had Guy sent this amazing bird to me to blow my mind even further?

It had to be Guy's doing – sent on a crazy mission … unless …

'Guy?'

Now I felt really stupid talking to a bird.

'Hello, Luke.'

Bloody hell. Take me to a padded cell. I'd lost it. Maybe I never had it!

'Guy? Is that ...' This was crazy. '... is that you?'

But then he didn't answer using words.

At first the magpie shimmered, as if the radio-waves transmitting a holographic image faltered for a few seconds; coloured lights shot out like fractals from a million angles then increased rapidly in mass until a person stood before me. Guy. A genie from a bottle.

What had I just seen? What had I just witnessed?

Chapter Sixteen

I stared open-mouthed and with new eyes at the boy now standing beside me.

'Maybe your friends are right. I'm a freak.'

'Is this some kind of joke?' My mind struggled to express my thoughts. 'Have you some kind of superpower?'

'Not superpower, Luke, just energy. We all could harness it if we only listened to nature.'

I so couldn't believe this crazy transformation I'd witnessed just a few seconds ago. I had to be dreaming. This felt unreal.

'This is ancient magic ...'

Magic? Yup, I'd just entered cloud cuckoo land. Goodbye normal world.

'Thousands of years ago all people lived closely with nature. Ordinary people had what we'd consider supernatural powers ... magic. But it wasn't anything out of the ordinary – not for them, because they lived with nature and listened to what it told them. The problem with our modern world is that we think we can control things, but we can't. Nature is always too big for us. We're not in control – we're just part of it. Animals. Creatures, like all the others we share our planet with. Our biggest error is in thinking we can harness or manipulate natural forces. Of course we can't. Nature will always be bigger, stronger, and beyond our control. Rather than master it, we should accept our part in it and learn its secrets and wonders.'

It was only then that I noticed he was naked. Although it made me feel uncomfortable, there was no sense of threat, and Guy just carried on as if nothing was strange or different.

I didn't really follow what Guy was telling me as it all sounded like a load of new-age hogwash, really.

'Where did you get all this stuff from?' I garbled, for want of anything more sensible to say. 'Who the hell are you?'

But Guy had clearly told me enough already.

'I need something to wear.'

Without another word I nodded and found him some old jeans and a jumper.

'Put your warmest clothes on,' he ordered. 'We need to sneak out of here without waking up your parents.'

'Do I dare ask why?'

'Showing you is so much more fun that telling you.'

'Why am I trusting you?'

He smiled and put a hand on my shoulder. For some reason I trusted him. I'd changed. In the old days I'd have punched his lights out for doing that.

Before I could wonder how we'd creep down the squeaky stairs and out the front door without waking up my Mum, Guy was already climbing out through the window onto the ledge overlooking our back garden. With light agility he stepped down to the fence and then jumped two-footed onto the lawn. My jump was less elegant, but ended with a roll onto the grass, which jarred my ankle.

'What exactly are we doing? Not looking for hedgehogs and badgers, are we? I could be curled up asleep in bed right now. I've had enough of animals for a few days.'

'Just wait. It'll be worth it. Promise. Atmospheric conditions are just right. We have to be patient.'

How could I say no to a boy who can turn into a bloody magpie? Everything in my entire world had changed in those few moments.

We walked for about ten minutes, and eventually got to the local park where we'd spent all that time previously looking at wildlife.

'Not more bats,' I said, disappointed.

'No, no. Although it's a shame you can't appreciate how cool they are.'

'I can only take so much,' I grumbled. I wanted to see him change back into the magpie. Now that was cool! If it had really happened. I started to doubt my own memory. Things like that don't really happen. Not really; in reality. A wind began to press against us as we walked.

'The swings!' he cried out to me.

'You've gotta be kidding me,' I now began to question his sanity as well as my own. 'You got me out of my bed to go on the swings?'

Guy shrugged and jumped on one of them. 'Trust me.'

I begrudgingly sat on the second swing, next to him and pushed off to get to the same level.

A strong gust of wind blew into my face as I started to gain height. Then it changed direction and an invisible shove gave me extra momentum.

'Higher,' Guy ordered. He was pushing hard on his swing until his head went above the level of the metal crossbar. I did the same and felt the wind suddenly strengthen as it swished through the trees. Within seconds a storm had erupted, with pelting rain cooling my face, and I was soon drenched as the winds drove against each rise and fall I made on the swing.

'Keep pushing,' Guy screamed. I could only just hear him so I followed his arcs and tried to keep level. By now the stormy winds were bending even the giant trees. 'Nearly there,' Guy called out.

Nearly where?

Thunder rumbled distantly. Was this it? Guy had brought me to come and play in a storm! Big deal. Big let-down.

'Grab my hand!'

I looked across and wondered if I'd heard him right.

'Your hand! Keep together. Get ready to let go.'

I placed my right hand in his and gripped onto the chain with my left as my legs swung up and down. My swing was not in perfect synchronisation with Guy's but we managed to stay together even though my arm got a bit wrenched.

'When I say "now", jump.'

'Sod off!'

'Just do it. But keep hold of my hand.'

Was this revenge for calling him a freak? I always used to jump off swings as a kid and remembered how much the sting hurt your feet. What the hell.

'Three, two, one. Now!'

I gripped Guy's hand tightly, scared of it slipping away in the rain. I felt my bum slide off the plastic seat and then waited for the searing agony. Please don't let my head smash on the concrete path.

We didn't crash. We only went and floated!

Instead of dropping we somehow soared to the top of the trees. The next part made me feel queasy. We were flung around and around as if caught in a circulating air current. Each time we hurtled towards the ground, I prepared for death, but then became aware of another rapid, stomach-churning ascent.

My hand still gripped Guy's but it was slipping down to his wrist. He looked over at me and smiled. I must have looked scared stiff.

'Relax,' he shouted. 'Put your other arm out – like a plane. Trust me.'

Just this simple action gave me much more control. Guy smiled as if this was a natural, everyday event for him. He pulled me close and shouted into my ear.

'We're riding the storm! Woo-hoo!'

I began to laugh manically – nervously. It was elation mixed with absolute terror.

'Climb onto my back and hang on tight. This could get rough.'

He jerked me towards him – giving me the chance to grab hold of his shoulders. I flung my arms around his chest and locked my fingers together, and refused to unlock them, even in the throes of intense cramp. Without thinking, I also wrapped my legs around his.

I was shrieking; swearing; cheering; wailing. Tears streamed down my face from the onrushing air. When we fell – hundreds of metres at a time – I couldn't hear myself scream. The sudden rise upwards left my gut behind and I dizzily clung on with my last ounces of strength.

'Thermals!' Guy yelled. 'We're birds! Woo-hoo!'

Then two terrifying thoughts struck me. What if Guy changed back into a magpie? He wouldn't be able to hold my weight. Then worse – how do we land?

Maybe Guy could sense my terror. Perhaps my tightening

grip had begun to hurt him.

'Had enough?'

All I could do was nod dumbly and hope he got the message. I wasn't sure if I'd be able to hold onto him much longer.

Guy stretched out his limbs and wheeled around a perfect arc. I finally got an amazing view of the sprawling network of lights below me. What a sight – the whole town at once. I started to relax a little, thinking about this freedom. How weird to be away from the ground – from my own town and home. This just wasn't real. It couldn't be.

Skilfully steering a path back over the houses and trees, Guy manoeuvred us back towards the park. I saw the lake ahead of us, lights rippling on its surface. Just as we approached its shimmering target I realised Guy had put one hand over his shoulder to grip my arm. Then in one sudden move he'd flipped me and himself so we faced each other. I clung to him desperately and he embraced me tightly. We were already falling. Very fast.

'We'll go for a soft landing,' he whispered into my ear. 'Brace yourself.'

I think I must have lost consciousness. There was an explosion, the loudest thing my ears had ever experienced. Then, when everything moved in slow motion, I wondered if I'd died and become a spirit in a nether world. I just remember shapes and shadows lunging at me. It went black and white. The slowness continued, until suddenly, another explosion led to a gasping of breath and an end to the agony. My body collapsed and I knew I was being held. Water splashed onto my face and I dragged fresh wind into my mouth. Air. Beautiful, life-giving air.

My heart was too big to fit in my chest and my lungs were boiling – about to burst. My eyes stung and my ears throbbed with echoes and drumming. My arms and legs didn't work. I was freezing cold. But I was alive!

Guy hauled me out of the lake – drenched, limp, and exhausted. I blubbed and howled in a cringing mess of bones and skin. Guy stood over me, grinning and hardly out of breath.

'How wild was that?'

I just lay on my back and laughed at the strangeness of the last few days. In all truth, what I'd just experienced was the greatest moment of my life so far.

Chapter Seventeen

'You know what he's gone and done now?' Simon asked as I reached my locker.

'What? Who? What you on about?' I shrugged melodramatically.

'Piss-pants. Freakshow. You know. The wee lad.'

'Oh,' I said with less enthusiasm. This was going to haunt me for the rest of my life. I'd created a monster. I dreaded to think how my original rumour could continue to evolve and spiral out of control.

'He's found some allies,' Pete added.

'Yeah, he hangs around with Cheryl and Taylor and that lot now,' Simon explained.

'They love him. He's one of the girlies.'

'Told you he was gay,' Simon added unnecessarily. 'He can chat about shoes and shopping with them.'

'Now Connor wants to fight him,' Pete said. Listening to these two was like watching a tennis match.

'Why the hell does he want to fight him?' I tried not to sound too alarmed or defensive, so I turned back to my locker.

'He thinks the freak is stealing our women,' Simon replied.

'But that doesn't even make sense. If you reckon he's gay then he's no threat.' I felt pleased with my argument, but I wondered if it was good to support the "Guy is gay" theory – especially if I was ever seen in his company. But then again, another part of me wondered if it were true. He had started becoming quite tactile, and when we'd been flying I'd been hugging him very tightly. I shuddered. Now I felt very confused.

'Whatever.' Simon deflected my comment nonchalantly. 'Anyhoo, Connor wants to beat the crap out of him.'

'What planet is he on?' I slammed my locker shut and spun

around. 'What's Connor worried about exactly? If Guy is gay then there's no problem. Or does he seriously think that the freak is going to shag every single girl in our school and turn them against him? What the hell is going on in that tiny brain of his?'

'Dunno,' said Pete. 'Why not ask him yourself?'

Connor appeared on my left and I couldn't be sure how much he'd heard.

'Hi, Connor,' Pete said. He gave me a quick glance and smirked. 'Luke here has something to ask you.'

'Thanks, "mate".' I shot him my best evil look.

'So what is it?' Connor said, standing his tallest right in front of me.

'I've heard you're looking for Guy.'

'Yeah. So?'

'Just wondered why you wanna fight him,' I ventured. It sounded limp but I couldn't think how else to broach the subject.

'Why do you care?' He rolled a grey blob of chewing gum between his tongue and top lip.

'Seems a bit unnecessary. He's not trying to hurt you.'

'Are you his batty boy or somefing?'

I suddenly felt in danger. Connor was unpredictable. He could lash out without warning.

'No, I'm not gay. Just a pacifist.'

'You sound well queer. Maybe I should teach you a lesson first.'

I stared back at him, trying not to blink. Connor blinked first, smiled, and looked down. I relaxed a little. Connor moved off and turned back to us.

'We can't have scrotes like him nickin' our muff, innit? We have to make a stand.'

He strutted away and I was left unsure whether Connor still meant to hurt Guy or not.

'Hey, lads,' Pete said, giggling childishly, 'his name is Guy, right, but we should just call him Gay, instead. Geddit? Guy. Gay.' He actually looked at us hoping we'd consider him a genius for his amazing wordplay.

104

'Yeah, well done, Pete. Whatever,' I said, striding off to the tutor room.

The next time I saw Guy properly was two nights later – a Saturday. He'd avoided being beaten up by skiving off school again.

I woke up with a start, unsure what had disturbed me. The clock said 3.09. I sat up and slipped out from under my duvet, instinctively making my way to the window, where I pulled back the curtain. Guy stood brazenly in the middle of the lawn, looking up at me. He was completely naked. Looking away quickly, I stepped back and let the curtain fall back into place. Oh crap! He was naked again. Part of me realised he couldn't have clothes on when he magically transformed into the magpie, although all this talk of him being gay made me nervous. What if this weirdo was trying to get off with me, though? Why was I being so stupid as to trust this relative stranger – this freak?

However, another part of me recalled the excitement of his company and the unbelievable things he'd shown me so far. Had they all been real? Or was I the victim of some strange delusion? The last week had been so unusual that I was finding it very hard to keep a grip on reality at the moment.

I had a decision to make. To go with this strange nature boy – this super-powered, shape-shifting wonder, or to end it all right now by sending him off or calling my parents. There was no knowing where he meant to lead me, or whether I could trust him. I had to consider what might happen at school the next time we met. It just felt that right there, right then, I had to make a decision.

Opening the window out wide I signalled dumbly, not even sure what I meant by the gesture, grabbed my dressing gown, and threw it out to Guy. I promptly got dressed, found my torch, then shimmied down to the fence and ended up inelegantly sprawled on the lawn. I'd made my choice.

'What's today's little secret?' I whispered.

'Something incredibly important,' he replied in his usual soft way. His voice sounded like a gentle spring breeze. 'Follow me.' He moved a few steps and stopped. I just managed to avoid bumping into him like some cartoon character. He whipped his head around towards me. 'Hope you're feeling brave. You'll need some courage.'

My mind reeled with trying to guess what hideous night-creature he had ready for me. We didn't have vampire bats or killer spiders here in Britain. Werewolves don't exist – I felt mostly certain about that. What else came out at night? Foxes? Badgers? Owls?

As he crept towards the shed I initially wondered if he'd caught something in there which I'd be forced to confront. Although nervous, I couldn't help enjoying the creepy sensation of anticipation giving me an adrenaline rush.

It didn't occur to me at first as Guy made his way to the back of the shed. I watched as he began ripping out handfuls from the top layer of the compost heap. I fumbled for my torch and tried to aim the beam where he was digging until he found what he'd been searching for and brought it out for me to look at.

Frisky!

The stiff and skinny body of our family tabby cat had been better preserved over these few weeks than I'd imagined. I expected something maggoty and skeletal, but this little corpse was still recognisably Frisky. My stomach turned and all the guilt I'd been hiding came back to me.

Chapter Eighteen

I had to look away. Eventually, I forced myself to look again at the corpse of our family pet.

Guy was cradling Frisky as if rocking him to sleep. He muttered something directly to the dead creature, and I even thought he was going to kiss it, but instead he carefully inspected the body. He found a small wound and with one thumb carefully pressed out a little pellet – the ball-bearing from my Desert Eagle. Then he carried the little dead thing over to my mum's herb rockery and tore off a cluster of leaves from one of the bushier plants there, crushing them between his fingers and rubbing the mulch over the wound.

'Lavender stops infection spreading,' he whispered.

At first I thought he meant to somehow embalm the body, but my deepest fear was confirmed in his next sentence.

'Do you want him back?'

At first I stared at him as certain now that he was insane. Then I nodded uncertainly.

'Good. Then you have to help me.' Guy placed Frisky on the grass and took my torch from me. 'Do you regret what you did?'

'Yes. Very much. But I didn't mean to kill Frisky. I thought it was a fox –'

Guy turned on me and hissed angrily. 'And what would have been your purpose in killing that creature? For food? In self-defence? Were you threatened?'

I shook my head. I knew the answer and it didn't need to be said aloud.

Instead, I gazed at Frisky, stark and motionless – legs outstretched and back curved around. Guy stroked the dead cat's back and picked out the various leaves, twigs, and chunks of dirt clumping his fur.

'So many creatures have suffered because of you.'

He was right. My head dropped down until my chin pushed against my throat.

'I knew them all,' Guy continued. This was an odd way of explaining it. I could sense him looking at me and I waited for the accusations and hatred. None came.

With a thorn from a bush he pricked his finger and poured a few drops of blood on Frisky's head. Nothing happened. Guy then looked up at me, waiting for me to meet his gaze.

'This is going to hurt, so get ready. It involves a transference of your life force into him. If you make a loud noise you'll wake people up and it won't work. Understand?'

I trembled wildly, wondering what the hell it all meant. What on earth did he have in mind for me?

'Sit down!' Guy pointed to the space opposite him on the other side of Frisky. I did so, facing him. Guy took my left hand and held it over the cat's body. He picked up a sturdy piece of wood which he must have found and placed there earlier. 'Grip this tightly between your teeth. Bite down hard when you need to.'

I felt terrified, but obeyed his directions.

He slowly pinched the little finger on my left hand and pushed my thumb into the palm and then wrapped my other three fingers over them. Then, before I could brace myself, he swiftly snapped my little finger backwards.

My God! The pain!

I bit into the wood, which cut into my soft gums and lips during the urgency and panic of the shock. Spit dribbled down my chin.

A bolt shot across to my shoulders and my head, which pounded horribly. Then I remembered my little finger and every single atom of me seemed to disappear, leaving only the searing agony all concentrated into that tiny point and part of me.

I kept in the desire to howl and scream. My breathing intensified until I thought I might black out. Dizziness suddenly took control of me. Everything went white and blurred. Then, unexpectedly, I felt something warm begin to swell from my abdomen, which moved slowly up to my chest and head, then

108

slowly down the length of my arm, to my wrist, palm, and finally to the epicentre of pain. From then on I remained aware of the ache, but now only as a distant stinging.

Something – perhaps adrenaline – had given me the strength to survive this ordeal. I now felt I could be slightly separated from the event itself. I looked at my finger still popped out at a jaunty and illogical angle. And I giggled. Like after the flying, I felt elated.

'Breathe in deeply,' a voice whispered. Who was speaking? At first I couldn't recall my own name or where I was, but then the whiteness shimmered into translucence and I could make out Guy's shadowy outline still holding my left wrist.

I became aware of my shallow breathing – like an uncontrollable shivering – so I concentrated on inhaling slowly.

'That's it. A few more times,' Guy encouraged. 'Good. Now I want you to close your eyes and focus on the feeling in your hand. Take in a very long breath and hold it until I say.'

Following his directions carefully, I filled my lungs with what felt like the sweetest air I'd ever tasted. My head spun and my body convulsed with the power it gave me. I managed to hold it in. Then I opened my eyes. Frisky's lifeless eyes and bristled fur floated a few centimetres away. Guy was holding him up and forcing open the jaws, previously locked by rigor mortis.

'Blow into his mouth.'

Then the smell hit me. Decomposed. Fetid. The smell of death. I shuddered, seized with the horror of what I'd done. Instinctively, I jerked away and coughed and spluttered helplessly – feeling like a failure.

'Try again!' Guy tugged at my little finger. The excruciating pain snapped me back into position and a new heightened awareness. 'Focus on the point where it hurts and let your life force fill you to bursting. Then hold it with all your strength.'

Closing my eyes, I repeated the motions – once again feeling the joy as my lungs became swollen. Just as I thought my head might explode I felt a cold hand being placed on each cheek. On opening my eyes I saw Guy move his own face close to mine and then tilt in the manner of a kiss. I stayed calm and trusted the moment. Guy placed his mouth over mine – but this was no kiss. He began to draw my breath out of me. It sounded like he drank from me with a straw. There was nothing I could do as he drained me of oxygen, and on my final wheeze, when I thought I might die, he stepped back and left me flopping about pathetically.

As soon as he withdrew I felt the enormity of my aching finger once more. It was unbearable. Uncontrollable spasms stopped me from thinking any of my own thoughts. The white sheen returned until I felt forced to stay lying down. Watching from my prone position gave me the chance to observe what Guy did next.

He held Frisky in front of him, with outstretched arms. The inert creature still had its mouth open in a yawn, its long tongue dried and useless. Proving himself braver than me, Guy then pressed his lips against the gaping mouth of the cat and slowly blew into the dark, narrow hole. This process took a few minutes to complete, all done with impressive concentration.

'Now you hold him! Keep him warm!'

The corpse was thrust at me and I grabbed it, mostly out of shame. Death lay here in my hands. Not knowing what else to do, and still glad to have something to distract me from my pain, I sat up and cuddled Frisky just like I had done as a little boy. For a few moments I remembered exactly how I felt as that small, lonely child. Then I returned to myself. Seeing my little finger out of joint disturbed me, so I used that hand to hold Frisky and my right hand to stroke his hardened, blotchy fur.

I couldn't be sure initially if it was my imagination, but Frisky had now curled into a ball, like a kitten; his previously outstretched legs now tucked in comfortably just like he had looked most evenings on our sofa. His fur appeared somehow less matted and blemished. Some parts around his ears and nose were patchily bald, but he certainly felt a great deal softer already. I gave him a squeeze. It came from a desire to pass on my warmth.

Guy sat down next to me and put a hand on the animal's back for a few moments, smiled, and nodded. Settling Frisky onto my lap Guy took hold of my left hand and stared at the little finger. It reminded me of the pain. He looked about for the bit of wood, which I must have spat out and placed it between my teeth again. He caressed the back of my hand a couple of times and then, placing his fingers around my small digit in his fist, he yanked it back into place.

The wood broke into splinters in my mouth and bile rose in my throat, hot and stinging. Turning my head away I spat out the mixture of wood and vomit, reeling with nausea and an acute headache.

Guy pressed Frisky back into my arms and this time I felt a little resistance to my embrace. Tingling little pinpricks could be felt against my skin on my arms and chest, which reminded me of a familiar sensation. I looked down and saw Frisky staring back at me – his eyes animated if somewhat sleepy. His ears flicked in response to the many night time sounds. The prickles were his claws. Of course, his claws were pushing into me as he stretched out his awakened limbs. Although he lay limply in my hands there could be absolutely no doubt about it – Frisky was alive again.

I raised him right up to my face and felt a mixture of horror and confusion. I've no idea how long I sat there, staring and stroking, but I quickly snapped out of it when a light came on, stretching right across the lawn, followed by the sound of the French window sliding open on its noisy rails.

'Who's out there? I'm calling the police!'

It was my dad. I jumped up in a panic and ran towards him with Frisky, my head rapidly clearing.

'Dad, it's me. Look! I found Frisky! I heard a noise and I came outside to have a look. It's him. Isn't that great?'

Dad clearly hadn't expected this. 'Um, yeah. Wow. Well done. Bring him inside. We need to look after him carefully and take him to the vet as soon as we can, just to be sure. He's probably hungry, poor sod.'

I also wanted to distract Dad so he didn't see Guy, so I encouraged him back inside. Just before I entered the house I looked back and could only see my dressing gown spread on the grass. As I stepped over the threshold I heard a hoarse chattering from a nearby tree, 'Chack-ack-ack-ack-ack-ack'.

Dad found Frisky's basket and I placed him carefully in it. He seemed grateful and content, finally purring as Dad started stroking his still roughened fur.

'Get him a bowl of water and some food. I'm glad we kept all his stuff. I'll go and tell Mum the good news.'

While Dad returned upstairs I shot back outside to retrieve my dressing gown and looked for the magpie with no luck.

Frisky seemed excited about the water, which he lapped up greedily. I guess being dead is thirsty work. He sniffed the cat food – some soggy jellied meat – but rejected it rather haughtily. I wondered if cat heaven had better food on offer and that bringing him back was actually a slightly mean thing to do.

Of course, both parents were overjoyed and we spent the next hour or so inventing theories about what must have happened to him. I had no intention of telling them the truth. How could I? Oh, um … well, actually, our cat is a zombie; the undead; Nosferatu; beast from the grave; reanimated. I did suggest we rename him 'Lazarus' which got a wry smile from Mum. Eventually, Mum and Dad agreed that he must have been trapped somewhere, like in someone else's shed or even a house while the owners were away on holiday. The next best theory was that he'd been in a fight and had slowly recovered somewhere until he was strong enough to return home. I voted for that one, which also explained his dirty, unkempt state.

It looked like I'd really got away with it. Thanks to Guy. I'd witnessed something miraculous that early morning; something which made me realise that there is so much more to our world than we can ever hope to understand.

In all the excitement and wonder, I'd forgotten about my little finger. Once Mum and Dad had taken Frisky to the vet I became aware of a throbbing ache and had to take two paracetamol. Using bandages, plasters, and a wooden lollipop stick I found in the cutlery drawer, I improvised a splint and made up a story about an accident in PE. It continued hurting – a lot – but I was beginning to understand that bringing Frisky back to life meant some kind of sacrifice on my part, and this seemed infinitely preferable to the sacrificial rituals seen in those mad old Hammer Horror films my Dad loved so much.

Frisky came back with a clean bill of health. He'd lost a bit of fur in small patches and the vet found certain cuts and bruises, but nothing that couldn't be explained by the usual behaviour of a tomcat. Somehow Guy had healed up the ball-bearing wound – or made it look like a bite or scratch. I also wondered if he'd done something to preserve the body. The vet reckoned Frisky had got into a fight with, perhaps, a fox and then hidden somewhere to recover. Apparently it happens all the time!

I waited for Guy or a magpie to appear all Sunday, day and night, but was disappointed. The pain in my left hand didn't help my sleep or concentration. But I had made an important decision.

Chapter Nineteen

He didn't appear in the playground at all on Monday. I asked various people in his classes if he'd been in. Nobody remembered him being there – but a few didn't seem certain if he had or not. How did he manage to miss so much school? I knew he was considered a school-refuser, but what did his foster parents say? Was the educational welfare officer on to him? As I sat in English pondering these things rather than completing the exam practice questions, I did glance out of the window beside me across to the mobile classes below my line of vision. On the roof amongst the general detritus of tin cans, crisp packets, and a couple of footballs, hopped a magpie, although I had no way of knowing if this was Guy or not. The bird seemed keen on the moss sprouting from the guttering – perhaps pecking it for insects and grubs. Although I did wonder why Guy might do this, knowing his odd behaviour at the best of times, it didn't make me any less or more certain either way. It did stop a few times, bobbing its head and angling it to look at me with one eye, but I'm sure I just imagined it. The magpie's tail gleamed metallic green and its wings were a sheeny blue.

On Tuesday I waited at the gates for Guy. Simon found me first.

'Come on, Luke. We've got some bangers – crow-scarers. They're awesome. Pete's gonna set them off on the field. We can still make it.' He ran off, looking back to check I'd followed. I remained where I was. He came back looking confused.

'You OK, mate?'

'Yeah, fine. Just waiting for someone.'

'But everyone's over on the field.' Simon looked genuinely confused. 'You've gotta come.'

'Nah, I'm all right. See you later, yeah?'

'OK, suit yourself then.'

'Yeah. I will,' I said, more adamantly than might have been required.

'Whatever. It's your loss, mate.' Simon actually pouted as he spoke and I realised for the first time how ridiculous he sounded. I was sick of people like him, Connor and Pete telling me what to do and making me feel bad if I didn't join in with their stupid pranks. The more I thought about it, the more determined I became. I'd made my choice and now I had to deal with any consequences. I have to admit I had many second, third, and fourth thoughts about it, but I wanted to see where my chosen new path would take me.

Simon gave a mocking sneer, with a sound like escaping gas, shook his head, and ran off without looking back this time.

I nearly gave up waiting as the bell had gone and I'd be marked late on the register, but just as I considered leaving, Guy arrived. He looked terrible – lank, greasy hair; scruffy drainpipe black jeans; a grubby untucked shirt; and a half-mast tie with the thin end on the outside.

'How's the finger?'

I held it up. 'Could be worse.'

'You need to drink a special tea of comfrey root and mouse ear,' Guy said, as if it sounded perfectly normal.

'I'm not swallowing some manky mouse's ear. What are you, a witch?'

Guy laughed. 'No, not ear of mouse – it's not a magic spell. Mousear, the flower – also known as chickweed.'

'Yeah, I'll just pop to the supermarket and get some of that then.' I laughed, but not in a mean way. Guy didn't look offended.

'I could sort it out for you later. Meet me at the roundabout after school.'

'Sure.'

We walked together openly across the playground, but I was aware of faces turned towards us, people pointing and sniggering. Then, as we entered the front doors of the main school entrance, I suddenly became aware of Mr Saddler's bellowing behind us.

'Get in there! All of you! You absolute idiots! You've really got it coming to you this time!'

At first I thought he meant us two for being late, but as I spun round I saw Saddler pushing half a dozen boys with fallen faces, including Simon, Connor, and Pete. Guy and I stood to one side as they stumbled past us, ushered menacingly by Saddler. Simon glared at me and pulled a face on seeing who I was with. He'd enough time to look me up and down before being shoved onwards and catching an earful from the rampaging Deputy Head.

Just behind Simon came Connor, who gave me a dirty look followed by the universal gesture for 'I'm watching you', pointing two fingers at his eyes, then one at mine. Even Saddler did a double take, raising one eyebrow as he clocked who I was standing with.

It turned out to be an odd day. Simon wasn't in my lessons, having been, I assumed, excluded with the others for their possession and letting off of bangers within the school grounds. It had been pretty stupid of them, even by their dumb standards. Part of me felt glad I hadn't got caught up in that escapade, especially with my own recent poor record. It would have been bye-bye school and hello very angry parents who'd probably keep me at home and teach me themselves. I'd be grounded forever.

At break time I sought out Guy, who was sitting with Cheryl, Taylor, and the trendy girls. He looked pleased to see me, and even relieved when I sat down next to him. This became a little awkward, as Cheryl and the girls all assumed Guy was gay – so me being friends with him was pretty much me announcing that I batted for the other team, at least in their eyes.

During lunch I sat alone to eat until joined by Cheryl, Taylor, and Guy.

'Shove up fatso,' I heard Cheryl say. She bumped me over with her hips and I laughed. As we sat together I felt Guy staring at me intently and wished he could have more self-awareness. I chose to ignore him and concentrate on chatting

117

with the girls, who surprised me with just how interesting they were. In fact Cheryl liked talking about football and films, which got us off to a good start. We nattered together for quite a while.

'Ooh, look at us. Like a couple of old women, we are.' She gave me a smile which dimpled her cheeks. I wanted to brush my finger against one of them to feel how soft it was. Guy tried to join in our conversation but didn't have any reference points for the two main topics, so he quickly got left out again. Cheryl kept bringing Taylor in for her own safety – seeing as I was still a relatively unknown factor to her. The whole experience of talking to Cheryl was rather wonderful. I never knew girls could be quite so interesting and fun.

Chapter Twenty

Walking home I couldn't help thinking about Cheryl – how she'd pressed her fingertips onto my arm, and even once on my chest, when I made her laugh. But best of all had been seeing the bright pink of her bra through her white blouse. I could only hope my gawping hadn't been too obvious; I'd tried my best to do it surreptitiously, making sure I looked into her eyes when she faced me.

I walked in something of a reverie. In fact, as Coney Island roundabout came into sight I came to with a start, as I couldn't for the life of me remember most of the journey; like I'd been teleported straight there.

By now, finding my way quickly to the centre had become second nature. A couple of rabbits scampered away as I crept through the hole in the undergrowth and into the little hollow. No Guy – much to my disappointment.

Over and above the traffic I heard a snap of twigs and what might have been a muffled cough. I peered through the brambles in all directions but could see no obvious movement.

'Up here, Luke.'

Way above me, sat there on the branches of a silver birch tree – one of many that grew in this mini-jungle – I could see Guy. Of course, he was naked, which meant he'd just transformed into human shape. I waved and shook my head in amusement as he nimbly sprung down, catching hold of the branch so his legs swung downwards, right over my head. It was still a long way down for him – about the height of an average house – and yet I watched him let go and plummet to the floor right beside me. He landed like a wild creature on all fours and promptly stood up as if this was completely normal, then held his face right up to mine and grinned. I couldn't help but laugh – things were never boring with Guy.

119

'Oh, man,' I said, still tittering, 'please put some clothes on.'

'Why? Does my natural physical being offend you?'

'Well, yes actually, now you come to mention it.' I spoke with a half-serious tone.

'But this is how I was born – how nature intended.' He wandered away and then posed in all his glory. 'It makes me feel more alive. I'm closer to nature like this without man-made garments. They only act like barriers to our real selves. We're animals too, and yet we separate ourselves from our true heritage.'

I looked away. 'Let's just say it's put me off cocktail sausages for life.'

'Do you find it offensive? You find your own nakedness offensive? Have people become so divorced from their own nature that they find their true form offensive?'

'I think it's a bit more complicated than that. It's more to do with sex and being decent, I think. Maybe I'll tell you about the birds and bees some time. Look, have you got something to wear? Please tell me you have, it'll make things easier for me.'

'Sure. I keep a bag of old clothes down here.'

He disappeared for a few moments and returned with a pair of khaki shorts in his hand. He pulled them over his feet and got them to half-mast when he suddenly stopped still and became acutely alert like a hunting dog; his head twisted around so he was practically looking directly behind himself. Then he tipped his head back and sniffed the air, swivelling his head until he looked right over my shoulder. Slowly, a finger came up to his lips. I froze. He suddenly pulled his shorts up and buttoned them as he nudged past me, diving into the thickets.

Shaking myself back into full consciousness, I followed his disappearing back, knowing I'd never be able to move through the vegetation as quickly as he did. Soon I lost sight of him, then heard an angry voice and what sounded like a scuffle between two people.

Someone else had been here.

I shoved through the thorns and whippy branches, feeling myself getting scratched on face and arms, and tried to follow the sound. I couldn't see Guy until I felt a hand on my back. It made me jump with terror.

'He's gone.'

I turned and felt relieved to see Guy before me.

'Who?' Then I noticed he was holding his bottom lip. He took his hand away and looked at the red blob on his fingertip. His lip was bloody and already swollen.

'Simon. I caught him, but he whacked me. Hard. Then he ran off like a coward.'

'Simon? What was he doing here?' I couldn't help wondering what he'd seen or why he'd come. Presumably he'd followed me. Guy had done enough to see him off, but had got hurt in the process. It occurred to me that this secret place was now blown. It was no longer a place to hide.

'You're hurt,' I said, stepping closer to take a better look at the damage.

'Ah, it's nothing,' he said with a casual wave. 'There's yarrow growing nearby. It helps to stop bleeding.' He turned and sidled through some gorse and beyond another silver birch and came back with some yellow flowers, whose stems he crushed and rubbed roughly over his lip. 'Now then,' he continued, completely undaunted. 'I got those ingredients together to make you that infusion to help heal your finger.'

'How did you find them?'

'I flew.'

No more explanation was offered or required.

'I've got some water,' Guy added, 'and the herbs. Just need to boil up the brew and we're done.'

Visions of Guy rubbing dry sticks together and making a primitive, blazing fire – the real danger of doing so didn't occur to me at first – were soon ruined as Guy heaved a primus camping stove, matches, and a bottle of bought spring water into the clearing. He even had a tin mug like soldiers use. In it was a small collection of flowers and twigs.

'What were these plants called again?' I asked, bemused with this slightly odd little ritual.

'Mousear and comfrey.'

The cup contained a couple of white flowers with thin petals and at least five centimetres of stem with numerous squishy leaves. Then I noticed that what I thought had been twigs were actually the reddish brown spindly roots of a plant – still a little dirty – thin and twisted like elongated talons.

Guy filled the cup three-quarters full with bottled water and placed it on the hob, which sparked into a blue flame when he triggered the dial. We watched the cup in silence as its already tarnished outside went from white to red and then a whole oil-slick of colours. Eventually we heard the water boil and the flowers and roots began to shift around in the bubbling, rising liquid. Guy turned it down and let it simmer for a while, stirring it with a birch twig and smelling it at intervals. Once the infusion had turned vaguely yellow, he twisted the flame off and lifted the cup. Using the twig he agitated it for a while longer, before hooking out and flicking away the various plants, one by one. He tasted it first.

'A little bitter, but I've tasted worse.'

'Yeah, I can believe you have,' I replied with a chuckle. 'I'm used to normal food and drink, though.'

He passed the cup over and I leaned forward to take the cup in both hands.

It hadn't occurred to me that the cup would be scalding hot. I tried to quickly take the handle between my thumb and two fingers, but the handle felt just as unbearable. I placed it on the ground, concerned about it tipping over on the uneven floor, shaking both hands in pain.

'Argh! Bollocks! That's hot!' I yelped. 'I think it's melted my fingertips.' I examined them closely and wiggled them to check they still worked.

'You can become a master thief now,' Guy said with a smirk. 'No need to wear gloves.'

So he did have a sense of humour.

'Don't be a wimp,' Guy continued. 'The tea is probably cooler than the cup.'

No it wasn't.

I stretched my sleeve over my hand and lifted the cup gingerly to my lips. The steam wisped hotly over my lips, which I moistened lightly. I gripped the rim of the cup with my teeth, curling back my lips like a snarling wolf, and took a little

122

sip.

Firstly, it tasted absolutely disgusting, nearly making me retch as its smell filled my nostrils and throat. Then its acid touch blistered my tongue and palate. In the panic of the next few seconds I chose not to spit it out – and that meant the burning sensation continued down into my gullet.

I had to open my mouth wide and inhale deeply, enjoying the relief of cool air filling my throat. Strange gargling noises forced me to look up and see Guy muffling his desire to laugh at me.

'Pass it here.' He stretched out to take the cup from me. 'I need some too, but I'll leave more than half for you to enjoy. Don't let it cool down too much as the effect will wear off.'

'Right,' I said, my mouth still agape. It hurt too much to touch my tongue on anything, and the roof of my mouth felt like it had been ripped to shreds. My tongue remained shrivelled and numb. 'Hey! You'd make a great doctor,' I said, trying to smile. 'Not so sure about your bedside manner, though. Might need a little work.'

I did finish the disgusting tea, and felt certain the next morning that it had worked. I certainly slept well.

School, however, was hideous. Easily the worst day of my life.

Chapter Twenty-one

I realised something was up when a group of year sevens walked past looking at me, then talking secretively and collapsing into fits of laughter. That brought others into play and I could see straight away that I had become the centre of attention, leaving me to wonder if my zip was undone, or whether I had something on my face or bird poo on my blazer.

A crowd from the year above me came past.

'Watch out, boys,' one of the tarty girls shouted. 'Keep your backs to the wall.'

'Yeah,' a floppy-haired boy added, 'make sure you don't drop anything.'

'Look out for the batty boy!' cried out a boy with a grey hoodie under his blazer, 'or he's gonna take you from behind!'

This was followed by a series of groans and exclamations of disgust.

The floppy-haired boy walked straight up to me and looked at me as if I was a freshly laid dog turd. 'So you're the little chutney-ferret, are you?' He stepped back and stared at me. 'So where's your boyfriend, then? Is he lost in a place where the sun don't shine?'

The group had grown and everyone listening fell about into all degrees of amusement, ranging from mild tittering to complete hilarity.

It was clear what they accused me of, and around a thousand of them were happy to see me as the target for all their deluded anger and hatred.

But why now? What was different today?

I moved away, realising there was nothing I could do against so many. Red-cheeked and holding back tears, I marched towards the front office, hoping to find a teacher to hide behind. Perhaps I could convince the school nurse I was ill and should be sent home. With head down I scampered past the front desk and found my way to the staff toilets. The disabled loo was vacant so I went in and locked the door.

All I could think to do was slump down with my back to the door, facing the porcelain toilet bowl. Tears flowed and my mind spun in confusion and despair, until after what must have been at least half an hour I struggled to my feet, unlatched the door, and poked my head around. It seemed spookily quiet for a school, although I guessed everyone was presently in lessons. I sneaked back in front of the reception desk again, hoping to get past to go straight back home, when I heard a booming voice.

'Luke!'

I froze without turning around.

'Luke?' The voice was softer this time and rising at the end in a question. I slowly gave myself up to my fate.

The lady at the desk stated my full name and I nodded. She picked up the phone and spoke softly into it.

Almost immediately, Saddler appeared. I could only groan inwardly – caught bunking after being caught in possession of a weapon … permanent exclusion for me then.

'Ah, Luke. There you are. We were worried.' Saddler put a hand on my shoulder and spoke in a comforting tone. 'We know. It's OK. Now I think I understand all that funny business from before. It must have been very hard for you, but I guess it feels good now, eh? To get it all out in the open. A big moment? That's it. Brave lad, I say.'

'Sorry?'

'No, don't apologise. Please never apologise. The problem is ours you see, not yours. It must be horrible to be so misunderstood by so many. It's important to me and to the school that we offer you all the support and help we can. Not that you need help – that's not what I mean at all. Sorry. I'm gabbling now. You must think me a complete fool.'

It seemed to me that I was better off staying silent as I really had no idea what he was blathering on about – yet he seemed to be being kind to me and offering me some hope.

'Would it help to speak to someone? Not me, of course, but someone more neutral who is trained to listen? The governors recently employed a new person to be what we call a "Pastoral Intervention Officer". She's here to listen and give advice. She's not a teacher at all. It's more one-to-one, do you see? No pressure but if you were keen then I could probably sort something out straight away and you could miss your first lesson ... if that sounds at all suitable to you, of course.'

This was certainly one of the most bizarre conversations I'd ever been involved in. Saddler seemed to be uneasy about something and his tone gave the impression that he couldn't do enough to help me. Had my dad threatened to sue him or something? As he'd mentioned something about missing my first lesson I nodded and mumbled. 'Sure. Yeah. That'd be great.'

'Excellent. Excellent. Come this way.'

He led me past the Head's office and through a large office with lots of clerical staff busily tapping away at computers, before pulling open a door on the other side of the room which led to a corridor leading up to a staircase. At the side and beneath the stairs was a little white door, bearing a legend scribbled in blue felt-tip: Pastoral Intervention Officer.

So it had come to this. They thought I was mad and were sending me to the shrink who worked in the cupboard under the stairs. What symptoms had I shown to be in need of psychiatric help, I wondered. I suppose having a gun might count as criminal and psychotic behaviour, so I guess I deserved all that came my way.

Saddler knocked and waited for a lady's voice to shout, 'Enter!' before ushering me inside.

'Sapphy, this is Luke ... you know ... the one I mentioned earlier.'

'Yes, yes, of course. Come in. Thank you.'

Then Saddler left me with a woman in her fifties that I'd never met before in my life.

'I'm Miss Mire, but you can call me Sapphy.' She stood up and pointed to the chair by the window. She waited for me to sit down before starting her spiel. 'So, you're the very brave little boy who should be given a medal, then?'

I tried not to react, but couldn't help pulling a slightly

quizzical expression.

'You'll find it very difficult at first, but give it time and people will soon get used to things and you'll find everything will settle down. You see, prejudice is like that. It's not the fault of the victim – the real problem is with the bully. Ignorance is what it is. Homophobia is rife in this school – as in any other – but people need to be re-educated.'

A penny dropped but I let her continue as I felt my heart sink deeper into an eternally black abyss.

'It's when brave people like you speak out and are honest that the rest of us need to shift our positions and reconfigure our scopes when we view the world.'

Even the teachers thought I was gay! My first thought then was whether they had spoken to my parents about this.

'Two of my best friends are ... a same-sex couple – married in a civil partnership – and they're very happy. They've adopted a child and lead a very fulfilled life –'

'Sorry,' I interrupted. 'Can I just say something?'

'Of course you can, Luke. And anything you say here is completely confidential. Feel free to open up and express your deepest feelings.'

'OK then. I'm not gay.'

Sapphy nodded earnestly, rubbing her tightly pursed lips. Then she clicked a silver pen and began scribbling something on her pad of paper.

'Uh-huh. Classic denial. Understandable in the circumstances. Are you being bullied?' She put down the pen and gave what she probably considered to be a chummy, sympathetic smile. 'You know, don't you, that I'm not a teacher. There's no hidden agenda here. I just want you to be honest, to be yourself so that you can be strong and become the whole beautiful individual soul that you were born to become.'

'Yeah, but I'm not gay,' I insisted.

'There's nothing wrong with being gay. It's natural and wonderful and perfectly normal. It's just the unfortunate prejudice that we're fighting here and together we can combat this heinous form of discrimination and just allow people to be who they were always destined to be.'

128

'Yeah, and I agree with all that.' My voice got a little tense and I knew this would possibly count against me. 'It's fine. I have no problem with someone being homosexual. Fine. No problem. It's just that … I'm not.'

'Sometimes, Luke, we have to step back a bit – metaphorically – and allow ourselves to just … be.' She beamed smugly. 'We must give room to our true selves so that we can form and grow, away from the narrow confines of society. We all have to throw off the shackles of our brainwashing socialisation and find our true, honest persona deep beneath the surface. Perhaps it's time that you delved deeper into yourself, Luke, to discover who is there under the surface of your nurtured ego, to find the embryo of your truly natural id. Then when you discover your new self, make friends, and even fall in love with the person that you really, truly are.'

I could see I wasn't getting anywhere so I stood up abruptly.

'Well, thanks for the chat then. You've certainly given me lots to think about today.'

Sapphy stood up, looking lost – as if she'd failed to get me to open up and 'find myself'.

'These things take time. I understand. You have lots of soul-searching to do. But remember, you're not alone. I'll book you in again for tomorrow at 10.30 in the morning. How does that sound?'

I hurried out of the room and found the nearest exit to the outside world.

Just my luck – it was break time and as soon as I hit the playground tarmac I had hordes of people running up to me. One sweet little boy got to me first and shook my hand, adding, 'I think you're great,' to which I didn't know how to respond. Everyone else made rude gestures, calling me 'batty-boy' or 'arse bandit'. I'm ashamed to say I ran. Pushing through the gathering crowd I took flight, not wanting to be seen welling up again. I put my head down and sprinted away from them all – through the staff car park and out the front gate.

I went home rather than going to Coney Island. I wanted to be alone, and I wasn't sure if going to that place was a good idea any more. Frisky jumped on my lap and I welcomed the company.

'You don't judge people, do you? You cats just accept us exactly as we are … as long as you get some food, eh?'

He purred, trod his claws into my leg and eventually settled down.

As I sat there my mobile signalled a text coming in. It was from Cheryl.

'u OK duck. Wanna talk?'

It seemed a good offer.

'OK cheers'

Then my ringtone sounded and Cheryl's voice sang out of my phone. Hearing her voice and laugh lifted my spirits no end.

'I heard what happened, my darlin' and I just want to give you a big hug.'

I wished she was sat on the sofa next to me – the thought of pressing myself against her chest made me feel excitedly wobbly. The depression soon allayed those feelings, though.

'Thanks, Cheryl. I might take you up on that offer next time we meet.'

'Oh, I'll hug you anytime. You poor little thing.'

I found her pouting sympathy oddly comforting, even though I knew I should be offended by her patronising tone. I wanted nothing more at that moment than to be mothered by Cheryl, and began to imagine what it would be like to feel my arms around her; her long hair caressing my face as she clung desperately to my shoulders. The thought of our bodies touching and legs entwining was too delicious to contemplate.

'Are you at school now?' I asked, hoping she'd offer to bunk her next lesson and come over.

'Yeah, it's lunchtime innit.' No offer was forthcoming, much to my disappointment.

'Do you know what's going on? What's happened?'

'It's all over the school about you and Guy,' she said tonelessly. Then I heard her talk to someone away from her phone. 'Look gotta go now. I'll send you the wotsit. Ciao, my love. Take care now.'

Wotsit? Strange ending to the conversation. I didn't feel I

130

really understood any better what was going on.

I lowered my phone and gazed out the window, trying to recall how Cheryl looked in her tight blouse and short skirt. This was interrupted by the sound of another text arriving. From Cheryl, it had a media attachment but no written message to explain. I clicked on the tiny picture and waited for the photo to emerge from the black screen.

At first it appeared out of focus – then two fuzzy figures cleared from the initial blur. One was me looking at someone else. While my face was clearly visible, the other figure was only seen from behind, but something significant about him filled me with both foreboding horror and a fearful understanding. It was Guy, and he stood before me completely naked. His scruffy, lank hair gave him away, while his buttocks, hairy legs, and smooth white back stood out in perfect focus. His hands were out of shot and held in front of him, implying some lewd gesture and my eyes could easily be conceived as staring straight at his groin.

I stood up suddenly, forcing Frisky to leap off me, leaving him on the carpet looking up at me, offended.

This photo explained everything.

It meant I could never go back to school; perhaps never leave my house again.

I looked at the picture one more time, groaned audibly, and pushed delete. I wondered how many people had seen this picture. Going by the reactions of hundreds of people who didn't even know me, I guessed the whole school had seen it. There was just no knowing how many Twitter, Facebook, Tumblr, or Google Plus accounts had pinged or been retweeted, shared, forwarded, tagged, or posted up.

It still didn't explain how my teachers had found out, though.

The only thing keeping me from jumping off the roof was the thought of Cheryl clasping me tightly to her bosom. She may well think me gay but if it meant I could be tactile with her then it seemed a sacrifice I'd be willing to make. Perhaps once

I'd gained her trust I could then convince her of the truth. At the moment she and Guy were all I had, as I couldn't exactly explain this to Dad – he'd disown me.

Simon. It was my so-called best friend who'd done this to me.

Chapter Twenty-two

I bunked off school the next day and nothing happened to me at home. It seemed that my parents knew nothing of this latest episode, and that school were too scared to question me, possibly for fear of being considered homophobic and intolerant. So just like Guy was left alone due to being a school-refuser, and with nobody really knowing how to tackle the problem, I was given time and space in order for the school to seem sympathetic to my plight. Which suited me. For now.

I took the rest of the week off and lied to my parents about homework and my progress in general.

Guy found me at home. I refused to go to Coney Island, which he assured me was fine, but I preferred not to take the risk. Simon, Pete, and Connor were still excluded and on the prowl. Guy didn't seem to really understand the problem. I tried to explain it simply.

'What, they think you and me ... do that? Together?'

'Yup,' I replied.

Guy's facial expression showed that he couldn't really comprehend the whole deal about sexuality. He understood mating for breeding purposes – I think – but the human emotion of lust wasn't something he appeared to fully understand. When I spoke of my emergent feelings for Cheryl he looked blankly at me.

Further explanation was wasted on him.

'They have a picture of you naked. I'm standing next to you.'

'So?' He genuinely couldn't figure out the problem.

'So I'm getting bullied because they think you and I are ... well ... having it off.'

'Huh?'

'Bonking.'

133

'What, you mean –?'

'Yes … engaging in sexual intercourse.'

'Why do they think that?'

It just didn't compute for him. You had to admire his complete innocence. If only there was more of it in the world. I'd have given him a hug if I hadn't been so self-conscious and scared of any misunderstanding.

'I need your help, Luke,' Guy said with an edge to his voice. I could see that my huge dilemma meant nothing to him – even though he was involved.

'What's happened?'

'I've run away.'

'Why?'

'Well, school have been phoning up every day, and now Celia and Ernest are being pushed by some official man to get me into school. This man – some kind of officer – keeps coming around and asking to see me. At first Celia and Ernest were very supportive and shielded me a bit, but the other day they told me they'd lost patience. I haven't been so friendly with them recently.'

'They're probably wondering where the hell you are most of the time.' I tried to imagine them finding his bed empty at night and getting worried about him.

'Then the officer man spoke to me and told me the authorities were going to take it to the next stage. Basically, I have to go to school. But I just can't, Luke. It's so awful and depressing.'

'And I hate to say it – things are about to get even worse for you there. And for me. Take my word for it.'

Guy stared at me expressionlessly. 'Just this evening, Celia and Ernest sat me down and told me they can no longer cope with me. So I'll go back into care and get sent away somewhere else – or end up in some sort of prison like last time.'

'Hmm, blimey, mate. You're right up that old metaphorical creek, aren't you?'

'Huh?' Guy's face screwed up into a look of confusion.

'So you've run away? What are you planning to do from here?'

'I don't know. That's why I need your help.'

'Well, you've certainly got the ideal disguise for escaping capture. I don't think they'll be looking for a magpie, do you?'

'But I can't stay as Pica forever.'

'Pica?'

'My *numen*. *Pica pica*. Magpie.' He said it in a tone that made me feel stupid for not understanding this simple idea. I realised it had to be the Latin name.

'What, you can't just become the magpie and wait for it all to die down?'

'No. I can only become my *numen* for a few hours at a time. And when I am Pica there is always the danger of being killed by a predator ... or shot by kids with airguns. Life is so much more precarious for wildlife than it is for humans.'

'But you could fly somewhere safe where nobody would find you.'

'Where? I'm sick of running. It's what I've done all my life. I can't take anything with me – I'll have no money or clothes.' He looked uncomfortable, fiddling with his shirt button. 'And you're the first person to really accept me for who I am. That's why I've trusted you.'

I felt bowled over by this confession and took it as the compliment it was clearly intended to be.

'OK. Then you'll have to accept that you need to go to school and live in a house with adults to look after you. I'm afraid that's what happens when you're a human child.' I said this warily unsure if Guy really was human or not.

He nodded, as if considering it for the first time. 'But school doesn't let me just be me. It's always trying to make me conform – so I have to be exactly like everyone else, which I'm not.'

'Ain't that the truth, bro,' I said, half to myself. Both parts of what he said were spot on. 'But sometimes we have to accept that we can't just do whatever we like.'

'But why do I have to be the same as everyone else? It seems so harsh. As if I'm not allowed to be me at all.'

'Yes, but most people are not like you, that's the problem. The rest of us have to accept that we need a job to make money to lead even a half-decent life. You're different, though. I can't do the amazing things you do.' I shrugged as if I couldn't explain it any other way.

'But you can.'

I flashed him a puzzled expression.

'You can do the things I do. You're just like most people who don't realise the full potential that exists within yourself.'

'Sorry, hang on a minute. No. I can't turn into a magpie. Neither can I fly. Or get animals to trust me and let me hold them like you do.'

'No, but you could.' Guy kept his piercing gaze on me. I stared back as if playing the blinking game. He continued undaunted, 'Everyone can. Most people have just forgotten how.'

This was becoming a little odd now.

'How can we forget if we didn't even know we could?'

'Your ancestors knew.' Guy often gave simple answers like that, assuming it all made sense to everyone afterwards.

'You spoke before about magic powers –'

'Not magic – just natural powers. Humans need to understand their place in the natural world. They are not the masters of the planet – just another species of creature within a very complex web. Once you accept your true nature you begin to see the world as it really is. I don't have antigravity power, but I do understand the rhythm and patterns of winds and thermals which can be manipulated and used to my advantage. It takes training.'

'It probably helps being half-magpie.'

Guy smiled. 'When I'm Pica I have wings. When I'm Guy I don't.'

'So who taught you all this stuff?'

'My mother.' His sad tone reminded me of her illness. I thought it better not to dwell on that subject.

'And the shapeshifting?'

'That's the best part. Humans have something no other creature possesses – a soul. A spirit. But we can share them with our fellow creatures. Your *numen* is your spirit animal. You have to find your own. Mine is Pica – the magpie.'

136

'So are you saying that anyone can do this?'

'Yes.'

'I have a ... *numen* then? A spirit animal of my own that I could sometimes turn into?'

'Yes.'

'So what's mine then?'

Guy shrugged. 'I don't know. Only you can discover that.'

'So I could do it now?' I froze and tried to focus my thoughts with a look of intensity, but then quickly stopped, worried that I just looked like I had constipation.

'No.' Guy shook his head solemnly. 'You need a guide. A mentor.'

'Like your mum?'

He nodded.

'Will she show me?'

'No.' Guy's eyebrows dipped in deep thought. 'But I can. There are lots of things to show you. I think you'd be amazed.'

'Now that I can believe.' I bit my bottom lip as I considered what to do. 'So, you need somewhere to hide. You can't go back to your foster parents because they'll just send you away again and you don't want to be caught and put back into care. Mum and Dad won't let you stay here. Mum'd just call Celia.'

'You're the only one who can help me.'

'So no pressure then?' Guy didn't respond to my ironic comment. 'You could stay here, somehow. Every time my parents come up though, you'd have to hide – I dunno – in the cupboard or under the bed.'

'When I'm Pica it's easier to hide. I wouldn't be here all the time. I need to fly.' His face revealed his sense of hope at this plan.

'Can you change at will then? Or does it just suddenly happen?'

'I choose when to be Pica, and when to be Guy, but it is very tiring for me. Then I need time to get my energy back.'

'Can you only become a magpie, or can you change into other creatures?' There were still a million questions I wanted to ask.

'That's something I'm working on.' He let a little smile

escape. 'I think we have the potential for endless transformations, but I might be wrong. Perhaps it depends on your *numen*, or your strength of character.'

'So what exactly do you need then?' I asked him directly. 'I mean if you stay here then what should I get for you?'

'Clothes.'

'You can use mine. Have you got stuff at your foster parents' house?'

'Not much,' he said with a grimace. 'I don't really own much.'

'Anything else?' I said, amazed that a teenager could survive without a mobile or games console. 'No toys, books, music, films?'

'No.'

Life for Guy really was quite simple.

'I can bring you some food – but only bits, otherwise it'll be obvious.'

'I don't need much food. Just enough to keep my body working properly. I can find most of the food I need.'

Just then I heard the front door.

'Mum's home. You need to make yourself scarce.'

Chapter Twenty-three

Before Mum had even taken off her coat, I watched in amazement as Guy suddenly froze, seemed to shimmer, change colour, and shrink rapidly. Then, within seconds, a heap of clothes lay empty on the floor. The trousers twitched a few times before a small, black head popped out from underneath the waistband, then the whole magpie followed, and hopped rapidly across my carpet with a shake of its wings. That was the first time I saw the transformation happen that way; it was miraculous. Pica disappeared under my bed and I kicked the scattered clothes out of sight as Mum jogged up the stairs.

'Hiya, sweetie. How you feeling today?'

'Yeah, a bit better, thanks.'

Mum placed her palm over my forehead. 'You seem fine. Maybe back to school tomorrow. Have you got enough work to be getting on with or shall I phone the school for more?'

'I'm fine, Mum. Honest.'

Continuing in an unresponsive manner, I impatiently waited for her to leave me alone, so I could interact with Pica. She eventually gave up on me and disappeared downstairs with a tut. I kicked the door firmly shut, then got on all fours, placing one cheek on the carpet so I could peer sideways under my bed.

He took a few steps forward and nodded his head, blinked, and turned his head sideways so that one eye stared at me. He seemed to twitch and his tail wagged up and down like a happy puppy, so I put out my hand and he hopped straight on, up my arm, and onto my back.

'Stand up, Luke.' The voice sounded like that of a small child trapped in a metal box.

I slowly got up and he cleverly balanced himself, using his wings and tail as I shifted position to finally stand. He ended up on my shoulder, like a pirate with his parrot. Without thinking, I reached out to stroke his head, but the beak felt hard and powerful as Pica snapped it a few times as if to warn me to keep fingers away. Putting out a flat palm before him, he stepped onto it and I carefully swung him round and down onto the windowsill so I could face him properly.

'Like a new pet,' I said without thinking.

'You don't own me, Luke.'

'No, sorry. I was joking.'

Of course, magpies couldn't smile. I wondered if birds even had a sense of humour, but then remembered that this was something Guy himself struggled with at times.

'I'm not really sure how Frisky's going to react when he sees you.' This new danger had only just occurred to me.

'Should be fine. Never know with cats.' Pica opened his beak and the words came out, sometimes closing and sometimes staying open – not like with cartoon birds whose beaks become 'lip-synched'. Speaking for birds must be like singing – it came from their throats.

'I'll try to keep you two apart then, just in case.' I also wasn't sure how a zombie cat would respond.

'Need to go out. Must fly.' The head kept changing angle with almost robotic, staccato movements. The sunlight streaming in through my window showed off his sleek, black head and some white speckles on his chin. The blue on his back was deep and vibrant and every now and then the green pierced through the darker colours. I noticed just how black the feathers were. Almost like an absence – an opposite of light.

Once I'd opened the window, Pica took to flight and soared over the trees beyond the houses opposite.

How strange my life had now become.

That evening I had a bath and it turned out to be another wonderful experience. I held my nose and slipped right under the warm comfort of its surface. I was only under water for a minute or so before I came gasping back up for air, but in that moment I once again connected with something awe-inspiring.

Water must have the ability to remember, because that's the only way I can explain my experience. I somehow tapped into

140

the 'memory' of water. All in a few seconds I lived the many incarnations of water; flowing streams, meandering rivers, gushing cataracts, expanding ice, voluminous oceans, still lakes and stagnant ponds. I fell miles as a raindrop and evaporated as steam. I rose in giant cloud formations and dropped as ice and snow, fluttering to the ground amongst happy children. I refreshed the dusty fields, brought relief to millions who swallowed me in thirsty gulps. I smashed, drenched, seeped, flooded, and surged in tides that affected the whole planet. I was the centre of life itself a habitat and a source of fertility. Fecund nature required my soothing touch to make life grow and flourish. No tiny drop must ever go to waste.

Then my lungs burst out for air and those 'memories' vanished – but I knew its significance. That fleeting experience had taught me a great deal. I understood.

Chapter Twenty-four

A photo of Guy appeared on the news and front cover of the local paper with the headline 'Police Puzzle Over Missing Boy.' The photo was one from a few years ago, which I hardly recognised as him – probably an official photo from one of his many previous schools. He wore a green tie and black blazer. The article remained vague and included an interview with Celia and Ernest. I read it carefully – twice.

"A search is underway for a teenager who has gone missing from his foster home. The police, school, and emergency services were contacted when the fifteen-year-old boy, Guy Tellumo, never returned to his Eastbridge Green home. He was last seen on Thursday by his foster parents, Mr and Mrs Parmenter, who believed he was on his way to school. When we contacted the school the Headteacher reported that the boy had not attended his lessons on that day, or for some weeks before.

'He's a quiet lad,' Mr Parmenter told us. 'He didn't have many friends and tended to keep himself to himself.'

Police suspect that he may have run away, and confirmed that the boy in question had a history of disappearances. The search has begun and the police have released a statement.

My parents quizzed me. Ernest and Celia came to visit, hoping I might know something.

'Just any little clue – a snippet. You might be able to think of something he said or did that we didn't know about. Perhaps a place he used to go to?'

I considered telling them about Coney Island, but decided not to in the end, although I'm not completely sure why. Instead I denied all knowledge and refused to admit that I had anything but a parting or fleeting acquaintance with Guy. I must have been convincing because the adults accepted my plea of ignorance.

Things went well for a few days. I brought Guy a little food and drink – just enough to avoid arousing suspicion. A few times I released Pica from my window and took a bus to an agreed point of rendezvous where I could hand him some clothes and a little money. He had to remain disguised or hidden when in human form, and at night he usually tapped on the window when he got too cold and I let him sleep under my bed wrapped in my thickest fleece and wearing my football socks.

Then something went wrong. Guy didn't appear one night. Initially unworried I was sure he could survive out there using his instincts. I wasn't his mum for goodness sake – not even his brother. Then I was awoken at about 4.20 a.m. by a familiar tapping sound. The taps were not strong or regular, but were persistent enough to be Pica – perhaps tired after a long flight, or maybe he'd just got lost.

I jumped out of bed, strode towards the window, and, tearing back the curtain, I made out a little forlorn figure behind the misted glass. Condensation ran down in drips as I unhooked the bar and swung the casement open. Pica made a chattering sound rather than use words and at first I wondered if the wrong bird had come in. In the gloomy morning light I peered closely at Pica and could see that something wasn't right; he seemed to be limping and one blue wing stuck up at a funny angle. His tail didn't flicker, but pointed down towards the ground, so I gathered him into my hands and instinctively brought him close to the warmth of my chest.

Then something suddenly pressed hard upon my hands and chest as Pica shimmered and expanded rapidly. The weight pushed me backwards and I just avoided hitting my head on the corner of my bed frame. The next thing I knew I was crushed underneath Guy's naked, sprawled body. He was sweaty and hot, his breathing shallow and uneven. With some effort I wriggled out from under his dead weight, his head thumping pathetically on the floor. With a real struggle, I managed to haul him up onto my bed, where I rolled him under my duvet for him to sleep. I wedged my chest of drawers in front of my door to stop Mum or Dad from just walking in and finding him there. I

144

sat on my chair, watching him breathe and splutter, wondering what to do next.

I must have fallen asleep in the chair, because when Guy's voice woke me, I came to with a start and felt a crick in my neck, which had been hanging to one side like that of a rag doll. My chin was soggy with saliva.

'Luke? Are you awake?'

'Yup.' I rolled my head round in a big circle, wincing as it clicked, and made loud gristly noises. 'Ow. You OK now?' I looked at him properly for the first time. His face was smeared with red and black streaks. 'What the hell happened to you?'

'I was attacked.'

'Oh my God!' I imagined Guy being mugged in an alleyway and him being too naive to understand why someone would want to hurt him. 'Who was it? What happened?'

'It was another male. I didn't know it was his territory. There weren't any signs – or I didn't notice them.'

What signs? Graffiti tags? Then it dawned on me.

'You mean another magpie?'

Guy nodded, wiping his eyes and scratching at the dried blood on his cheek.

'I didn't hear the warning call. Probably too much traffic or noise. I was just inspecting a broken bin bag when he dive-bombed me.'

I pulled a face, trying to imagine the scene.

'The first dive was to scare me. I tried to show him I was not a threat, but he just screeched and came at me again. Perhaps he thought I meant to take his mate or attack his nest. On the second dive he caught me with his claws on my wing as I attempted to get out of the way. Then he attacked again and again. His beak and claws ripped my flesh. In the end I was forced to defend myself, but then I managed to get away and hide in an open-topped lorry nearby. The other magpie seemed too scared to follow me and the lorry drove off. Because it was warm and safe, I slept and even changed back for a while, just hoping I wouldn't be found. Luckily, I wasn't disturbed and I managed to rest for a few hours.' Guy paused for a moment.

I wondered what would have happened if some burly lorry

driver had checked the back of his truck and found a naked, bleeding boy. Or perhaps worse, seen a shivering magpie in the corner. Would he have killed it? My head filled with this horrific image of some ignorant lout stepping on Guy with his size twelve boot, or whacking him viciously with a plank of wood. It was a grizzly thought that I shook away. Here he lay in front of me – alive.

'When I felt my strength return I changed back into Pica and flew here. It took all my energy.'

'I didn't know magpies could be so violent.'

'Pica's a crow, you know. *Corvidae*. Scavengers. And can be predatory when necessary.'

'Really? What, like a bird of prey?'

'Well, we're not as big, but Pica eats young birds as well as insects, snails – that sort of thing.'

'Yuck.' The thought of eating creepy crawlies made me gag. 'I never thought of you, I mean Pica, eating other creatures.'

'It's no different to you eating beef, chicken, or fish.'

'Well, I suppose –'

'The only difference is you don't do the killing.'

This made me think of Frisky, so I changed the subject.

'You need to clean yourself up. You can have a bath once my parents are out. I'll get a bowl of water for you to wash your face. What about the rest of you?'

I pulled the duvet down to his waist, horrified to see more bloody streaks across his chest and shoulders. The sheets were stained too. I screwed up my eyes, hoping reality would change in those few seconds but my sight was met with the same view again. There was nothing else for it; I'd have to get them washed and dried and back on the bed before Mum returned from work.

The cuts must have been from being pecked and on his back he showed me the tiny scratches from sharp talons, as if needles had been scraped across his flesh. The wounds were sharp and precise, and although they seemed tiny on Guy, they must have been more serious on the much smaller Pica.

'I'll find that stupid magpie and wring his neck if you like.'

'No, don't be silly.' Guy put his hand on my arm. 'It was

just following its instinct. That's what they do. It's a natural reflex. Animals don't have a conscience like humans. They just follow their gut feeling. It's intuition. Impulse. A kind of natural perception that they're born with and never question. That's all they have to live by. Humans were like that once but now we've forgotten what it's like because now people don't live with their numen. It's a great loss. It means most humans are not being their true selves.'

I became aware of my parents' alarm. They'd be slowly coming around to consciousness now and I had to be alert. Guy nodded his understanding when I put my finger to my lips. I began to get dressed into my school uniform, even though I had no intention of going in. Dad's footsteps passed my door on his way downstairs to feed Frisky and make the first cups of tea. Mum knocked on the door on her way to the shower as she always did, but never came in.

'Hiya. I'm up, thanks,' I called loudly. I heard her call out, 'Good morning.'

I had to pull the chest of drawers back away from the door quickly and without too much noise.

Guy had curled up onto his side in a foetal position when Dad returned and knocked on my door. I quickly darted forwards before he could enter, making sure I opened it just wide enough to receive the mug of tea. I needed to block Dad's view of my bed for obvious reasons, and that I had my school shirt on, half buttoned up, showed him I was getting ready.

'Oh, good lad. That's the ticket.' He turned away as I thanked him for the drink.

Once gone, I put down the tea and shook Guy gently.

'You need to hide in case Mum and Dad come into the room. You understand? Then once they've gone you can relax.'

'You OK, Luke?' Mum's voice startled me. I whipped my head around to see her opening my door. She obviously hadn't showered, then. 'Who are you talking to?'

I stepped hurriedly towards her.

'No-one. It was ... the radio.' I stood directly in front of her, probably too closely, as I had with Dad. 'I was just turning it off.'

147

'Oh, OK. Just checking you're not going mad or that you didn't sneak someone in. A girl, for instance?' She said it in a way which sounded like she'd be relieved if I had done – or was I just being paranoid?

She leaned forward to look over my shoulder. I relented and turned to let her past me. I'd never be able to explain this. The police would get involved; it would create horrible tensions with everyone. I'd have to explain it to everyone at school …

But as I turned to look at Guy, he'd gone. The bed lay empty, except for a tiny lump in the middle, which I could see, but would Mum? I even saw it move slightly.

'Only being daft, love.' She tousled my hair, gave me a big smile, and turned to leave. 'You having toast or cereal this morning?'

I gave my choice and closed the door, before sliding down it and onto the floor. The duvet moved and Pica fell onto the carpet, feathers all bristled and jutting out. He shook himself and began preening slowly and carefully.

That cup of tea tasted extremely good right then.

Chapter Twenty-five

So I pretended to go to school. This meant actually leaving the house at the right time and walking around the corner where I waited by some garages, hoping nobody had seen me or would come and retrieve their car. I doubted if any were kept in these garages; probably all storing furniture or stolen goods. No-one disturbed me. I had to trust that Mum didn't go into my room and poke about. I had closed the door firmly to make sure Frisky didn't go in! Once it got to 8.45 I felt certain they'd both left and returned to the house. Seeing both cars gone I knew it would be safe. I opened the front door and closed it quickly behind me, hoping the neighbours weren't watching, ready to report all to my parents.

At first I couldn't find Guy and I panicked that he'd been found by my parents or Frisky. He was certainly not strong enough to have flown off. After a proper search I found Pica asleep under my bed, tucked into the far corner behind a stack of old comics. I decided to leave him, as sleep could only be the best thing. My movements and sounds hadn't disturbed him. Even though I did think the worst initially, I could see him breathing and twitching as he slept.

Tiptoeing and being as quiet as I could, I stripped the bed linen and took off the duvet cover, gathered it into the smallest bundle I could manage, and carried it downstairs to the washing machine. How difficult could it be to operate?

I pushed the dirty laundry straight in through the round hole and stooped down to look at the dials and controls. What the hell is a 'prewash' and 'rinse hold'? There were lots of numbers on a dial from 30 to 95 and then a choice of larger numbers: 700 to 1600. It meant nothing to me. Another button offered me the options of 'Super Rinse', 'Heavy', and 'Skip'. I wondered where the 'Punch Hard' and 'Head Butt' switches were situated.

I had a brain wave and decided to look for labels. They'd help me sort out this dilemma. The duvet cover was a new one with dark colours and patterns. It was bound to have a label – but I couldn't find one anywhere. The sheet said 40 degrees centigrade, but would that remove blood? Vaguely recalling that hotter washes shifted more dirt I went for the highest numbers on both and selected 'Intense Wash' for good measure.

Pressing 'Start' made it click and whir, then I heard water gushing into the machine. All seemed well.

Telly always showed crap programmes during the day; probably to deter kids from bunking off school. That was my theory.

After an hour, the washing machine was still rumbling round and round and I just had to hope this was normal. I had no idea if it was, to be honest. After another ten minutes or so of worrying it suddenly stopped and began beeping at me, loudly and persistently, as if shouting for me to come and sort something out. Perhaps it had broken down.

I tried to see if the dials or buttons were giving away any clues. Perhaps the contents were ready to hang up, although putting up the washing-line-whirligig-thingy outside wasn't really an option with prying neighbours, so I considered using the hairdryer. I tried opening the washing machine's front-loading door, but it wouldn't budge. It seemed to be locked. I shook the whole thing quite hard and then kicked it, hurting my slippered toes in the process. Peering closely into the round window I could see the machine was still filled up to near the top with water – I could see it slopping around. How the hell did you get the water out? If I had opened the door it would have flooded the entire kitchen.

I then spotted a dial labelled 'Spin Cycle'. I turned it randomly and then pressed lots of other buttons, angrily hitting them and grazing my knuckles as I did so. Miraculously, the machine suddenly came back to life and the unmistakeable sound of draining water made me feel elated. The level definitely went down and the faster motor of the spin dryer whizzed into action, and I felt a great sense of relief and a little pride that I had – albeit inadvertently – managed to work out how to wash my own sheets.

With a smug feeling settling upon me I went up to check on Guy.

A human leg stuck out from under my bed and, as I approached to see if he was comfortable there, I saw it move.

'Luke? That you? Give me a hand.' Guy's hand reached out and I crouched down and pulled on it with both my hands. The whole bed moved with him. 'My legs have gone to sleep. Pins and needles. I often get it after changing.'

I tugged with all my might and the top half of him emerged. I put my arms under his armpits and leaned backwards. After his legs appeared we toppled comically backwards, although Guy had a soft landing – me.

Seeing the state he was in I remembered what was required.

'I'll run you a bath.' I paced to the bathroom, where I turned both taps on full before squeezing lots of gloopy bubble bath under the running water. At three-quarters full I turned off the taps and called him. Preferring not to see him naked yet again I returned downstairs to see if the spin cycle had finished yet.

It hadn't, but I did spot a 'Pause' button, which I pressed, and watched as the whole machine juddered, screamed, and wheezed to a halt. Once the barrel had stopped rotating I waited a few more seconds before trying the door, which opened easily and I triumphantly pulled out the clean linen.

Except something was wrong.

The duvet had been dark and colourful, but I was certain I had put the clean white sheets in with it – and yet nothing I pulled out looked in the least bit white. All the material slowly spilling from the washing machine was decidedly dark. Then the horror dawned on me – the colours had run. Never mix colours and whites. I recalled my mum saying this now – she always asked me for my whites or my colours but I'd never really considered it before.

'No-o-o-o!'

The sheets were ruined – now streaked with black, grey, and dark red. I'd made them worse than before. What was I supposed to tell Mum and Dad? Should I lose the evidence and find some new sheets for my bed and hope nobody would see? As if Mum wouldn't notice.

I sat for a while in a daze, trying not to panic. First, I had to come up with a story to explain why I was washing the sheets. I could just say that I wanted to be helpful; I am turning over a new leaf, after all, and I wanted to save Mum a job. It didn't sound very plausible. It looked dubious that I only washed them and not the other things in the laundry basket. Then it occurred to me that I could say I felt really ill and had wet the bed, then due to being really embarrassed I had tried to clear up and got it wrong. Surely Mum and Dad would understand and even compliment me for doing the right thing. They always went on about how important it is to 'do the right thing'. And now I had.

As long as they didn't suspect me of harbouring a runaway and of lying to them – even though I was guilty of both … but that wasn't the point.

By the time I had gone back upstairs Guy was standing in my bedroom wrapped in Mum's fluffiest pink towel. I rifled through my drawers for some clothes, finding my oldest boxer shorts, a faded T-shirt, and some ripped jeans, all of which he caught gratefully.

'When my mum and dad get home you have to hide.'

'Sure,' Guy said with a yawn. 'I'm feeling much better, thanks. I might even go out for a bit later.'

I guessed he meant as Pica. It would have been a bit patronising of me to argue with him. He's big enough to look after himself.

We chatted about magpies and birds for a while, until Guy announced he felt tired and immediately fell into a trance-like sleep. I suddenly remembered I had left the ruined sheets on the floor downstairs and wandered down again, vaguely considering my options. Best to just confess and give the bed-wetting explanation, however humiliating it sounded. I watched a few films until Mum returned just before tea, by which time I had learnt my lines by rote.

She nodded and tutted as I told her my story, smiling kindly.

'Hmm. I'll have to teach you how to do it properly, won't I? Perhaps doing the washing could be one of your jobs you do for pocket money.'

This alarming suggestion wasn't quite what I'd had in mind, but I couldn't exactly argue.

When I said about being ill and wetting the bed, she nodded thoughtfully and said something a little odd.

'I think I understand what you're telling me. It's perfectly normal, isn't it, for boys your age? Don't you worry about it. It's natural and healthy.' And she wandered off to the kitchen to start getting tea ready. I left her to it, slightly puzzled, and went to my bedroom. Guy sat on my bed, stretching his back and rolling his shoulders.

He got up and opened my window. Just as I heard Mum's footsteps ascend the stairs, Guy transformed. The clothes fell to the floor and Pica got to the window sill, poked his head out into the cold air, and then disappeared.

A few moments later Mum tapped lightly on my door.

'Could you remember to pull the plug out the bath and clean up after yourself next time?'

Guy must have left the water in and I imagine all that dirt would have left a grubby ring around the edge. Stupid me, forgetting to check. If I remained that careless then we'd be caught. I must think and be more cautious next time.

'Sorry, Mum.'

'OK. I'll have to put the water on so I can have a good soak later. And why are those clothes lying all screwed up on the floor? Honestly!'

When Dad got home I heard their conversation, which explained Mum's weird comment, and which grossed me out completely.

'I think poor Luke was the victim of adolescent fantasies last night,' I heard her say.

'Eh? You what?' Dad was being his usual dim self. Subtlety didn't work with him.

'I caught him washing his sheets and duvet.'

'Um, yeah. That's good isn't it? He's become so much more helpful recently.'

Mum's voice sounded a bit exasperated. 'What I mean is, I think he was trying to hide something from us.'

'Really? What would that be?'

'Oh, for goodness sake, you were his age once. What's the polite way of saying it? Teenage nocturnal emissions? Wet dreams?'

'Oh, I see! I see what you're getting at now. Right. Yes. That. Hmm.'

'The same thing must have happened to you.'

I turned away from the door and fled upstairs. I couldn't bear to hear any more.

Chapter Twenty-six

I didn't see Guy for a few days, but I tried not to worry. Sure enough, he returned, full of life and looking in good shape. I remembered his knowledge of herbal medicine and I guessed he'd found the right plants to use to get his health back up to full strength.

School had contacted my parents to ask when I was going to return, which made for a very awkward discussion. I admitted to bunking.

'But why, Luke?' Mum asked with a pained expression in her eyes. She was *that* close to telling me how disappointed she was in me. 'There's usually a reason for this sort of thing. Please tell us.'

I remained silent. Dad just sat staring at me with a look of puzzlement fixed upon his face, the sort of look he has whenever he hears any hip-hop or rap.

Unfortunately, my mouth proved itself quicker than my brain.

'I'm being bullied.'

'Ah. We finally get to the truth.' Mum seemed pleased as she looked at Dad.

Dad just gave me the full 'disappointed' look. All his dreams of proudly nurturing a tough, sporty son were shattered in that one moment. His silence became poignant, but I was trapped on a runaway train.

'Have you told school?'

I nodded meekly. The last thing I wanted was for my parents to march me down to school. This was going horribly wrong.

'Yes, they're dealing with it. I don't want to make a big issue of it. I can handle it.'

Dad suddenly shook himself out of his despondent trance. 'That's it, son. You need to stand up for yourself and deal with this your own way.'

'Fighting back will just get him into trouble, though,' Mum retorted.

'It's a dog-eat-dog world out there, love. Experiences like these teach you how to survive. We all have to take a punch every now and then. School of hard knocks and all that kind of stuff, you know. Let Luke deal with it. We can't always be there to protect him. He's growing up.' Dad stared beyond me.

On the one hand he was helping me out of a difficult situation – but on the other he was basically saying that a good beating might be good for me. Make a real man out of me. Cheers, Dad.

'Well, Mr Saddler has asked me to take Luke in and have a meeting to get him back into the daily routine. Like a fresh start. We're meeting him tomorrow morning at 8.30.'

'I can't,' Dad said. 'Too much on at the office. We're snowed under.'

The next morning Mr Saddler beckoned Mum and me into his office at precisely 8.30 a.m. Just as the big digital display on the wall flicked onto 8.30, his door opened to reveal him filling the rectangular frame. I sat on the plastic chair while he and Mum had softer chairs, forming a triangle in front of his desk. Mr Saddler hugged his right knee, which he hooked over his left thigh.

'Now, I think it's important to start by saying that Luke is not in trouble as such. I don't want you to feel this is some kind of sanction or disciplinary hearing. It isn't.' To my horror he leaned towards Mum and cupped a hand over her shoulder. She bristled slightly and gave a less than natural smile. This seemed to please Saddler, who moved back into his original position. 'Now, I assume he has told you about his unique situation and indeed his courage of late?'

Mum's eyebrows dented. 'Yes, he's told us everything.'

This clearly wasn't true but I assumed Mum didn't want to be caught out as a bad parent who didn't listen to, or understood, her own child. So far so good.

'Splendid. Then we're all singing from the same hymn-sheet, as it were. Good.' He gave a self-satisfied nod. 'So, as Luke's situation is a unique one, we're willing to overlook the absences, but need some reassurance that he will be fully committed to his studies from now on, so that he can get back to meeting his target grades and realising his true potential.'

'Yes, I'll make sure he gets to school every day. My boss is willing to give me flexitime so that I can drive Luke to school each morning and watch him walk through the gates.' Now it was Mum's turn to look pleased with herself. This was news to me.

'Marvellous.' Saddler gazed admiringly at Mum with increasing intensity and it occurred to me that the old perv probably fancied her. The thought made me wince.

'If only all parents could be as dedicated and as compassionate as you.' Then he leaned forward to clasp her shoulder as before. Mum froze and didn't smile this time. Saddler released her and sat back deeply on his chair with his hands on his knees. 'I feel sure Luke will get through this difficult stage with your support –'

'Yes, and my husband's too,' Mum added emphatically.

Saddler's lips twitched somewhat before continuing.

'So even though Luke is a bit different, I feel very certain that he can –'

'I beg your pardon?' Mum intervened.

'Sorry?' Saddler's head moved forward in isolation, like that of a tortoise peeking out of its shell.

'You said "different". In what way is Luke different?'

'Did I say that?' Mr Saddler's voice tensed into a panic. 'I don't think I did say that. Did I? What was it? Different? No, no. Luke's not different at all. He's the same as everyone else. We're all the same. He's not different in the least.' The pace of his words increased. 'Are you sure I said that? I'm positive I didn't. No, no, no. He's exactly the same as all our pupils. Not at all different. We're all equal; alike; identical; one and the same.'

I was nervous that he'd let on about the whole ridiculous gay misunderstanding and I was just glad that Dad wasn't here. Explaining it all to Mum would be difficult enough.

'We treat all pupils the same at this school. No prejudice or favouritism – ever.' He was back-pedalling now and I was waiting for him to fall down his self-dug hole.

'Glad to hear it,' said Mum, sounding a bit annoyed and bored now. 'Perhaps you were merely referring to the fact that he's become something of a victim recently.'

'That's it! Yes. That's it. Entirely. That's exactly what I meant. I said it in sympathy of someone being victimised.'

'So you admit you did say it then?'

'What? No, I don't think so. I just meant if I did say it, which I didn't – then I would have said it – although I didn't – for the reason that you just explained. That's all. You can't prove it otherwise.' He looked at his watch. 'Now then, if you don't mind, I have other appointments to attend to.'

Mum shuffled on her chair. 'So I have your word that Luke will be safe and properly cared for here?'

'You have my word.'

She didn't look overly impressed but stood up anyway. Saddler held out both hands towards her as if hoping for a hug but Mum moved in the opposite direction towards the door. 'I'll leave Luke in your safekeeping then. See you later, love,' she added, touching my head affectionately. She left the door open and I listened to the sound of her heels striking the polished floor of the corridor.

Giving a little wave to her back, I stayed in my seat to await my orders from Mr Saddler. Perhaps being considered gay had its benefits. I felt certain, though, that it wouldn't be the case once I got to the classroom.

'Right then, young man. Follow me.' He thrust his hands in to his trouser pockets and strode ahead of me, on the familiar path to my form room.

As I followed closely behind him he spoke without turning around.

'You don't feel we've treated you any differently, do you? At all?' This was clearly concerning him. Not replying seemed to make him more anxious. 'Because we won't be seen to tolerate prejudice here. It doesn't matter what your ... um ... inclinations ... or ... um ... well, leanings are.

You know? Your, um … orientation. It matters not in the least. Not one jot. And you won't be treated any differently to anyone else. Because you're exactly the same. As everyone else in this school. The same. Exactly. Full stop.' We turned a corner and made for the white door labelled 13A – my tutor base. 'Here we are, Luke. Remember what I said, and if you ever need to talk you can always speak to me, Mrs Fuller, or indeed the school counsellor and we'll be behind you all the way.' He suddenly spluttered and spoke rapidly again. 'Well, you know what I mean, I'm sure. Good day.'

Like a soldier he did an exaggerated about-turn and scuttled away in a half-run.

I braced myself for the dramatic entrance to come, and pushed open the door.

'Oi, oi. Backs ter the wall, lads. Here's batty-boy!'

'Where's your boyfriend, Gay-guy?'

I ignored the taunts and walked towards my usual seat next to Simon.

'You can't sit here, you queer.' Simon gave me a dirty look. Others were giggling and smirking as I stood there feeling lost and empty inside. Mr Fairclough looked up.

'Ah, Luke. Welcome back. Sit down, lad.' He gestured for me to sit. 'Good to have you back again.'

Ignoring Simon, whose feet were on my chair as a warning to keep off, I sat down anyway. He sneered and moved his feet away.

'Don't touch me. I don't want AIDS.'

Mr Fairclough ignored us, more intent on peering at his laptop, which meant my former friends could continue their sudden torrent of abuse. Eventually, the tutor snapped his laptop shut and wandered over towards me, completely oblivious to the enmity aimed at me from all directions.

He called for everyone's attention. 'I just wanted to say, welcome back, Luke. I realise it's been tough for you. Mr Saddler tells me you're coming back initially on a half timetable. The rest of the class here have promised to help out and get things quickly back to normal.'

'He ain't normal, sir.'

'Um, thank you. We'll have none of that. We're a team, remember. Like one big happy family and we should always pull together. It's not easy for Luke. Help him out, folks, and go easy on him for these first few days.'

'Sounds like he needs to man up a bit, sir.'

'Yeah. He just ain't man enough.'

'Have you got any man in you? 'Cos I bet you'd like some!'

The whole group exploded into jeers. Mr Fairclough tried and failed to retain some kind of order until, to my relief, the bell rang, signalling for everyone to get up before being told to. Half the class had already gone, with Mr Fairclough still shouting over the noise of scraping chairs and raised voices.

I was left alone with him. He smiled sheepishly, looked like he wanted to say something, but then walked past me.

'Have a good day. See you later, Luke.'

Getting through that day proved a matter of survival. I remembered a picture that, ironically, Simon had sent to my phone of a fox marching surreptitiously in the middle of a group of hunting-hounds with the caption, 'When you are in deep poo, look straight ahead, keep your mouth shut, and say nothing!' Good advice. I hurtled through the day, ignoring all comments and lurching from one lesson to the next.

This must have been exactly how Guy had felt every day at school, and it really made me appreciate the weekends even more.

It felt like it would never stop. Each day was going to build on the one before and compound the problem, resulting eventually in abject misery. When complete despair and loss of all self-worth possess you, it's impossible to see a way out, even when parents and teachers tell you to 'Hang in there' or try to persuade you it'll be over soon and you'll look back on this time one day and laugh. None of that eases the pain because you simply don't believe it's true. Feeling wretched about yourself is the worst sensation. You start to believe what people tell you. Perhaps I am worthless and disgusting.

I kept an eye out for Cheryl but didn't see her. She'd not been returning my texts.

160

Connor was the worst of all. After school he found me and pinned me to my locker. He had a big crowd of tough lads around him and as he shouted he spat all over my face, his voice full of unexpected malevolence.

'Shirt-lifters like you make me sick! You need to learn how to be a real man. You should be ashamed of yourself, gay-boy. All you queers should be shot, man. Put down at birth. It's a disease! You keep your gay-boy arse away from me. My dick is only for the babes, you get me? And there's plenty of them seen it in action. You ever talk to me or touch me, I'll kill ya.'

Then unexpectedly, he wrenched my head to one side, cricking my neck painfully. Connor had my hair in his fist and had jerked my head right down. His mouth came within an inch of my eyes. I watched it open and shut angrily but couldn't make out his final words as it took all my energy to overcome the agony. A white sheen flashed across my eyes and I realised that I was about to faint, so I shifted my stance haphazardly and groped for something to hang onto. My hand felt only shoulders, hands, and blazers. The crowd scattered quickly amid cries of derision.

'Ugh! He's trying to kiss me!'

'I think he wants to shag you!'

'Get out before he bums us all!'

'Run for your lives!'

Within seconds I was alone with just enough energy to lean light-headedly against the lockers. I closed my eyes and breathed heavily, the white fog gradually dissipating until my sight fully returned. I tipped forward, which pushed me away from the wall, to give me some momentum to begin my slow trudge home.

Chapter Twenty-seven

'I think I've done it!'

Before hearing what he'd done, I felt quite keen to persuade Guy to put on the clothes I had ready for him. The transformation occurred once more before my eyes – a miracle; as if his very being, or essence, changed into a gas, and then condensed into a liquid before finally solidifying.

It was two in the morning and I hadn't seen him for a while. I was glad he was OK. He didn't seem too keen on the jeans and T-shirt I held up for him, although he nodded vacantly when I reminded him about being quiet and being ready to hide or change.

'I can be more than just Pica! Yesterday it finally happened. I changed into Bufo.'

'Bufo?'

'Watch.'

He closed his eyes, yet nothing happened immediately. He crouched down on all fours and began making a noise like he was going to be sick. His cheeks blew out and I saw his skin begin to ripple and spasm, and the familiar shimmering and discolouring occurred just before he vanished.

No, he didn't vanish. He just shrunk quicker than my eye could follow. Then there on my carpet, about a metre away from my bare feet, sat a squat, slimy creature with warty, lumpy brown-grey skin. A toad.

Stooping right down I placed a hand on the floor before him and he waddled awkwardly onto it. I'd expected him to hop. For a few moments I watched his throat pulsate in and out. His back throbbed at a different rate to his throat. His eyes were yellow with black slits.

Then he belched. It sounded like a bubbly fart. He repeated the sound. The third time sounded vaguely different and I held

Bufo close to my ear.

'Window,' he seemed to rasp. Then again I heard, 'Window.'

It was still open from when I'd let him in as Pica. I placed him on the window sill, noting that his skin didn't feel slimy. He flopped towards the open window and I was concerned that he'd jump or fall out, but he settled himself in the gap and I watched him for a few minutes, before I realised he was eyeing a large moth which had landed close by on the adjacent window. It must have been a good ten centimetres away. Bufo shuffled slightly, and with a sudden jump it released its spring-coiled tongue in a flash and was suddenly munching on the moth, whose wings now hung limply from the toad's jaws. A few jerks of his head and the long wings disappeared. I left him dining on insects for a while, trying to ignore the crunching, crackling sounds.

I crept back into bed, glad to rest and lie down as my body still ached from my tiring and soul-destroying day. I must have dozed off, as the next thing I knew Bufo was belching next to me. And he stank.

'I want you to help me find my *numen*.'

I'd been thinking about this for days – wondering if Guy was just a freak or whether we all had the same potential.

Then he transformed before my eyes. I reached out for the previously discarded clothes. He sighed but seemed to understand my reasoning, then he sat at my feet, leaning his back against the wall.

'You want to find and become your *numen*?'

'Yeah.' I sat up too, unable to pull the duvet with me to keep warm as Guy was weighing it down. 'I want to find out which animal I'm spiritually linked to. Is it just one, or do I have many? You have Pica and now Bufo. How come?'

'There's one which we are all naturally attuned to. For me, it's Pica. But there are other shapes that we can also become as we become more sensitive and adept. I was certain I can recall my own mother becoming more than one animal, but I was never sure and never had the chance to ask her.'

'How long has she been ill?'

164

'For years now.'

'Do you still see her?'

'Not for a long time.'

A silence encircled us and for a while seemed appropriate.

With my lamp on I noticed how wiry and wrinkled Guy was; old before his time. His craggy face was not that of a boy and the angle of the light accentuated these lines until I couldn't be sure if it was an optical illusion or not.

'How do I go about finding and becoming my *numen*?'

Guy considered this deeply.

'By searching inside your own soul.'

I grimaced and twisted my mouth to one side.

'O-K ... But what does that mean? How can I do that?'

'By working out who and what you really are, and by experiencing the elements of nature.'

I nodded, as if doing so would help me make sense of these vague instructions.

'Yeah, but how can I do that?' I tried not sound too exasperated.

'Rock, air, water, fire, vegetation, and then animal.'

'What? I have to become those?'

'In a sense.' Guy had become unhelpfully enigmatic.

'What, a literal or a metaphorical one?'

'In a real sense.' He closed his eyes as if starting to meditate.

'So I have to become a rock and a vegetable? Right, I choose to become a stick of rhubarb, then. Or maybe a potato. At least it'll be quiet underground and I won't have to put up with your pretentious crap any more. That is, before I get cut into quarters, smothered in tuna mayonnaise, and eaten in my jacket.'

'You need to be like the rocks and become a part of the world. Be a tree by slowing down and being patient while you listen to the ancient truths. Fly through the air to feel the power of nature. Become like water as you flow over different strands of the truth, connecting with all parts of creation, and then you are fire as you die of yourself and transform into the shape of another; your souls uniting and melting together. Once you've done these then your *numen* will become alive in you and you in it.'

As no sensible response to this occurred to me, I kept quiet. I thought through his words. They kind of made sense. The idea that I might get the chance to fly again filled me with excitement. This time I might be able to appreciate it a bit more.

'So what's the first step then?'

'You've already taken it,' Guy replied quickly.

'Oh. Have I? When?'

'When you decided to listen and chose to learn how to tune in to yourself,' Guy answered. 'You were kind to me and allowed me to be myself. Because you've seen this in me, you've changed and now want this reality for yourself. That's the first step.' Guy scratched his chin thoughtfully. 'You're beginning to realise that you are not just an individual with your own struggle through life. You are a part of this world. An essential part of a much greater whole. What happens to you affects others, and what happens to them affects you. You exist because other people and animals and plants and elements exist. You are not on your own – but part of something living. You are an element of nature just like any animal, plant, mountain, air molecule, cloud, or grain of sand.'

'I think I'm beginning to understand,' I said, lying back down. 'But what can I actually do? Practically, I mean. You need to show me what to do next.'

'Once you've accepted that you are an animal – a creature like an ant, an elephant, a magpie – then you need to understand how to be a human. Humans have imaginations; an ability to empathise and show emotions. They can love and be selfless and not just out of instinct or self-protection. People can create complex inventions and put theoretical ideas into practice and apply ideas to different situations. People communicate and write down ideas for future generations to learn from. This has created something unique called our soul or *numen*. But they are not just for us. We must use these gifts to give something back to nature. We do this by sharing our soul with other living things.'

'Other animals.'

'Or plants. Or stones, or drops of water, or flames.

Everything in our world is alive, just in ways we can't always understand.'

'Religions talk about souls or spirits. Is that what you mean? Believing in God? A creator?' I did my best to keep up with Guy, but I was quickly losing his drift. I said this to show I was thinking it all through carefully.

'Sure. If it's a way to help you understand it, that's fine. But I'm not sure believing because you're scared of being pitch-forked into hell is very useful.'

'So where does God fit into this?'

'Wherever you want him to. Although once you get into religious beliefs all the little rules and regulations start to get in the way of the truth, don't they?'

I wasn't sure as I only had a rudimentary understanding of the various religious faiths from school assemblies and RS lessons. Guy didn't strike me as weirdly religious anyway. Weird, sure, but not a religious nut. He'd never mentioned God before.

'Right, then,' I said, attempting to sum up what I understood from all this so far. 'I've done the "rock" thing by accepting my place in nature. Right? So now I have to be a tree, yeah? So grow really tall, lose my leaves, and drop fruit on passers-by?'

Once again, the irony was lost on Guy.

'You need to learn the patience and inner strength of the mighty oak, who listens to the wind and the rain. His roots stretch far outwards, reaching for the truth and soaking up elements of nature. Then he's inhabited by birds, mammals, and insects, who all confide in him their unique stories for hundreds and thousands of years. The oak waits and observes and never casts judgement.'

'But I can't live for hundreds of years.' I was starting to sound moody, and felt my frustration returning.

'You can by being patient.'

'So how long will it take?'

'Until you fully understand.'

'How do I know when that is?'

He actually smiled at me before replying. 'It will be when you stop having to ask me such stupid questions.'

I couldn't help but laugh. We actually shared a moment of laughter.

'Fair enough. I think I'm ready to try the next step then.'

'Good.' Guy stood up and changed into Pica. 'I'll return in a few days.' He flew out of the open window, which I shut quietly before returning to bed.

Chapter Twenty-eight

The weekend afforded me some quiet time to reflect on the way my life had changed in the last few weeks. I still had some time to go before half-term. How school days dragged. Thank God for weekends. I spent a bit more time with Mum and Dad and even started to enjoy walks with them. Dad took me to a wetlands bird reserve and explained the many species of wildfowl and waders; it was completely fascinating. I was so engrossed I didn't want to leave, and enjoyed the magical sound of the names of the birds. Peewit. Turnstone. Merganser. Avocet. Gadwall. Smew. I repeated these like a mantra. We saw skylarks rising vertically then hovering as they warbled and shrilled beautifully; he pointed out buzzards and yellowhammers whose song sounded like a lunch order; 'A little bit of bread and no cheese!' How stupid had I been, not appreciating these wonders?

The way I looked at the sky and the horizon had also changed. The clouds were beautiful and peaceful, like whales floating in a tranquil sea. The shapes of the trees intrigued me, as did the outlines and patterns of the leaves which looked like giant fingerprints. Had I been blind before now?

I continued to appreciate Frisky too. There was no knowing how long we'd have him. Would he die again at some point, or live forever?

Then Cheryl called me on Sunday morning.

The shrill ringtone made me jump. Nobody had called or texted me for a few weeks now. In fact, sometimes I didn't even bother to turn my phone on. Yet now Cheryl's name flashed on the display and I contemplated leaving it unanswered, but then changed my mind. I felt I could take her on.

'Hiya, darlin'. I've missed you, sweetie.'

This comment disarmed me completely.

'Hi, Cheryl. I wasn't sure if you were still talking to me or not.'

'Yeah, course, darlin'. You're my new BFF, intcha? Just had a bit o' me own business to sort out.'

'Really? Oh, OK then.'

'You wanna meet up later?'

'Sure.' I was excited to hear from her and I had to remember she viewed me as her gay friend, and try to keep it cool. 'I'm free from two. Shall I come round to yours?' I pictured myself sitting in her bedroom surrounded by her underwear.

'I'll meet you in town. By the war memorial at two thirty. See ya then.'

I didn't say anything, but she'd already rung off. Two thirty it was then.

Even though I was nervous about seeing others from school, I walked confidently into town. On the way it occurred to me that this could be a set-up. Perhaps Cheryl was tricking me and she had Connor, Simon, and the others waiting to pounce on me around the corner.

Keep going, I told myself. *I can't hide indoors forever. Face your fears. That's it.* I became aware that I was muttering loudly to myself and getting some strange looks from passing strangers.

The outskirts of town were already densely populated, meaning the centre itself would be packed. The gates to the mall were right by the tall war memorial, and I was nervous about being recognised by someone from school. It seemed inevitable. As I waited I kept my head down and wondered if Cheryl would be alone or with her gaggle of hangers-on. Panic swept over me when I felt a hand on my shoulder. I spun round and swapped panic for relief on seeing Cheryl – alone.

She even kissed me on the cheek and took my hand. A wonderful moment.

'Shall we go straight in or have a drink first?'

'Let's shop,' I replied, hoping it was the right response.

She seemed pleased and we strolled around the corner to New Look and entered the shop displaying a 360 degree array of tops, skirts, and accessories. The colours and choices overwhelmed me slightly.

'Should I go for dark or light?'

She gazed at me, waiting for my answer. As her supposedly gay friend she was expecting a knowledgeable response. I knew nothing whatsoever about fashion. She would rumble me straight away. I stared back intently and half-closed my eyes as if concentrating hard. I then scanned the tops hanging up – most of which seemed to be dark autumnal colours. I glanced back at what she was already wearing, hoping it might give me a clue. The clothes she had on were mostly dark, so I went for it.

'Oh, definitely darks.'

She gave me a hug. 'Correct. You're a fashion guru. You have an eye for this sort of thing. I knew I could rely on you.' She pulled me to one of the walls full of blouses that all looked the same and selected three. Then I felt myself being dragged towards the changing rooms.

'Come on, fashion guru.'

A surly girl who looked about sixteen stopped us at the entrance of the changing rooms.

'He can't come in.' She jabbed a finger at me accusingly.

Cheryl snorted a laugh. 'You can let him in, darlin', he's as bent as nine pound note. Or dontcha believe in gay rights? He's expressing his feminine side, innee?' She bent her wrist and pouted. 'One of the girls, you know.' The shop worker shrugged and checked her watch.

We marched past her confidently and entered a curtained booth.

I couldn't believe my luck as I helped Cheryl pull her top off over her head. She handed me the warm garment to fold up and place on the chair. Her black lacy bra pushed her cleavage together and it took all my inner strength to not reach out and touch her lovely firm roundness. I had to consciously not stare. Instead, I grabbed the purple blouse and held it open for her to slip her arms in. I even started to get a bit over-confident and did her buttons up for her, lightly brushing my fingers against her bosom. She actually smiled as I did this and I had to breathe deeply to control myself. Once done up, Cheryl took half a step back – which was as far as the cubicle allowed her to – for me to take in the effect.

'Beautiful,' I murmured with genuine pleasure.

'Does it go with my skin tone?'

'Definitely,' I nodded. 'I was about to say exactly that!'

She stepped forward and gave me an awesome hug. 'Lukey, my definite BFF.'

I wanted the B to stand for 'boy' rather than 'best', but felt certain that wouldn't happen. If she found out I wasn't gay after all she'd be screaming and calling me a pervert. I'd be chained up and put in a dark cell somewhere. If George Orwell's *Nineteen Eighty-Four* came true I'd be profoundly guilty of many 'thoughtcrimes'.

To my delight, however, I helped Cheryl try on the blue and black blouses too, biting my tongue when I felt the urge to suggest she try one without her bra. I did receive another hug and enjoyed the warmth she radiated through the long, touching surface we created with our bodies.

'So?'

My mind went blank. *So what?* Had I missed something she'd said just before? By now she had her original top back on and was holding up the three blouses for further inspection. I guessed right.

'I'd say the purple.'

'You mean indigo?'

'Well, obviously, yes – I meant the indigo one. It's a mysterious colour, regal almost. Just fitting for someone so beautiful and enigmatic.'

'Dunno what the hell you're on about, love, but you make it sound good. Indigo it is then. C'mon, BFF.'

I followed her out of the cubicle, even though I wanted to stay in there with her. I should have pulled her back and kissed her right there. But I didn't.

We did shoes, jumpers, and she even tried on a few hats, but we sadly never strayed near the underwear sections in any department store. Throughout the day she continued to refer to me as her BFF rather than use my name which began to grate, because I wanted people to look at us and consider us a couple rather than see me as 'one of the girls'. Things went further downhill when she met up with her coven of friends and they all rattled off into their gossip and chatter, which I didn't understand in the slightest and couldn't keep up with as they constantly changed subject. After half an hour of feeling pushed aside I got up to leave.

'You off somewhere?' Cheryl pouted and got up. Frantically searching for an appropriate excuse I nodded, with my mind remaining completely blank.

'Oh, OK then, lover.' This name brought me a great deal of pleasure; then, to my increasing delight, Cheryl flounced over to me and gave me a histrionic kiss and a hug. Still reeling from that, I also got a few pecks and squeezes from some of the others, and by the time they'd all finished I waved at them as they all chorused sorry goodbyes and I walked off with my head full of startlingly 18-rated images.

At home I attempted to think about my *numen,* but couldn't get beyond Cheryl's cleavage. Guy had suggested, rather obliquely, a way of finding my spirit animal. The process seemed complicated, something about being like a tree, water, and fire. Somehow. The tree bit didn't fill me with a great deal of excitement, but fire and water sounded a bit more dynamic. I needed Guy to help me out as it all felt a bit distant and overwhelming. Instead, I lay down, gave in, and allowed my imagination to return to those images naturally dominating every part of me.

Chapter Twenty-nine

I saw Pica and Bufo a few times that week, but not Guy; so I had to assume he was finding his own food and shelter. I began to empathise with all the poor creatures, especially knowing how cold it got outside. Then one night I was woken by him in the silent darkness.

'I'm freezing.'

I opened my eyes and saw his human outline in the gloom. I usually left the window unlatched and he had worked out how to access my room directly without me having to be present.

'It's frosty out there. I need warmth.'

Groaning slightly, I firstly insisted that he put on some pyjamas before letting him under my snug duvet. I turned my back to him and let him wriggle in beside me. He held me for warmth – not for any other reason; I knew that and it only seemed fair. Once he'd regained a proper body temperature I kicked him out with his own blanket and he scuttled underneath my bed and curled up happily. Sometimes I regarded him as a peculiar pet, and he often obliged by acting exactly that way – perhaps I should have let him curl up at my feet.

Can you hear me?

It didn't actually sound like a voice speaking. The words entered my head, but were not mine. I often silently spoke to myself, but these words came from elsewhere.

I'd finally gone mad! I was hearing voices. Perhaps it was God or an angel; maybe a fairy or an alien? I'd lost it. Gone completely doolally.

Luke? Can you sense me?

It knew my name! I was lost forever.

It didn't have the same quality as a voice – no sound went through my ears. The words existed in my head somehow. My schizophrenic mind had finally divided into another personality and I now possessed a second me completely independent of my Luke-self. Oh God! I needed a psychiatrist right now. Just not Miss Mire – she'd find a way of making the whole experience dull and ordinary. This felt like a mystical experience, the sort of thing that when you try to explain it to someone in the cold light of day makes you appear like a right weirdo, and the more you explain it the less convinced you become. But as the voice entered my mind again – however it did so – I knew this wasn't madness or a delusion.

Guy wasn't in my room. At least not as Guy. I wondered if Pica or Bufo was hiding somewhere and talking to me from a secret place. But even that didn't make sense because it didn't come from any particular direction – I couldn't locate its source. I did look under my bed and in the obvious places to no avail.

Luke. Sit down and take heed.

That was a strange phrase. Why not just 'listen'?

It was this which convinced me my instinct was correct – no voice was actually speaking. The words were manifesting themselves inside my mind, but independently of me. I'd seen lots of science fiction films and wondered if some alien creature was telepathically communicating with me. Or was I being possessed by a demon?

Neither and both, it seemed.

Luke. This is Guy. I have become part of you.

Of course it was Guy. But the voice sounded different. I had to remind myself that it wasn't a voice – more a new thought inside my head. A thought placed there by someone else. How strange it felt to have another creature in there – someone other. This was an invasion of personal space in extremis.

'How did you get there?' I said these words aloud.

I have found a third form for my numen. I am a parasite. You are my host.

That idea seemed very scary.

'You mean you're a virus or bacteria?'

No. I'm protozoa. I'm sharing your food, but so little of it you'll never notice. I'm not infectious but I live inside your

176

cells. *Being so small was a problem at first, but I found a way.*

'Great place to hide.' I couldn't express my feelings about this invasion of my bodily particles. Just the thought of it appalled me.

'So if you're inside me …' I continued speaking aloud, uncertain if that was necessary for Guy to 'hear' me. 'What happens if you suddenly turn back into a human?'

I imagined myself exploding in slabs of bloody meat across the wallpaper, with Guy, naked and gory, emerging from a cage made of my bones and sinews. How the hell did he get inside me anyway? Which orifice …? No. Some things are better left unknown.

I promise not to stay for long.

That didn't make me feel any better.

'So you can get out easily?' I wanted to sound hopeful, but I think Guy realised I wasn't happy.

I'll leave you soon and speak to you outside. Tonight you need to meet me in the park.

'OK then. You'll help with the next stage?'

No reply came, so I wondered if he was attempting to exit my cells. What a freaky experience. It also occurred to me that Guy could enter me or any other person he wanted to without them ever knowing. Perhaps he might even find a way of influencing the host and changing their thoughts. I feared I might not be in control of myself any more. It was a frightening thought.

Was Guy the only one in the world or were there others? The idea that he could teach me how to do this filled me with a mixture of fear and excitement. But I was never going to be exactly the same as Guy – even though he said we all had the potential to possess these skills.

Just as I was assuming he had left my body, I felt something cold and lumpy fill my mouth. Something was alive inside my mouth! I choked, unable breathe as it pressed against my teeth, guns and tongue. But before I could raise my hand to pull whatever it was out, a large slimy wet thing jumped out and landed with a thump on the floor. Bufo.

'You stupid gimp!' I was annoyed and felt somehow

violated. 'I thought I was gonna choke to death. Don't ever do that again!'

Bufo stared up at me with bulging eyes, making farty noises. I couldn't stay angry and soon cracked into laughter. 'You stupid git!'

Then I saw the shimmering air flicker into colours and shapes until Guy appeared vaporously in human form a few feet away from me.

'Oh my god! That is some trick.'

'My mother was right. We can transform into many shapes and sizes.' Guy grinned stupidly, as if he'd discovered the secret of life itself – which he possibly had. 'I never thought I'd achieve it.'

'Is that the hardest of all? Becoming so small?' I sat down on the floor as Guy started pacing energetically. Shape-shifting always affected his behaviour and immediately afterwards he seemed frantic and twitchy.

'Not necessarily,' he said, waving his arms with unnecessary vigour – his fingers shaking and his lips flickering. 'Becoming a creature like a mammal is difficult because of its complexity and detail, whereas an amoeba is simply constructed. I suppose the difficulty is in changing from one life form to another.'

'How do you choose?'

'You don't at first. Only through practice can you master the skills. Like learning a musical instrument; like anything really.'

I got up on my haunches and put out a hand to stop him pacing.

'So you used me as a host for your experiment? It could have gone wrong then?'

The disturbing image of my innards splattering across the wall as Guy wrenched my ribs apart to release himself returned. I even heard the sound of my bones splitting and tendons snapping. I felt sick.

'No. I've learned how to control changes with Pica and Bufo. Protozoa is the same. If anything its simplicity of structure gives me even better control.'

I remained unconvinced – if impressed.

'See you tomorrow.'

178

Before I could even nod, the air around him rippled and twisted inside out. I opened the window for Pica to make his exit. He looked at me sideways, snapped his beak, and disappeared.

Chapter Thirty

Guy reappeared at 1 a.m.

'You're ready for the next stage, Luke.'

'What's that? Flying and swooping through the air? Exploding into the fire of eternity?'

He stared at me as if I had special educational needs.

'No. You need roots first, to help you understand the eternity of things.'

'Uh-huh. Well, my roots are here. I was born here and lived here all my life –'

'No, not like that.' Guy became impatient and forgot to whisper. I worried that he'd wake my parents up and I figured I'd have to tell them I was talking in my sleep or some other nonsense.

'Then what?' I gestured for Guy to keep his voice down.

'Outside,' he replied simply.

It didn't seem to occur to Guy that wandering about at night could be dangerous. It was OK for him – but I couldn't fly away from any potential danger.

Glad, in the end, to have an excuse to get where we couldn't be heard, I put on my warmest clothes and offered some to Guy, who refused, and in a blink became Pica. I let him out first and then shimmied down to the fence and into the garden. Pica flapped over the roof of the house so I went through the side passage to the front, assuming we would go to Hillgate Park again and walking in that direction. With nobody about it was easy to get to the park without being seen. Passing cars never stopped or cared, while the odd stranger always looked as guilty as I felt or was more interested in their own affairs to give me a second look. This was an exciting kind of freedom – exciting in the sense that I had no idea what to expect.

The park somehow seemed darker than I'd ever seen it

before. When the moon shone it glowed with a silver brilliance, as if covered in shimmering cobwebs, but tonight, with the cloud cover, it was a giant shadow between the lamp-lit streets; the blackness felt welcoming rather than sinister. I found Guy there before me in human form.

'Let's go to the forest,' Guy said tapping my arm. 'The big oak tree.'

Everyone knew the big oak tree. All kids climbed it as a rite of passage. The bark on one side within reach from the ground had worn smooth. It had survived being struck by lightning and continued growing. Some of the giant lower branches were thicker than the trunks of most of the surrounding trees. It dwarfed all the other trees around – including the other oaks, and was even taller than the spindly, narrow pines which appeared to be more concerned with height than with spreading outwards – as if stretching up on tiptoes. The big oak tree, with its complicated panoply of boughs and leaves, was probably as broad as it was high.

Guy scampered up it with squirrel-like agility whereas I dragged myself up heavily, so that by the time I reached Guy I was out of breath and clutching on for dear life.

'Find a position that's comfortable and then press yourself as closely as you can to the branch or trunk.'

There was no point in taking issue so I obeyed him, shifting myself this way and that until I felt secure and balanced. I wrapped my arms around the trunk and pressed my right cheek to the bark, trying to make sure as much of me was in contact with the tree as I could manage.

'OK. What now?'

'Now listen.'

My ear was against the trunk, so I tried to listen to any sounds inside it. Of course I heard nothing at first.

We both waited in silence for a long time. My mind wandered – thinking about Cheryl or my parents. Then my heart lurched again as I remembered how everyone had seen that picture of me and Guy, making me reconsider whether being Guy's friend was really worth it. It'd be so much easier to just go back to how things were. Life was simpler then.

With no idea of the time or how long I'd been there, I'd reached the stage where I was getting cramp in my thighs. However, as I hadn't moved for so long it seemed daft to suddenly move now. My body would get used to it eventually. The pain was temporary and would disappear; I just had to block it out with my mind, grit my teeth, and fight through it.

Guy's voice made me jump.

Imagine you're part of the tree. Be at one with it.

I couldn't see him but the voice was very close; a part of me, in fact. I wasn't too sure if all my thoughts were my own now. This couldn't be right – surely.

Why was I losing grip of normality? Now I couldn't be sure about reality itself. Up to this point things with Guy had been exciting; a buzz; something to live for. Now I wasn't so sure.

The sensation was freaky and it happened much more quickly than I had expected. At first it affected my face. Where my cheek lay against the rough bark I could feel my face turn soft, like liquid, and slowly seep into the thin runnels, grooves, and swirls. The tree accepted me and my face collapsed willingly into a mulch – skin, muscle, bone, sinews all melted and spread slowly over a vast distance around the trunk. But I felt absolutely no pain as this seemed, somehow, normal.

Then I felt my hands stretch and entwine the trunk as my fingers turned into tendrils, snaking around like ivy until they too dissolved into the tree. Once I got through the bark I reached the hard wood, which was more difficult to penetrate. The pores were so tiny that I had to split and fragment into millions of particles; yet oddly it still didn't hurt. I was strangely aware of myself sitting on the branch, clasping the tree, but my sense of being was larger – magnified and elated. My head was now completely devoured by the tree as I sank deeper and deeper into its heartwood. The rest of me flowed and trickled from my clothes until empty material flapped on the branches 'outside' of me.

I had entered the mighty oak.

While my senses didn't register, I could still 'feel' in a non-physical way and remain aware of myself as me. And yet I had become part of the tree. Where was up? Or down? I couldn't tell the difference.

As I permeated through the wood and knotty root system I had a sensation of vastness, with my extremities reaching through and beyond and within and far away. Tiny twigs and leaf buds became as vital as colossal roots which delved, twisting, grasping, and mining the ground for goodness, while establishing a permanence; stability for the enormous existence above. Then my essence became the water, the sap, the knots, the buds, the deadwood, the luxurious blossom …

And I understood.

I understood the ancient wonder of nature.

I felt billions of years of existence overwhelm me. The knowledge and emotion of aeons passed through me – burning everything else away – as if what I knew as a human was ridiculously trivial and so pathetically … temporary. I experienced creation; destruction; transformation; extinction; resurrection; burning; freezing; explosion; implosion; then stillness. The stillness lasted for centuries, millennia. I could sense the geological and meteorological shifts and counterbalances. The planet turned relentlessly; grinding its way through infinity as nature continued its struggle to survive on its surface and within.

And I laughed wildly. No longer weak and tiny, I thrilled to be part of creation, released from all pain and fear.

Suddenly the sound of howling erupted into my head. It was my own voice. I was midway through separating my physical being from the tree – extracting each atom and molecule from the wood and rough bark – when I heard myself. I pulled away from the oak trunk so abruptly that I lost my grip and fell from the branch.

My hands hit the floor first with a stinging agony that ripped through my arms. Then my shoulder jarred into the rock-hard earth just before my body slammed with a sickening thud. I rolled over onto my back, spitting dirt from my mouth. When I closed my eyes it seemed that the ground itself swayed gently, rocking me from side-to-side. Then sick came up into my mouth, burning my throat. I turned my head to one side to spit it out. It slimed down my chin but I had no energy to wipe it away.

A throbbing headache in my temples forced my eyes closed, but even rest and darkness couldn't bring relief. The pounding blood in my head and ears stopped me from drifting into unconsciousness. Instead, I relived the enormity of the oak tree. I recalled what it felt like to be gigantic, important, to be still and ancient; what it was to know and understand nature itself. Such knowledge, gaping over eternity, which I had been lucky enough to glimpse and taste.

I couldn't be sure how long the experience had lasted. It could have been a second or a few hours. It didn't matter. It was real – and more than just a vision or hallucination. The gigantic scale of what I now knew remained with me. From now on I would be different. Of that I felt certain.

Something sharp prodded my chin and I became aware of a light moving object creeping over my chest. Summoning any reserve of strength I managed to swat a limp hand which bashed my own face. It touched something soft, which moved and then chattered angrily, springing up to avoid the hand before landing back on top of me. I felt pin pricks through my jumper.

'Get up, lazy.'

Laughing helplessly while also dribbling, I raised the same hand slowly and located Pica's head. He nudged against it. I grinned and let my weak arm fall back to my side again.

Pica hopped onto my belly and then fluttered onto my forehead; his tiny claws scratching my skin gently.

'You did well.' Pica snapped his beak and returned to my chest. 'How do you feel?'

I took a few breaths and tried, but failed, to open my eyes.

'I need sleep.' I tried moving my legs and they seemed to work fine. However, a spasm ran through my back and up to my shoulder blades. It felt like my spine had broken. It took everything I had to not scream aloud.

A hand took hold of mine and tried to pull me up – and failed. Guy stood over me, looking concerned.

'You need to get home.'

I don't know how I managed to struggle home, but anyone who saw us would have assumed I was drunk.

Chapter Thirty-one

School just seemed so unimportant now after what I'd experienced. None of the teachers could ever hope to show me a fraction of what I'd learned from Guy. Unbelievable secrets.

So many of my lessons were uniformly dull. Merely sitting in a classroom was no real education. Sure, there were books to read and basic theories to learn, and lots of writing – we never went on trips, or enjoyed outdoor activities. And every lesson had become the same – we always had a predictable and patronising starter activity that often had nothing to do with the rest of the lesson, but I assumed was given to us to shut us up while the register was taken, then every teacher used a PowerPoint presentation which whizzed about with colours and shapes but were only glorified worksheets. Like my dad always said, 'Form over content'. Then we always ended up with a class discussion when we had to explain in ninety-seven different ways what we were supposed to have learnt in that lesson, which was always bloomin' obvious because the lesson's aim was written at the top of the interactive whiteboard screen. What I hated was when teachers made us stick our thumbs up to show we understood the learning objectives as if we were five years old. And as for those flippin' self-evaluation sheets we had to fill in every day – there is only a certain amount you can write about a lesson before you repeat yourself ad nauseam.

School became difficult for me because my so-called (or rather ex-) friends decided to punish me for changing my allegiance from them to Guy. The gay-bashing got worse and became the focus of their hatred for me until it appeared the whole school had turned me into its victim and public enemy number one.

On one hideous day some year sevens shouted out the usual

offensive stuff. I did my best to ignore it.

'Yeah, walk on, fag.'

From the giggling and whispering behind me I guessed they were mincing behind me. It had become the school joke that I skip about waving my hands in a camp way. I'd never bloody done this in my life and I made a point of shuffling with my hands in my pocket.

'It's OK, you can call him anything you want,' a year seven girl said to her friend as they walked along with me. 'He never replies or retaliates.'

'Maybe he's a bit of a spaz as well,' her friend replied.

'Mm, probably.'

Obviously bored with my lack of reaction they left me to cope with the stairwell on the way to the science labs.

This was the gate to hell.

I knew what was coming, but kept on anyway. As I reached the bottom of the stairs I blocked out the name-calling and waited for the bombardment.

'He's there. Go.'

This time a shower of random objects spilled down upon me. Pens, rubbers, balls of screwed up paper, pebbles, a bread roll, and the contents of a crisp packet.

Wiping the crisps from my hair, I attempted to keep a blank mind, which is so much harder than it sounds. How I wanted to punch one of those little runts.

I reached the classroom door without being tripped up this time. Names and insults echoed and swirled around me.

A group of year nines in my class stood back to let me into the room, giggling suspiciously. I didn't care.

As I grabbed the door handle, my hand slipped off, and I realised something gooey and wet was now on my hand. The laughter turned into screams and howls.

What the hell was it that stuff on my hand? It was yellowy brown, and smelt disgusting. Once in the science lab I washed my hands and took my place at the front desk.

Outside, Cheryl was screaming at the crowds.

'Leave him alone, you losers! He's my boy and he's braver than all of you put together.'

It went quiet, even when Cheryl opened the door to join me, but the sniggering returned as the door swung to again.

'What a buncha tossers, eh, Lukie?'

She reached out to embrace me, and even let me rest my face on her squishy bosom as she fiddled with my hair, which only forced me to endure a very different kind of agony.

She told Mr Saddler about the victimisation and I was sent to Miss Mire again. This time I just nodded and accepted the leaflets she gave me. Any other response was a waste of effort.

'Here's the gay guy,' quipped Simon one time, 'who likes to get gay with Guy.'

The jibes and teasing were really starting to get on my nerves.

'You must miss your little bum-chum, you bender.' Connor approached me with an ugly frown fixed on his face. 'Unless you're hiding him somewhere.' Connor grabbed my shoulders and spun me around before I could fight back. The others all made a big show of looking at my backside and calling Guy's name.

'Yoo-hoo! You can come out now!' The lads all fell about laughing and were soon joined by a number of others. Just before it got completely out of hand I heard Cheryl's voice.

'Leave him alone, you prats! You are such a load of dickheads!' she screamed. It had an astonishing effect. The younger kids scarpered as if she was a teacher and the older boys all looked up dumbly as if unable to argue. Connor and the older boys wanted to impress her; to them, she was an opportunity to lose their virginity. Connor always bragged about his sexual conquests, and even though nobody believed him, no one was stupid enough to argue with him, so he carried on boasting.

'You bunch of saddos aren't half the real man Luke is,' Cheryl said. I didn't like to intervene, although I began to wish I'd had the guts to. 'See, Luke knows who he is and he has the bottle to tell the truth about himself, even though you've all turned against him.'

Connor dared to respond first.

'Yeah, well, I've shagged ladies twice your age – that makes me a real man, 'cos I shag real women.'

'He's got bigger balls than you have, boy.'

I couldn't help wishing Cheryl hadn't brought my testicles into this discussion. I couldn't see how this intervention was exactly helping my cause, but at least the lads weren't threatening me for a few moments.

'Just because he bats for the other side and doesn't fancy girls isn't reason to hurt him,' she continued, unabated. 'He's such a sweetie and he's my friend. If I see you lay one finger on him then you'll have me to answer to.'

I winced at the word 'sweetie' and saw Connor snigger at the idea of a girl protecting me.

Then Connor squared right up to Cheryl.

'I don't take no orders from a ... girl.' He stared at her, unflinching. 'A bitch is only good for one thing, innit? And I know you want some, babe.'

Cheryl moved with supernatural speed, slapping his cheek hard. He stood upright, shocked beyond belief. His face had already gone red from both pain and embarrassment.

'Not interested in you, ugly. Anyway, I hear you don't have much to write home about.' She stuck out her little finger, all droopy and crooked. 'You're such a sad case. See you, boys.'

She blew me a kiss and waved to the remaining onlookers, before disappearing outside to join the smokers by the back gate.

Unfortunately, that left me with the pack of snarling bull terriers. Connor's hatred for me seemed harshly irrational as I'd never really done anything to hurt him. Pete and Simon's anger, I assumed, came from their reaction to my friendship with Guy, which they saw as a rejection of them. The others were just mean-spirited pillocks.

'Are you looking at my dick?' Connor strutted towards me menacingly. He pointed down towards his groin with his fingers. 'I tell ya. This big boy is only for the ladies. You geddit, homo? Don't even look at me, gayboy!' He pressed his forehead right up against mine and continued spitting in my face as he spoke. ''Cos if I catch you even looking at me or any other bloke I'll castrate you with a rusty blade.'

Snot started running down my nose but I couldn't do anything about it.

'You dirty queer!' he screamed, and moved slowly away from me. I quickly wiped my sleeve under my nose, but I just felt the snot smear across my cheek. Then without warning he put his head down like a rhinoceros and butted into my midriff. I was winded and on the floor, doubled up in pain. I felt myself being hauled over the cold floor and outside onto the back fields. Forcing me onto my feet and surrounding me, the gang of boys pushed me behind the cricket nets and through the small allotments as far away from school as you could get while still on school grounds.

I'm not sure what their intentions were after that because I suddenly became aware that the beatings had stopped. Raised voices filled the air and I was alone for a few moments. Looking up, I could see why they had scarpered. Mrs Fuller was marching towards me with Cheryl jogging behind her. As they got closer I could hear Cheryl reciting to the Head Teacher all the names of my assailants.

I saw the school nurse and was given the rest of the day off. Dad picked me up, and said very little in the car. It remained an awkward, tense journey home and I felt like I'd let him down somehow. He clapped me on the back at one point and told me to keep my chin up. Mum was more sympathetic and gave me lots of hugs, which I accepted gratefully. I definitely preferred Cheryl's, though.

My girlfriend (as in my friend who happened to be a girl, and sadly not the other kind) rang me later.

'Connor's been excluded, innee? He's a goner an' a loser and we say goodbye ...' She broke into an improvised and tuneless song as she regaled me with this news: '... to that sad, stupid muppet – now sod off and die ...'

Not the greatest song in the world, but her sentiments were kind – at least to me.

With that, I made the mistake of thinking it would mean an end to those particular problems.

Chapter Thirty-two

I didn't go into school the next day, and with both my parents at work I stayed at home alone. When the front doorbell rang I initially considered leaving it as it was bound to be a salesman trying to get us to change our gas provider or the like.

I certainly didn't expect Connor.

Before I could close the door, he'd barged it open and was inside. Right behind him came Simon and another boy, Carlton. They bundled me to the floor and jammed what must have been a plastic bag into my mouth. Then they tied my hands behind my back and hauled me up to my feet.

'Now we're gonna go outside. You walk in the middle and don't do anything stupid. If you do, you're dead. Understand?' I could only nod to Connor's command. The bag in my mouth hurt my jaw, saliva filled my throat, and I began to gag. It took a huge effort to stay quiet.

Simon pushed me roughly outside and I walked with Simon holding one arm, Carlton, the other, and Connor behind me with something digging into my back. A knife? A gun? I had no way of knowing. I desperately wanted to plead with them that this was unnecessary. I had no idea what they planned to do with me or how much it would hurt.

We walked for about fifteen minutes, until we reached some private garages. Connor had the key to one, and flipped up the large, square, metal doorway. The heavy counterbalance weights moved as the door flipped outwards. I was shoved inside with enough force to make me stumble and fall to my knees, which grazed on the rough concrete floor. They stayed outside. My hands were still tied so I couldn't use them to balance or even grope around in the darkness that surrounded me as the garage door slammed closed. I tried kicking the metal to alert any passer-by – although if it was locked, what could they do apart from call the police? It seemed unlikely that I'd be rescued at all. The noise made by the resounding metal sheet became horribly deafening, so I gave up and fell on my rump.

The bag in my mouth began to make me choke, making it difficult to breathe. The musty reek in the dark garage added to my stifling sense of panic. Bile filled my mouth and began to dribble down my chin. Trying my best to breathe through my nose, I stayed calm and used my tongue to gently ease the bag from where it had got stuck between my teeth and where it jagged up into my gums. With patient prodding, and by pulling a series of extreme faces, the bag got dislodged and I eventually spat it out, allowing me to gasp and breathe in the dusty, thick air.

Then I concentrated on untying my hands. The binding was strong and so tight that the string cut into my wrists, and pins and needles began to tingle through my forearms.

'Bloody hell! How stupid is this?' I hissed into the darkness. What gave those prats the right to drag me here? The more I thought about how unfair it all was the more I seethed. What had I actually done to deserve being imprisoned and treated like a criminal? In fact, criminals are treated better; they get a bed, food, and exercise.

I got up onto my feet again – which was difficult without hands to push myself up – and walking sideways, I tried to feel around with my bound hands to find out what was in the garage. My fingers were numb. It was while I stood that I realised how much I needed to go to the toilet. My bladder already ached and while I had no qualms about emptying it in this garage, I couldn't actually manage it with my hands tied behind my back. From that moment, the desperate urge to urinate dominated my thoughts. I stumbled about a bit, tripping on heavy objects and scraping past sharp things sticking out at every angle. Anger throbbed in my brow; the darkness made me feel anxious. The pain in both arms spread to my shoulders, neck, and now pounding head; my aching bladder needed relieving …

I screamed as loudly as I could and charged, shoulder first, at where I could just see a square of thin light framing the garage door. As I barged against the unforgiving sheet of metal, my head also slammed against some concrete block jutting outwards at exactly head height. My mind went momentarily blank as I fell, and I felt my ear and cheek thud against the gritty and very solid ground. I couldn't move. I lay there wondering … why me?

First, I became aware of something scuttling over my face and very close to my open mouth. This made my entire body squirm as if being pricked by a million pins. I blew out between pursed lips and shook my head vigorously, yet couldn't get away from the sensation that bugs were crawling over my face and up my nose.

Then it happened; I felt the wet warmth trickle down my thigh. I was a baby, no longer in control of my own bodily functions. How humiliating. As it had already gone this far, I relaxed fully, finally glad to release the build-up. The feeling of relief was immense and improved my outlook on things considerably. That was one problem out of the way. Now for my numb arms. How long would it take before they shrivelled and fell off from lack of blood?

I lay still and ignored the pain, blanking out any silly fears of insects eating into my flesh, and surprised myself with how calm and lucid I felt at that moment. I even laughed aloud at just how stupid this whole situation had become. If I was going to die here, then so be it.

A new thought occurred to me in that instant.

'Guy?' My voice was broken and dry. 'Are you there, Guy? Now would be a really good time to appear. I don't even care if you're naked. Please come and help me.' Then I started to giggle inanely. It came from an instinct inside me. Not that I'd given up – but more that I wouldn't let those boys, or this daft situation, beat me. At that precise moment I had nothing to fear. My mind remained calm and my faculties were working well – better than ever. I was either experiencing a peculiar moment of inspiration, like an epiphany. Or this clear-sightedness signified the onset of complete insanity.

But as I lay prone on the floor, my arms and hands no longer ached. My head and shoulders felt fine. Inside, I became aware of a real power renewing me. I could smell every object in the enveloping darkness. It seemed my eyes had finally adjusted as I could now make out objects on the floor and walls around me. The stench became overwhelming.

Strangely, I noticed that my hands could now be pulled free from the binding, slipping out easily as they relaxed and contracted. I brought them around in front of me and shook each limb carefully. Then I rolled slowly onto all fours.

I would wait for them. A new determination gripped me and made me glow inside. I would wait for them to come back and I didn't care how long it took.

Chapter Thirty-three

Two voices woke me up. I heard them advance towards the garage, two distinct footsteps and two loud voices, so I readied myself by climbing onto a big box that sat to one side. They wouldn't see me straight away, which would give me an advantage. The voices and movements of both boys identified them. As the door slowly opened I knew Connor would be standing on the left, nearest me, with Simon on the right. I crouched right down with hunched shoulders and head perfectly still.

A clunk and a vibrating rattle preceded the influx of daylight as the door rose up steadily. Initially, the glare blinded me but I launched myself anyway. Animal instinct helped me find my target. Connor's eyes widened in fear as he saw me attack his face. He shrieked as my claws dug into the soft flesh of his cheeks.

I knew I moved too fast for him as he limply swatted his hand at my shadow. I used his shoulder to propel myself forwards, before jumping on top of the garage, and up a nearby tree.

Watching the two boys through a gap in the leaves I was filled with a confidence I'd never felt before; an arrogance and self-belief never experienced. I had changed.

'What the hell was that?' Simon sounded bewildered. 'You OK?' Connor was sobbing loudly and holding his face, now red-streaked and torn. 'Was that a cat? Flippin' psycho moggie. Must have been trapped in there.' He peered inside the garage – presumably looking for me. 'Where's Luke got to? He can't have escaped.' Simon went right inside to investigate. 'He has, you know. He's got away. How did he do that?' Simon stood in front of the still-whimpering Connor. 'Do you want me to get some help? God, that looks sore. Just missed your eye.'

'I'm fine.' Even though Connor mumbled in a cracked whisper I could hear him clearly. I marvelled at these new heightened senses I'd developed. 'Just a stupid bloody cat.'

'I think you're the bloody one, mate.' Simon winced as he examined Connor's face. 'Gonna have some nasty scars.'

Connor went back to nursing his stinging cheeks.

'That cat looked desperate to get out. Must have been trapped in there,' Simon continued. 'No wonder it was desperate to get out if Luke was trying to shag it.' He broke into a braying of guffaws, which fizzled out when he saw that Connor wasn't laughing. 'I think I should get you home, mate. You might need to go to hospital or something.'

From the safety of my tree I watched Connor trudging slowly away, with Simon uncertain whether to put an arm round him in public or not.

I'd done it!

This was even more amazing than I could have ever imagined. But why a cat? I sprung effortlessly down onto the garage roof, and without a moment's doubt, right down to the ground, even though the drop must have been more than ten times my own length. It felt like gliding. The power in my haunches made me some kind of superhero – except I was a cat. What was better was that I was still me; I had an awareness of being Luke – a human – but with the physical appearance and reality of a cat.

I couldn't believe my luck when I saw the garage door had been left open. Even though I'd been careful to pull my human clothes out of sight once they all slipped off me during the transformation, I felt glad Simon hadn't spotted them when he'd gone in. Now I had to think what to do. Perhaps I could tug them with my teeth and hide them carefully behind something. I padded into the garage and found them in the corner where I'd managed to drag them.

But as I considered what to do I felt an unbearable spasm in every muscle and sinew. Some parts of me splintered and collapsed, others bent and began to remould themselves into a different length and shape. The pain forced me to collapse and I gave in to the throes of agony surging through each cell and atom. For those few moments I lost my new-found strength and agility and succumbed to torment. How long would this last? When something that acute racks your whole body, even for a few seconds, it seems like eternity stretching out in your mind.

I swear I heard bones crack and snap into place. Like having a fit, my body got thrown into strange angles and shapes as limbs and torso rebuilt thcmselves. Fur melted and I had a new desire to stand upright. Then I became aware of the cold and how I stood in a strange garage completely naked, my entire frame stiff and aching. Every muscle groaned with cramp and all my joints clicked back into place. In this weakened, numbed state I attempted to put my clothes on, which became a struggle. They were also cold and damp. But once clothed I checked around to see that no-one had seen this bizarre event. I quickly lowered the vertical door with a minor crash and limped off home, hoping not to meet too many people on the way – especially Connor.

I gratefully reached home without a problem. Once home I crept upstairs and curled up under my duvet where I slept – like a cat.

Chapter Thirty-four

After that, I felt like a different person. While the experiences were hazy in my mind, there was no doubt that I knew more. I simply understood. The things Guy had told me made much more sense now. I could see beyond myself and this paltry world. Being alive meant being a part of nature, not a species fighting against it. Humans always seemed to want to destroy and control and manipulate, or prove themselves better than nature, while animals were disrespected or put up with. Land was possessed and used only for the good of other humans. We were like spoilt little children unwilling to share a possession that we'd found and claimed as our own. This was what Guy had been talking about all this time and now I finally understood the enormity of what he meant.

The whole *numen* thing made this sharing even more pronounced. Now I saw things as an animal might see them. Not as a pet, but as a wild creature fending for itself. While instinct to survive became important, so did seeing your place within a complex system and learning how to be the best you can be within that system. Well, it made sense to me.

Now I had completed my initiation – I had flown through the air and known the freedom of my own thoughts; my changing into Felis being the equivalent of fire because of the pain required for each transformation. Fire melts metals into new shapes and my own body had been resculpted in the shape-shifting flames. I'd been part of the earth itself and knew the freedom of water which flows and touches everything, slowly understanding as it moves and spreads in its never-ending cycle.

Everything changed. How could it not? To begin with I had no control over the changing. The only way I could make it happen was by sitting in silence for about an hour, really focussing everything mentally and physically – which is a great deal harder than it sounds. Just concentrating for more than five minutes is difficult.

Guy helped me. He woke me up that night. In the darkness I couldn't tell if he was in my head or next to me. Then I felt his weight press down on my feet and I knew he'd be sat there naked, cold, but too polite to get under the duvet with me. He knew my feelings on that subject now. I switched on my bedside lamp. He already wore my dressing gown and had slipped his legs under the bottom of the duvet just below my feet.

'I should call you Felis Catus from now on,' Guy whispered. It felt so strange. There was a whole part of me that I hadn't known existed. At that moment I didn't fully understand the difference. 'I just hope you'll remember not to catch and eat any magpies or toads. We could become enemies.'

I smiled at him.

Guy taught me how to control the changes. One time I woke up and, at first, I thought Guy had turned into a giant, cradling me in his arms with his massive face close to mine. But he hadn't grown – it just seemed that way from a small cat's perspective.

'There's a good boy. Aren't you beautiful,' he whispered. I couldn't tell by his tone whether he said this ironically, although the mischievous look in his eye followed by a grin gave me a good clue. 'I really prefer you like this to when you're human.'

'Put me down or I'll scratch your eyes out!'

My *numen* could talk!

'Shame it hasn't improved your personality, though.' He put me down on the floor. 'There you go, Cuddles.'

'Sod off, or I'll change my mind and have magpie for breakfast.'

I nearly slipped in my paltry attempt to jump up onto my bed, and then remembered I had claws to help me hang on. Although I'd never practised, something in my instincts told me that the leap up would be relatively simple. I hunched down and sprang up. On turning around for a reaction I caught Guy shrinking down to become Pica, who immediately took off through the open window with his stuttering flight and long steering tail. The sun was rising and the night was nearly over.

My biggest concern was that if I went to sleep now my parents might come in and see a cat instead of me. How would they react?

I needn't have worried. A few hours later I woke up as a human; naked, but definitely human. I'd have to ask Guy what had happened to my clothes next time I saw him. I expected to be stiff and aching with muscle pain, but after a good stretch I felt vibrant, and much more well and alive than I'd felt in ages.

My mother was right.

'What?' I jerked my head around, making it crick and sending shooting pains through my neck. Behind me sat the usual classroom full of bored pupils. Another day; more lessons and humiliation. Each classroom had become a dungeon, every corridor a black hole, and all pupils became hissing demons. Now I sat in yet another lesson. All lessons melted into one another, into a spiral of boring crappiness.

Guy was inside me. I couldn't get used to the idea. As a parasite he could somehow put his voice or thought in my head. No privacy for me, then. I couldn't talk aloud without getting told off and dragged away for being insane – not to mention bullied for the rest of my life.

'Luke! Turn around,' screamed Miss Blewitt.

I controlled my thoughts and phased back out of the droning lesson.

Can't you get the hell out of my head?

No, Luke. I'm dependent on you as my host.

My eyes widened. I hadn't expected an answer. I really had been invaded. At least it saved me the humiliation of being seen to talk to myself. I really could exist in my own world. So when Guy "spoke" to me it involved more than just sound, and more to do with an exchange of thoughts. If my mind hadn't been blown already then this certainly finished the job.

My mother's dying. The words conveyed no tone or emotion, as they were being relayed without a voice.

Do you know where she is? Is she in hospital somewhere?

There was a long silence, during which I tried to listen to what Blewitt was saying and hoping my name didn't come up. We were supposed to be writing something down. I picked up a pen and pretended to write. She'd never come to check and today wasn't the day to give in books to be marked so I'd be OK. I could copy off Cheryl, who sat on the other side of the room. She saw me looking in her direction and waved. She was texting someone on her mobile under her desk – she could text with one thumb superfast and without looking at the screen. I hoped she wasn't texting me because I couldn't remember if I'd put mine on silent.

I need to find her, Luke.

How?

I don't know.

This seemed incredibly odd. How could he not know where his mother was? But then I remembered he was in care and being fostered, so perhaps she had abandoned him or he'd been taken away for some reason. Abused? I didn't really want to think about it.

You said something about your mother being right. What do you mean?

About you.

Me? Does she know me?

She sent me out to find you.

This came as a shock. I didn't know his mother and yet she had picked me out.

What the hell are you chatting about, Guy?

She told me there was someone who was more sensitive than the rest ... who could harness the energy. It's you. Nobody else could've found their numen so quickly. You're strong. Only the strong ones become mammals. Being a cat shows the strength of your spirit.

So did that mean my 'power' was greater than his?

It just means we're different.

I'd forgotten Guy could read my thoughts.

We have different purposes. I am a guide and a channel. You are a leader. You are being prepared for something greater. I was sent to find you and help you to find yourself.

And this is to do with your mother?
She is your mother, too.

I carelessly snorted aloud in derision. Everyone turned to look at me.

'Luke! Stand up!' Miss Blewitt screeched. 'Is my lesson not good enough for you? Are you one of these know-alls who doesn't need an education, then? Some children in other countries would give their right arm to get free education, but spoilt brats like you just take it for granted and have no appreciation. I suppose it's your right, is it?' She signalled double quotation marks with her fingers as she emphasised the word 'right' sarcastically.

I had no idea what she was talking about. My face took on a perplexed sneer.

'Detention with me today – lunchtime and after school. You dare be one minute late and I'll get your parents in.' She waved for me to sit down again and carried on pointing to the interactive white board, whose whizzing sentences and images wafted before me in a complete blur.

Chapter Thirty-five

I went round to Cheryl's the next evening and although I assumed Guy was still with me, he had the sense to keep his host happy by remaining quiet.

Cheryl's parents allowed me to spend as much time with her in her bedroom with the door closed because she'd obviously told her parents I was gay, so they wouldn't worry. While her father eyed me suspiciously, her mum treated me like one of the girls and I felt happy imagining the countless hours to be spent in Cheryl's boudoir.

'Blewitt the Bag has it in for you, innit?' she said casually as I watched her changing into a freshly ironed T-shirt. Today she was wearing a white bra with embroidered flowers, red and blue.

'Oh yeah. I need to copy out the work from today.' I looked up hopefully.

Her face dropped. 'I was gonna ask you the same. I didn't do anything in that lesson. No idea what she was on about.' She stretched her mouth out widely and put an index finger to her lips. I remembered she'd spent the whole lesson texting.

'Didn't you see me getting told off?' I asked, surprised. 'I had to do two detentions.'

'Yeah, so I thought you'd get all the work done then, so I could just copy it.'

'No. She set me extra work on top of that. She said if I didn't hand it all in tomorrow then she'd get my parents in.' Her casual assumption annoyed me slightly.

'Oh. So you ain't got it then?' She didn't appear too concerned about my doomed fate. 'Who else can I ask?'

At first I felt hurt that she'd have to go elsewhere, but then realised getting the work from someone else could be mutually beneficial.

'Then we can both copy their work. Thanks Cheryl – BFF.'

'Um, yeah. Yeah, course.' She began texting manically.

'Flippin' school, eh?' I said, groaning.

'Yeah. Well moody teachers making our lives a misery.'

'All just a bunch of psychopathic sadists who want to take out their own problems on a bunch of defenceless kids.'

'Sadies?' Cheryl shook her head at me, still texting. 'What the hell's that? God, the words you come out with.'

'Sadists. It means they like hurting people. They take out their own angst and neuroses on us lot.'

'If you say so, darling.'

'It's what Guy always says.'

Cheryl stopped texting and stared at me intently.

'What?' I put on a bad American accent and waved a hand in front of her eyes. 'Hello? Talk to me, girlfriend!'

'You know where he is, don't you?'

'Huh?' She caught me off guard, I had to admit.

'Guy. You said it as if you still see him and talk to him, otherwise you'd have said, "That's what he always used to say".'

I panicked, not having expected such lucid deduction from Cheryl. 'Uh, it's just a figure of speech. That's what I meant to say … what you just said.'

'I can tell by your eyes when you're lying. You're a really crappy liar, Luke. You know where he is. You're always talking about him. And I know why.'

She gave me a coy look and I could feel my face stretch into an ugly expression.

'No, I don't.'

'It's because you're in love with him. He's your boyfriend.'

'No, he isn't.'

I'd got myself trapped in one of those conversations where the more I argued, the more defensive and guilty I sounded. Cheryl started laughing at me; not pleasantly – in a sneering way.

'You keep telling me I'm your best friend, but I'm not. It's him. It'll always be him, won't it? Well, that's fine. If he means more to you than me then go. Go to him and get all the manlove you can. 'Cos from now on you're not my BFF. I thought I could trust you. I thought we had something special – a connection. But you just think about him and talk about him all the time, and I get sick of hearing how amazing he is. Go on! Go to lover boy if I'm not good enough for you!'

Where did that come from? How irrational did that just sound?

Cheryl's eyes were challenging and uncompromising. My mind went completely blank. What would sound right just at that moment? I wondered if Guy was there to help me. Then she did the girly thing of crying as if I'd caused her some great emotional pain.

'You've got it all wrong, Cheryl. I am friends with Guy – or I was. But you're my best friend, honest.' Even I knew this sounded insincere. Whenever anybody ended a plea with 'honest', you could guarantee it wasn't true; just like 'But it wasn't me'. I decided to confess there and then. 'Look, Cheryl, I've got something important to tell you. I might as well tell you now. Please, don't get angry with me, but … I'm … not gay.'

Her face twisted into something unattractive, especially with the smudged eyeliner glooping down her face. Then her face broke into a smirk – as if the idea of me being heterosexual was too difficult to contemplate.

'Of course you're gay, don't be stupid.' Flecks of saliva collected round the edges of her lips. The black rivulets leaked further down her face.

'I'm sorry, Cheryl. I've been lying to you. But I really do like you –'

'What? You like me so much that you've been lying to me – every day now!'

'It's not like that. Our friendship means a lot me. I really, really like you, Cheryl.' My mind spun, but this train wasn't stopping now.

'What you trying to say, Luke?'

'I went along with the gay thing because I enjoy your company and it gave me the chance to spend time with you. I really fancy you –'

'But that would mean you just pretended to be gay so you

could watch me getting undressed and letch all over me!'

While there was a certain element of truth, it didn't really tell the whole story.

'Nah! I don't believe it.' She looked me up and down and snorted with laughter. 'You haven't got the guts to do something like that. No, you're definitely gay, honey. We got photographic evidence, remember? Connor calls you The Bum-Bandit.' She laughed mockingly.

'Connor?' I spluttered. 'What's he got to do with anything? He's a complete knob.'

'We're going out, if you wanna know the truth.' She was full of surprises today.

'What? You and Connor?' Disbelief wasn't the word.

'I got a bit drunk at his party last week.'

'Oh my God! But … Connor?' My world imploded.

'He's a great kisser and he's really misunderstood. Poor little love.'

'You're going out with Connor?!'

'Yeah, what's wrong with that?'

'Well … because it's Connor, that's why. The guy's a complete moron.'

'He's more of a man than you'll ever be.'

'No, no, no, no, no. This is all going wrong.'

'He was right about you being a crap friend.'

'What? He said that?' I replied, gob-smacked.

'Yeah. He warned me about you. And now I know he's right. He might be a crap boyfriend with anger issues but at least he's not a liar and a … a … bitch like you.'

'What have I even done wrong?'

'You're always on about Guy. Guy this. Guy that. Well, sod off then and be Guy's BFF. Looks like you've made your choice.'

'But I really like you, Cheryl.' This was hard to say at the moment with her black starfish eyes and ugly frown, but I kept getting images of her bra and knickers in my mind and couldn't help thinking I'd missed out on something. My mind wasn't working properly. 'I really fancy you. I was waiting for the right time to ask you out.'

210

'Nice try, but you don't fool me. And even if you were straight? You? I wouldn't fancy you. Eugh! You were lucky to be my friend for so long. But I've had enough of you now. I think you should sod off – once and for all.'

Her phone beeped.

'That's Connor. He's on his way round. I could tell him your story about perving and stalking me if you really want me to. And I'll tell everyone that you know where Guy is!'

I looked at her ugly face and shook my head slowly. With as much dignity as I could muster, I grabbed my coat and left. I passed her mum on the stairs and let myself out, leaving the front door wide open.

Chapter Thirty-six

What the hell would happen to me the next day at school? I tried feigning illness but Mum saw right through me. Then I considered truanting and going to Coney Island but I'd only get caught out and punished; I was still on report to make sure I attended all lessons. No, I had to face up to my fate and get through as best I could. In the cold light of day, the worst I could be accused of is lying and being a bit of a perv. Guilty on both counts, m'lud. Perhaps when the lads worked out the advantage of my plan, they might finally give me some respect; although if Connor was now going out with the girl I'd been stalking then I might just be dead meat. Perhaps being killed was the best thing all round.

And why was Guy so quiet? Was he OK?

That night, once my parents had gone to bed, I experimented with learning how to become Felis. It seemed to take a great deal of concentration and clearing of my mind for me to learn any kind of control, yet after hours of patience and intense focus I only had a piercing headache to show for all my effort.

I crept downstairs to get some headache tablets and a glass of water, remembering to give Frisky a quick pat as he uncurled slightly on the stool, making that weird pigeon noise which is half-purr, half-meow. Then I sneaked back to my bedroom, grateful for the supportive softness of my mattress; rolling up my pillow behind my neck, drifting in and out of consciousness as if in a hypnotic trance.

As the headache slowly seeped away I enjoyed that goose-pimple moment of liberation and light-headedness. My entire body melted into a liquid of relaxation and at last I found the ability to focus. Now I could imagine myself with the streamlined body of a cat as my limbs became slender yet powerful and my senses heightened beyond human experience.

I could extend and contract my claws at will; 'see' in the darkness – not only with brighter eyesight, but by the sixth sense of my whiskers that allowed me to feel the size and shapes of objects close by. I could even judge movements in the air around me through these sensitive strands attached to my face. And my hearing! My ears detected sounds completely unfamiliar to me. Suddenly my bedroom filled with a cacophony of noises; echoes of everything, however small, collecting in my brain for further analysis. Then the new smells. Each breath drew in layers of tastes and aromas – some pleasant, others rancid and making me recoil.

I stood up on all fours and found my claws sticking annoyingly into the pillow and duvet with each step. I was about to leap off the bed and test my new-found agility when I smelt something strong and heard a noise that sent my instincts into defensive mode. The fur raised on my back, which became arched. Something other than logic had sensed a problem before my mind managed to work it out. The noise increased in volume behind me; a high-pitched growl that became a hiss. I leapt up and round to see a shadow just a few inches from my face. I thrust out a paw, but was too late. The attacker had already clawed my face and was now prone and hunched before me, ready to spring again. I yowled in pain and leapt off the bed to give myself a few seconds to prepare for the next strike.

Now I could see Frisky on my bed, creeping right up to the edge, staring at me wildly. He had the advantage of height. His reactions were not surprising. He'd just encountered a strange cat in his house – his territory – so this behaviour was natural and instinctive. I'd been stupid enough to leave the kitchen door open and he'd come up innocently to sleep on my bed. Poor Frisky had never expected this.

Unfortunately, I knew nothing about fighting. I had to let my feline senses take over. The human urge to use rational thinking served no purpose here. This fight was animalistic – about survival and use of natural skills. Frisky had more experience than me. He leapt at me again, without clawing at me this time. Now we stood face-to-face both trying to look as big as we could – in a crazed stand-off. His throaty yowl deepened as a warning to me. If I could I'd have turned and scarpered, but he'd cut off my only means of exit. I wondered if there was a cat way of showing respect and submitting. He certainly had the advantage over me and I would have been willing to yield to his superiority as a cat. Just as he lowered his haunches with his ears folded right back and face a demonic mask, a thought occurred to me in those fleeting seconds – I could regain the advantage as a human. I needed to stop panicking, overcome any fear inside me, and focus on my transformation. That's what Guy would tell me to do.

I inched closer to Frisky – which was counter-intuitive, but caused him to remain wary of me. This bought me a few moments to concentrate. When nothing happened I had to quell my fear and try again.

Frisky seemed to sense something unusual occurring. In fact, it wasn't until he started backing away with his growl getting deeper that I realised I was changing again. The whole room shrunk until I stood above Frisky, who stared then dashed suddenly out of the door and rushed downstairs, yowling his head off.

I stood stock still with my feet refusing to move. Sounds from my parents' room indicated that the noises had disturbed them. The whole fight must have lasted less than a minute, but Frisky's terrified meows had echoed through the house.

Mum reached the landing first.

'It's OK. It was Frisky,' I explained as she came into my room.

She turned on the light, which half-blinded me.

'God, what's happened to your face?'

I'd forgotten about my wound in all the excitement.

'Oh, er, I'm OK. It wasn't Frisky's fault. He somehow got out and was on my bed. I woke up suddenly and startled him.'

'And he scratched your face?'

'Um, yeah. He was asleep on my pillow. I must've turned over suddenly and woken him up.'

Mum and Dad accepted the explanation and whilst Dad went down to secure Frisky back in the kitchen, Mum dabbed Savlon onto my cheek.

'That cat's a liability. He could've had your eye out.' She squeezed another small blob onto her index finger. 'Maybe we should think about getting rid of him. He's becoming expensive anyway and I'm tired of clearing up his sick and poo all the time.'

'No, Mum,' I implored. 'He's part of the family. You can't do that. This is his home and he needs us.'

'Oh. OK. I didn't think you really liked him much. You always used to complain about him and I remember you being horrible to him at times.'

The cream was stinging now, which meant it was working its magic on the wound.

'Well, I've changed a lot recently. I don't think like that anymore. Animals like Frisky need our help and protection. We should be looking after animals and the world.'

'Right. Well then.' She screwed up her face. 'Glad to hear you have such strong feelings about something worthwhile. Good.'

My little speech surprised and impressed her. She finished with my cut and kissed me on the head.

'I'm really proud of you, Luke. You've really changed and your Dad and I very much like the new you. I know you don't like me saying this, but – ah – sod it. I love you. I really do.'

The Savlon had a powerful stench, but I could also detect the separate smells of my mum: soap, faint sweat, yesterday's perfume, hairspray, and bad breath. I felt that I would never react towards people I knew in the same way again.

That night I woke up, scared I was dying. At first I couldn't breathe or even cough. My head and lungs were about to burst. My spluttering became a series of gasping moans. Vision blurred as my eyes rolled about beyond my control.

Death was painful. It burned. I flapped around, desperate to cling to life.

Air. I needed air. Water. Anything to stop the burning in my throat. My neck bulged out at the side, and my jaw was wrenched open as something hard clacked against my teeth. Sharp points scratched at my lips and tongue.

216

Suddenly a small gust of air entered my mouth. I had to eject the object blocking the way. I poked my fingers into my mouth and felt something there, soft, wriggling, alive. It thrashed and wriggled.

Coughing and spluttering in agony, I finally ejected the writhing, fighting creature, and became aware of claws and wings flapping furiously.

Pica was back.

'You stupid, freakin' bastard!' I hissed, still choking on bits left behind on my tongue. I spat to one side and wiped my tongue with my fingers.

Pica hopped onto my bed's headboard.

Miscalculation.

'Really? You don't say. You could've killed me!'

You wanted me out.

'Yeah. Thanks. Mate.'

We're all learning as we go along.

Bloody hell, I was learning a lot. And most of it the hardest way possible.

Chapter Thirty-seven

I arrived at school late after dawdling via a very long route, and even survived the first lesson unscathed with the absence of Cheryl, Connor, and Simon. I tried to hang around at the end of the lesson, but the teacher clearly wanted me to leave so he could have a cup of tea in the staff room. Avoiding my locker, I found a place to loiter unnoticed by the car park and waited for the bell until strolling to my next lesson, which was maths – the same set as Cheryl. As I entered the room, she turned her head away from me as if in a very dramatic huff. This, I could handle. If she kept quiet then I could see a way through until home-time. I sat alone – as had become the case in recent weeks. In fact, nobody spoke to me for the whole day, which was lonely and embarrassing, but at least I wasn't in hospital with broken limbs.

Simon found and confronted me at lunchtime near where we used to play football.

'So is it true? You know where Guy is?'

'Uh? Course not.'

'It's what Cheryl reckons.'

'So what? Who cares what any of you think?'

Simon looked at me pitifully. 'I can't believe we used to be mates. Did you fancy me then? When we played together as kids?' He puckered his lips and his eyes shot to the side as if remembering a particular moment. 'I just thought you liked me 'cos I owned a football, but all that time you were just checking out my packet ... I really thought we were just friends.'

It was a terrible thing and I realised from my position just how spiteful, judgemental, and downright nasty they could be. Simon was also displaying incredibly arrogant reactions by assuming I found him attractive anyway. Even if I was gay, surely I could be friends with another boy without having to

219

'fancy' him. How stupid and irrational he sounded. Simon was betraying the pig-ignorance, selfishness, and lack of empathy for another human being which came with any kind of discrimination.

I shook my head and turned to go.

'Yah! You poof! That's it. Walk away like a big fairy.'

It wasn't Simon's voice this time. Connor.

I turned to face him and had to dispel the sickening images of him and Cheryl snogging, heavy-petting and swapping saliva. By doing this I realised that my hatred for him was mostly jealousy: I so wanted to touch her naked flesh, but now this git had ruined my greatest fantasy.

As Connor advanced, Simon stepped back as if deferring to a person of greater status. How had Connor gained such power? Mostly, it seemed, by being a cocky, gobby ego-maniac.

He turned to Simon. 'Cheers, mate. I can handle it from here.' Simon flicked his head and jogged away. 'Let's go for a little walk.' I checked he was talking to me.

'Nah, I'm all right, thanks.' I turned and began to move away.

'Scared, are ya?'

I should have just kept walking. Unfortunately, I allowed myself to respond to this pathetic challenge.

'What, of a stroll round the park picking flowers?' I heard myself chuckle.

'I thought that sort of thing'd be right up your street – or should I say back passage?'

'Oh, God,' I groaned, looking up to the skies for strength. 'OK, whatever.'

We headed for the front school gates, which were always wide open and never manned. I began a fast pace and Connor had to half-skip to keep up with me, which pleased me greatly. At first he didn't say anything and I wondered which abandoned space he'd take me to this time. Would he be alone or with rent-a-crowd? We were only just outside the school gates when he pushed me into a corner where two high wooden fences met at right-angles. The stench of creosote invaded my nostrils. I trod on a can and some plastic, colourful crisp bags that had gathered there amongst the nettles. He caught me off-guard and I saw his mates appear around the corner – in fact, a huge group of kids had followed us to watch this altercation. Before I could react he'd grabbed my shoulders, making my head clatter against a concrete post.

His face loomed right up before mine, with his eyes stretched into intense slits and his lips thin and white. Wondering if he'd start with a punch or a head-butt I considered getting in the first blow – recalling that offence was the best form of defence. However, with Connor merely staring at me, moving his head slightly from side-to-side, I could only imagine he was copying some gangster film. Many animals played with their prey before the kill, so I let him indulge in this prelude to pain. The anticipation from waiting for the blow became unbearable – or perhaps he'd back off if he saw I wasn't scared.

But he didn't back off – just kept on staring. I have to admit to being unnerved. Before it escalated into something nasty I decided to take control of the situation. With some velocity I shoved him away and he stumbled over, looking surprised and hurt. There was a vocal reaction from the sizeable crowd.

'Piss off, Connor.' I took up a defensive pose. 'Leave me alone.'

How I keep getting myself into these scrapes remained beyond my understanding.

Connor got up and dusted himself down. His soft eyes had turned into slit, glaring ones. 'Bloody faggot!'

'Why won't anyone believe me? I. Am. Not. Gay.'

'You're a sad little bender.'

Laughter ensued. Connor stood in front of me, a little more cautiously this time, so that I felt I had the upper-hand – for the moment, at least.

Then he smiled and stepped closer to me.

'I bet you'd like a piece of me, eh? Do I turn you on?' He grabbed his groin with his hand and shook it up and down a few times. 'You want a bit of this? Or do you prefer the other side? Yeah. You love it, don't ya?' Now his hands were up, beckoning me towards him.

I quickly took a big stride towards him, grabbed both his hands before he could react, and kneed him hard in the balls. He sprang back, shrieking, and doubled over. I legged it as fast as I could, shoving on-lookers out of my way. The crowd offered no resistance – bunch of cowards. My head pounded in time with my feet slamming against the paving stones. My throat burned with the rasping dryness of my heavy breathing.

The school gate came into view and I ran in gratefully, merging in with a passing crowd of year eights who seemed oblivious to what had just happened the other side of the fence. Finally reaching my tutor room, I sat down in the corner, where I would just be ignored by the rest of my group as they streamed in.

During my History lesson that afternoon I became aware of a magpie flying around the playground outside. It landed on a fence nearby and cocked its head at me as I stared. The teacher didn't seem bothered that I spent most of the lesson observing Pica outside. I somehow knew it was Guy.

Chapter Thirty-eight

As usual I was the last to leave the classroom at the end of the day. I preferred to go to my locker once the crowds had died down. This time was no different; I passed a couple of teachers who both looked pleased to have reached the end of another day without having a breakdown. So instead of going to my locker there and then, I found an empty classroom and got out my history homework. I was glad of the peace and quiet, to be honest. Then, once completed, I returned to my locker through the eerily quiet corridors.

I emptied my locker for the weekend by sweeping everything into my bag, then I slung it over my shoulder and stepped out into the daylight. This door led to the field and to the back gate, which I'd found to be much more anonymous as an entry and exit into school.

But as soon as I passed through the doorway, I was confronted by a figure in a black hoody. There stood Connor. He stared at me coldly, daring me to say something.

'Look, Connor. Let's come to some sort of agreement, yeah?' I even tried a half-smile, but his expression was fixed. 'How about we just leave each other alone? You do your thing and I do mine. We just ignore each other.' I held up both palms towards him. 'You're going out with Cheryl, and that's good. I'll step back and –'

The attack he launched was savage and abrupt.

His fists battered my face. He kicked my shins with his hard boots. The pain made me lose my breath. I lost my sense of direction and it felt like I fell slowly, but in fact I was already on the floor when a boot slammed into my ear and forced my head to one side. It felt like the tendons ripped in my neck. Then he was stamping on me; my hips, kidneys, groin, back, thighs – all battered and crushed. A white sheen filled my vision and mind, making the pain temporarily stop.

When I opened them again, parts of me throbbed but the attack had stopped. I looked up to see a gigantic boy gawping down at me. His mouth hung open, drooling saliva. It was Connor. He hadn't grown; I had shrunk.

'What the freakin' hell?'

I was Felis.

My human clothes were no longer required.

His reaction of startled paralysis gave me a chance to scamper away, but my limbs were heavy and hurt. I didn't possess my usual springy sprightliness. I'd been hurt.

'What the hell is going on?' Connor still looked astonished. 'I saw you change.'

He stepped cautiously towards me, where I still struggled, dragging my numb back legs behind me. I needed to lick them and get some life back into them, but I had to stay alert and watch this threatening creature who could now kill me with one kick.

'I dunno what freakin' weird crap is going on here, but I know you're Luke. So this is your secret, is it? Some kind of magic or superpower? Well, you've just made it easier for me, you little prat.' He took off his hoody and threw it over me.

In my new-found darkness, I writhed and struggled as much as I could. My claws tore against material, but I felt myself being squeezed into a ball and even though my spine and bones were flexible I hated being so confined and unable to move. Then something slammed into me. He was either clubbing me to death, or by the swaying movements before each blow, he might be bashing me against a wall – swinging me inside the hoody like a sledgehammer.

Then the beating stopped and I fell a short way to the ground in my bundle. I waited. The anticipation got the better of me. I frantically ripped my way through the material, snagging my claws painfully but eventually tearing an opening. I peeked out of the hole. A few metres away I saw Connor running in the opposite direction for a few paces then stop. He waved his arms about him as if swatting at a bee. Then he did a little jump-turn and swivelled his head around, all the while looking up into the sky.

My peripheral vision caught something moving in the sky to my left. I saw it before Connor did and I immediatcly recognised the awkward flight and long tail of Pica. The magpie flapped right over Connor's head, then went streamline, diving towards the boy. Pica folded his wings back and became an arrow, sharp beak glistening downwards. At the last second, Connor saw him and began flailing his arms around crazily, more in hope than with any skill or judgement. Pica avoided the wildly thrashing limbs and I heard the sound of his beak hitting the boy's skull. Pica slashed his talons at Connor's screeching face, before falling to the floor and rolling over in a tumble of feathers and wings. Connor caught sight of the motionless bird and ran towards him. I had to do something.

Ignoring the painful, lifeless parts of me, I summoned up enough energy to scamper in front of Pica before Connor reached him. I hunched and sprang up at the boy. I only reached his waist, but with claws out I managed to shred his trousers and draw blood from the soft parts of his upper leg. I let go and ran off, except my legs wouldn't work properly and they tangled beneath me. Connor ran towards me and when he was one pace away from my unresponsive body he lifted a foot back and then followed through with an almighty kick, which connected to my side. As I blacked out, I genuinely thought I'd die.

It was when I realised I hadn't died that the anger started. I was losing control of my feelings when instinct took over. My fury triggered something beyond the control of any one creature. This worsened as I watched Connor stride towards Pica. He bent down and lifted the magpie up to his face. Then without warning he gripped Pica's head in one fist and snapped his neck. The bird's head lolled down beside its body. Connor threw it down. Small and twisted, Pica's mangled body lay motionless upon the grass – his head looking in the wrong direction, beak open to reveal a thin, pink tongue.

Before Connor could advance towards me, Pica transformed. As his life force slowly drained away, so he returned to his natural state. A human body – all life gone from him. Guy's corpse lay there before us. Inert, naked, grotesque.

My hatred turned to rage. My feline body couldn't cope with the intensity and I felt myself grow and change back to human form. Connor watched on fearfully. His whole world-view had just crumbled and shifted beyond his understanding. I trembled in spasms; falling over onto my face. Lying there, my body continued to shake and twitch as I felt my feet and fingers dig into the earth beneath me. Then my tongue, nose, and eyes extended from my face and stretched downwards into the ground, skin stretching and ripping as muscles, veins, and sinews tore away from my body and began penetrating the soil. I howled and shrieked as the earth itself began to quake and undulate. I slipped right in through a crack which appeared on the surface. My skin, my bones, my blood, my guts, and vital organs became part of the Earth. My atoms mixed with water drops, sap, air molecules, bacteria, and other microscopic life-forms.

The world crashed around me. The school building warped and began disintegrating – rubble cascading like waterfalls. Tree roots burst through grass and concrete, expanding rapidly in thick, coiling cables around anything in the way. Tree branches leaned down and slashed at the roofs and upper storeys, obliterating stone, bricks, and mortar and showering us with fine dust. Tree roots meshed with brambles and bindweed, writhing and tangling – covering everything in its path. Tendrils and creepers shot out with a whiplash fury, entwining and engulfing everything. Connor became trapped in a mass of ligneous foliage. It wrapped around again and again until he couldn't move. The walls kept collapsing until the school became a bomb-site.

Then, after the first wave came the cavalry. It began with rats. So many that they covered the entire field in seconds. Then I became aware of flying insects; swarms; black flames licking into every minute space. The din of the buzz and clicking became deafening. Connor disappeared inside a whirlwind of wasps and flies. Then worms, maggots, and creeping, squirmy things flowed like rivers, rising and falling – bursting over. They went into Connor's mouth and ears and nose, and ate into his flesh. A bewildering mass of animals followed – beasts large and small: deer, foxes, weasels, rodents, reptiles, amphibians. They fell over each other and bit and fought amongst themselves. Then came the birds.

The sky went black. Our world lay in shadow; so many birds that they blocked out the sun. Billions and billions of them swooped, dived, soared, screeched, flapped, and pecked. Millions were forced to land due to the numbers, and they got caught up in the madness on the ground where everything was immediately crushed, torn, or bitten. Mayhem. Pandemonium. The noise was unbearable. It made every single particle of my body and soul vibrate and explode.

I realised I couldn't control the chaos I'd unleashed. My wrath seemed to be the energy directing this horror. But now I wasn't sure if I was Luke or Felis or something new entirely.

As suddenly as it began, it stopped. The birds and insects still alive flew off in their swarms, bringing light back to the world. It was carnage. The ground still moved with animals, now scampering, wriggling, and jostling. There were so many that they crawled over each other, sometimes pushing up into hillocks that rose and quickly fell again. Eventually, the land animals disappeared too, leaving only the carcases of their crushed companions. Amongst the death and destruction Connor lay lifeless, still swathed in branches and roots, which were receding much more slowly than the fauna did.

A chill made me jolt. I was back on the surface, but unclothed and exposed.

I dragged my way slowly across to where I had last seen Guy. His body had been protected from any further damage by a canopy of thick tree boughs. As I reached out, the wooden canopy slowly shifted to give me a glimpse of the body. I climbed into the gap and shook Guy's shoulders. His lolling head gave no reaction. I pressed the side of my face to hear for, or sense, any sign of breathing. None. I desperately tried his pulses, not really knowing what to do, but I realised it was hopeless. Guy was dead. I had failed to save him and knew it was my fault.

Chapter Thirty-nine

Without the idea even forming properly in my head, I propped his body up and wrapped my right fist around the little finger on my left hand. I yanked it one way and then another. The searing pain made me feel weak, but I couldn't stop. With gasps and howls I kept tugging and wrenching until the joint jerked out of its socket. Then I bit it viciously and ripped my hand away so that the entire finger came away in my teeth, the taste of blood making me retch. I snatched the finger from my mouth, brandished the trophy above my head and let the blood trickle onto Guy's head.

I was aware of the pain, but something else – something more important – made me ignore the searing agony.

I remembered about breathing into his mouth. I let the pain fill my being and then blew out that energy into Guy's face and mouth, which I forced open with my good hand. I forgot the recoiling pain and just screamed for Guy to come back to me.

'Wake up, godammit!'

I took another deep gulp and breathed my life force into him. It had to work, even though I had no real idea what to do next.

I felt desperate. How would I cope without Guy? How would all this be explained? This was a disaster of the freakiest scale imaginable. The school was destroyed and I had no way of knowing if anyone else had been hurt. There must have been people still in the building when it collapsed. It was only half past four.

While cradling Guy's head, I tried to stem the blood now pumping out of the place where my finger had been. Deciding to lie Guy down, I tried to find something to hold against it. I saw my clothes scattered among sticks and leafy debris. Quickly putting on my trousers and jumper I used my white shirt as a bandage, winding it around my hand tightly and pushing it up against my hip. The wound was raw and stung mercilessly.

I returned to Guy. By now, most of the roots and branches had either slithered away like serpents, or had snapped and broken off. Guy and I remained hidden behind our canopy of broken branches. As I shook and cajoled Guy, giving one last deep breath, I heard shouting and sirens. I looked up and saw distant figures moving around the ruined building. Fire engines and ambulances arrived.

'Come on, Guy! You can't leave me like this. I need you.'

I began slapping his face frantically and pulled his hair.

Luke?

'Guy!' I wept with joy. His lips didn't move, but he spoke to me.

I feel so weak.

'No, Guy. Your *numen* is strong.'

You've given me your life force, Luke. Thank you. His face remained a mask with its fixed expression. *My mother was right about you.*

I looked around. 'People are coming. They'll find you. I don't know what to do.'

Go with them – back to your home. Don't tell anyone about what happened. Don't say anything about me.

His human body flickered for the very last time. Guy shrunk and transformed into Bufo. The small amphibian body lay motionless on the ground. I wanted to see it twitch. It didn't. Then, as I covered him up with leaves, Bufo's form vanished too. Racked with my own physical pain, I slowly stood up to make myself visible to the rescue services, waving my arms while allowing myself to sob uncontrollably.

The medics insisted I lie down on the stretcher as they examined me and saw to my still bleeding hand. Something cold and hard was forced into my mouth to help me breathe. My legs went numb and floppy.

Then I remembered Connor and garbled something, waving my right arm in the general direction of his body. The gas and air filling my lungs made everything a haze and the momentum of the stretcher being carried and swayed rocked me into a daze.

230

How the hell would I be able to explain it?

The local newspaper had a photograph of Connor and his family mourning their loss. My guilt was insurmountable. His death was my fault. Two teachers had been hurt and taken to hospital. One had concussion but was otherwise deemed physically fit, while the other had an arm broken when a ceiling fell on her. Lucky is the word. I might have been the cause of more deaths otherwise. Others in the building had escaped before the true damage was done. My legs were severely bruised with some tissue damage, but my finger had gone, and they had stitched up the flaps of skin over the knuckle.

The cause of the incident became an enigma, giving us a similar status to Loch Ness. Psychics, scientists, religious leaders, government officials, weirdoes, and the mildly superstitious all made public comments, but with no really sensible conclusions. 'The School Earthquake' with its bizarre plague of 'birds, beasts, and bugs' would be talked about for years. There is even a YouTube video of the sky becoming black, which someone caught on their mobile. Some experts suggested the earthquake was exacerbated by volcanic activity in Iceland. Green activists blamed fracking and drilling for oil. Others created outrageous conspiracy theories. Reporters and cameras became a fixture in the local area for weeks afterwards.

An earth tremor combined with an extremely localised, and not to mention unpredictable, climactic shift caused a freak change in atmospheric conditions which temporarily affected the balance of the natural world. Witnesses claim to have seen unprecedented flocks of birds and insects fill the skies. Mr Bostock, a local taxi driver, told us, 'I thought there'd been an eclipse of the sun. It suddenly went dark. I don't just mean cloudy and grey. The world suddenly turned black.'

The freak atmospheric conditions alongside the earthquake caused animals to stampede and act aggressively, which may well account for the death of schoolboy Connor Tennant. Large branches from surrounding trees were broken off in the storm and the weight and velocity of these boughs are thought to have been the cause of the destruction of parts of Crowstone

Comprehensive School. A spokesman from the Borough Council confirmed that the buildings were old and in need of repair. The students will be temporarily placed in neighbouring schools until a more permanent solution can be found.

I got a few mentions in articles in the papers and on lots of websites, but I declined the offer to speak on the local television news programme, claiming to have lost my memory of all that had happened that day. Of course, nobody suspected me of foul play (why should they?) so I just became one of the names in a list of survivors of this inexplicable local tragedy. I had crutches for the first few weeks and physiotherapy helped me to get my legs strong again. Everyone remarked upon how quickly my body seemed to heal itself. Relearning how to use my hand with a finger missing was hard work, though.

I felt like a murderer – unable to sleep and constantly haunted by images of Connor dying. In the small hours of each night I relived each second and wished I could go back in time and change the way I reacted. Sometimes I wondered if it actually was all down to me. Did I really have that kind of power now? The idea scared me witless. I often thought about Guy. Had he survived and was he still out there somewhere? There was no telling how long I would have to wait patiently for my only friend to make contact with me. Or if he would at all.

Chapter Forty

I never suspected your numen would be so strong.
The voice in my head startled me, but it was also the only thing that could have cheered me up.

'You're alive.'

Thanks to you, Luke. The voice was hollow and distant, but distinctly Guy.

'Oh, thank God you're alive.'

My joy became overwhelming. It had been over a month since I'd had any sign that Guy was even alive. My health was almost as good as before, although my mind was still haunted by what I'd been through.

'How is Pica?'

The voice betrayed no emotion: *I will never again be Pica. Presently, I can only exist in my simplest form.*

'But what about your human body?'

You'll never see that one again.

This was hard to accept. Guy was alive but not as I would remember him.

'Bufo?'

When my full strength is back I will find a different numen.

At least I had Guy here to help and guide me. I'd just have to get used to the new circumstances.

'I'm so glad you survived,' I uttered with complete sincerity.

To be able to control nature that way ... I thought only my mother could do that, but it seems you also ... Guy spoke as if he, too, were trying to understand it all.

In the ensuing silence I waited for what I assumed was a chance for him to gather his complex thoughts. I shivered in the coldness. It was night-time and I'd left my bedroom window open because of the lack of air indoors – but mostly in the hope of Guy returning.

I got up and felt an urge to look out the window, beyond our little garden in suburbia.

You brought me back. I owe you my life, Luke.

It felt like an atonement for the death of Connor … sort of. Contemplating life without Guy in human form seemed unbearable now. In that sense, I'd lost my best friend.

'You'd have done the same.' I felt certain of this.

Do you understand what happened that day? Understand exactly what you did?

I shook my head, and sat on the edge of my bed to listen to him, pulling back my curtains fully to reveal the darkened windows.

You have learned, very quickly, how to unleash the powers of nature; or at least how to be a stream through which nature can flow. For nobody can control nature – as you've already seen. You tapped into it but it is too powerful for humans to have any power over it. Nature is dangerous – beautiful and life-giving – but dangerous and deadly too. Nature gives life but also takes it away. You have a great power, but you also need help to keep this power under control. Without my help next time who knows what catastrophe you might unleash on the world.

I sat upright and stared at myself reflected in the glass, the image of my face translucent – transposed over lights and the distant objects of the outside world.

Somewhere inside me existed Guy. Would he only ever now be a voice inside my head?

A twinge of pain jolted through the wound on the knuckle of my missing finger. I stared at it and then shook my hand. It made me recall what strange adventures I'd been through. But what next?

No reply came.

I smiled to myself, and felt the new strength ripple through my entire being. With an effort of concentration, I transformed into Felis and slipped out of the open window and into the unknown shadows outside …

234

Accent YA is an exciting new list of young adult titles which launches in spring 2016. Accent YA works with readers, bloggers, vloggers – online and in schools – to make sure that our books are as good as they can be!

If you'd like to be part of our Editor Squad or our Blog Squad and get to see early material and give your feedback on things like cover design and even which books we should publish, please get in touch. You can also sign up for our newsletter – and you could even contribute to it...

http://accentya.com/contact/

or email

info@accentpress.co.uk

With Special Thanks to

The Accent Press YA Blog Squad

Alix Long;

Anisah Hussein;

Anna Ingall;

Annie Starkey;

Becky Freese;

Becky Morris;

Bella Pearce;

Beth O'Brien;

Caroline Morrison;

Charlotte Jones;

Charnell Vevers;

Claire Gorman;

Daniel Wadey;

Darren Owens;

Emma Hoult;

Fi Clark;

Heather Lawson;

James Briggs

With Special Thanks to

The Accent Press YA Blog Squad

James Williams;

Joshua A.P;

Karen Bultiauw;

Katie Lumsden;

Katie Treharne;

Kieran Lowley;

Laura Metcalfe;

Lois Acari;

Maisie Allen;

Mariam Khan;

Philippa Lloyd;

Rachel Abbie;

Rebecca Parkinson;

Savannah Mullings-Johnson;

Sofia Matias;

Sophia;

Toni Davis

With Special Thanks to

The Accent Press YA Editor Squad

Aishu Reddy

Alice Brancale

Amani Kabeer-Ali

Anisa Hussain

Barooj Maqsood

Ellie McVay

Grace Morcous

Katie Treharne

Miriam Roberts

Rebecca Freese

Sadie Howorth

Sanaa Morley

Sonali Shetty

Luca, Son of the Morning

Tom Anderson

The water is warm ... but can you be in too deep?

Luca loves reggae, hates his parents' rum habit, and wishes his dad could get a proper job. He also loves Gaby (though he'd never admit it to her face) so upsetting her is enough to push him into a dark place. Retreating to the local beach, as he always does when he can't sleep, watching the waves gives his life some sort of rhythm.

One night, as he lets the tide lull him, a group of figures emerge from the water and walk past him, unseeing. Spellbound by these impossible sea-men, Luca holds nightly vigils at the beach. Until one night the sailors beckon him to follow them back into the sea...

For fans of Mark Haddon and Neil Gaiman, *Luca, Son of the Morning* is a haunting book about imagination, delusion and the grey places in between.

Rosie Goes to War

ALISON KNIGHT

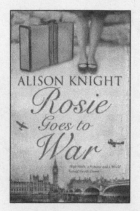

Stuck at her gran's house all summer with nothing to do, fifteen-year-old Rosie goes searching through some old junk and comes across a mysterious suitcase. It's full of vintage clothes, but when Rosie tries them on she finds herself suddenly flung back in time – into the same house in war-torn London.

With no idea of how she got there or how she can get back, she is soon caught up in a whirl of rationing, factory work, and dances. But Rosie comes crashing back to reality when she realises that if she can't find her way home, she may never be born at all ...

THE DEEPEST CUT

natalie flynn

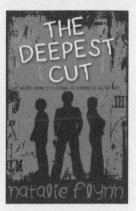

'You haven't said a single word since you've been here. Is it on purpose?' I tried to answer David but I couldn't ... my brain wanted to speak but my throat wouldn't cooperate...

Adam blames himself for his best friend's death. After attempting suicide, he is put in the care of a local mental health facility. There, too traumatized to speak, he begins to write notebooks detailing the events leading up to Jake's murder, trying to understand who is really responsible and cope with how needless it was, as a petty argument spiralled out of control and peer pressure took hold.

Sad but unsentimental, this is a moving story of friendship and the aftermath of its destruction.

THE SEA SINGER

SHOME DASGUPTA

There was a voice once that sang the ocean to sleep...

March is born in April, just as the sun is setting. A singing baby who cannot sleep, she sets Kolkaper on edge. The Town Council orders scientists to take her away and study her at the Cave Forest, a place for freaks like her. Acting quickly, March's parents send her away to the distant town of Koofay. But March's destiny is tied to that of Kolkaper. She must return to save the city from itself.

An enchanting fable about love and faith and accepting the odd ones among us.

á

For more information about **Jeff Gardiner**

and other **Young Adult** titles

please visit

www.accentYA.co.uk